MURDER BEGETS MURDER

The presence of a troop of cavalry would put a halt to any danger that the Utes might start a war. The army could get here, sure. They just could not do it soon enough to thwart a massacre.

They could clean up afterward, but they could not keep it from happening in the first place. In order for that to be done, Longarm was going to have to do it himself. Somehow.

Longarm hadn't yet reached the limits of Harry Baynard's "jail" when the excitable thief came running to meet him.

"What's the matter now?"

"There's . . . there's . . . ," Harry paused to gulp some air, "there's been a murder, that's what."

"Another one?"

"Y-yes. 'Nuther one."

"Damn!" Longarm prodded the bay into a lope, leaving Harry behind, standing doubled over with his hands on his knees while he tried to recover his breath.

TABOR EVANS

LONGARM

AND THE TALKING SPIRIT

JOVE BOOKS, NEW YORK

LONGARM AND THE TALKING SPIRIT

A Jove Book / published by arrangement with
the author

PRINTING HISTORY
Jove edition / April 2004

ISBN: 0-515-13716-2

A JOVE BOOK®
Jove Books are published by The Berkley Publishing Group,
a division of Penguin Group (USA) Inc.,
375 Hudson Street, New York, New York 10014.
JOVE and the "J" design
are trademarks belonging to Penguin Group (USA) Inc.

PRINTED IN THE UNITED STATES OF AMERICA

10   9   8   7   6   5   4   3   2   1

Chapter 1

There is nothing that smells as good as coffee boiling on a crisp and clear mountain morning. Well, almost nothing. But there wasn't a woman for miles around, so Longarm had to settle for the second best smell, which was the coffee.

"Put a couple more sticks on that fire, will you?" he said.

"Damn you, Long, I ain't your fucking servant."

"No, but you're my prisoner and you might wanna keep in mind who's going to tell the judge 'bout how you've behaved yourself." He grinned when he made the threat though. After all, Harry was a good old boy. A thief and a scoundrel but all in all a good old boy. He swore he hadn't known there was a mail pouch on the coach he robbed, and Longarm believed him.

Longarm had known Harry for . . . three years now? Four? Something like that. This was the third time Longarm had arrested him. At this point the two of them were downright friendly if not actually friends.

"Unlock these bracelets, will you, Long? I got to take a crap."

"I swear, Harry, much bother as you are I oughta go ahead an' shoot you."

"Then who would build up the fire an' make your damn coffee in the morning?"

"You got a point, it's true. And you do make good coffee." Longarm chuckled and fished the handcuff key

1

out of his pocket. He tossed it to Harry and said, "Don't lose that. It's the only one I got. An' don't go far, you hear? Not outta range of my rifle, say."

Harry Baynard gave the fire a poke with a bit of pine limb and stood, yawning and stretching. He took his time about removing his handcuffs, then laid the key and the 'cuffs onto a flat stone beside the fire. "Coffee's about done," he said. "How's about you go ahead an' pour one for me too. I'll be back in a minute."

"Damn, Harry. That means I gotta crawl out from under this blanket, an' it's cold out there."

"You want I should wrap you up in it an' carry you on down to Denver 'stead of it being t'other way round?"

"No, I expect the boss wouldn't like that a whole hell of a lot," Longarm conceded. "Go on now. Take your dump. Just mind you watch where you squat. There's snakes up here, and I damn sure ain't gonna suck out the poison if you set on one."

Baynard laughed and sauntered off a way into a into a clump of low, spreading juniper. Joshing aside he was careful to pick a spot where his head and shoulders were clearly visible from the campfire. He knew better than to give Longarm the idea that he was trying to slip away.

While Harry was occupied with his bowels, Longarm sat up and rubbed the sleep from his eyes, then jumped upright and walked in circles stomping his feet and swinging his arms to get his blood moving.

Deputy U.S. Marshal Custis Long stood over six feet of lean, sun-bronzed muscle. He had wide shoulders and narrow hips and a craggy face that was not exactly handsome but which certainly seemed to intrigue the ladies. And this morning he really would have preferred to wake up next to one of them instead of Harry Baynard.

He stepped over to the bole of a young aspen and took a quick leak, then came back to the fire and poured the dark, steaming, aromatic coffee into Harry's trail cup and his own. Longarm wrapped his hands around the steel cup to warm them.

He could see his breath as clearly as if he were exhaling smoke. It was that cold. And it was June.

Down in Denver it would be warm at this hour and hot by midday. Up here in the high country not three days' ride from the city on the plains it still felt like winter. Patches of dusty, crusted snow lay on the north-facing slopes or blanketed beneath rocks and trees where the sun could not reach.

"You make a good cup of Arbuckles'," Longarm said when Harry came back to the fire.

"I used to be a cook, you know."

"Really?"

"Oh my, yes. I was General Ulysses Grant's own private cook. Not since he got to be president, mind. This was when him and me was in the army. Right up until Vicksburg, then I got wounded and invalided out. It's true." Baynard nodded. "The general, he did dearly love the way I fixed his eggs. I scrambled them. Used to add a thimble of water and another of sherry for each egg. He loved that. Yep, true as I stand here."

Longarm's experience with Harry was that when he got to saying something was true it almost certainly was not. But what the hell. Lies that small were harmless. Old Harry just wanted somebody to look up to him about something, almost anything.

"We don't have any eggs today so we'll settle for the hardtack and jerky leftover from last night."

"Dammit, Long, you're a piss-poor feeder."

"They only give me but a little to feed you on, Harry, and if I go an' waste it all on you I won't have anything left over to pay for my high living and debauchery."

"Hell, I never thought o' that. Excuse me all to shit, will you?"

Longarm grinned. "There's no excuse for the likes of you, Harry, but if it makes you feel any better there's a mining camp up ahead about a half day's ride. We'll stop there to buy a proper meal and lay in some more supplies."

"You coulda done that before you set off, you know."

"I did," Longarm said, "but you, damn you, hid out so

3

I thought I wasn't ever gonna catch up with you."

"Wouldn't of hurt my feelings none if you hadn't," Harry told him.

"Aw, you know they miss you down at the prison."

"You don't think they could send me off to prison down to Texas, do you? Stone walls get awful cold in the winter time. Be warmer down there."

"Why don't I ask the judge to send you to Yuma?" Longarm suggested.

"I said I wanna be warmer. I never said nothing about baking me like a possum. Did you know that possum is one of General Grant's favorite dishes? It's true as I'm standing here, I tell you."

"That's interesting, Harry, it surely is," Longarm humored him. He brought out a pair of cheroots and offered one to his prisoner, then trimmed and lighted the other for himself.

Harry had to make do with his teeth to nip the twist off the end of his smoke—Longarm had taken his knife away from him first thing after the 'cuffs went on—and light it with a spray of pine needles that he dipped into the fire.

They smoked in companionable silence for awhile, then Longarm stood and tossed the stub of his cheroot onto the coals of the dying fire. "Let's clean up and get around," he said, standing.

Harry got up too and held his wrists out for Longarm to clamp on the irons. Most prisoners had to suffer the unpleasantness of having their hands cuffed behind them, but Longarm trusted Harry—up to a point, that is—and allowed him the much greater comfort of having his hands in front so he could scratch his nose when it itched or adjust the set of his hat.

Longarm kicked dirt over what was left of their fire, and they were in the saddle before the bright yellow disk of the sun cleared the next chain of mountains to the east.

Chapter 2

"Oh, quit your bitching. It's only about another half mile, and we can get ourselves a proper meal soon as we get there."

"I ain't bitching. Exactly. I'm uncomfortable, that's all. There's a rip in the seat of this saddle, and it's rubbing me something awful."

"Next time you go to robbing, Harry, get yourself properly outfitted for your getaway beforehand."

Baynard grinned. "If I coulda afforded to outfit myself better, Long, I wouldn't've robbed so close t'home. I'd've gone down to New Mexico an' robbed Meskins. The local law down there don't hardly care as long as it's only Meskins get robbed, and you wouldn't of been after me."

"Hindsight, Harry. It's always perfect, isn't it."

"Perfecter than foresight," Harry agreed. "Which reminds me. You don't think there's any chance we could stop for the night someplace where I can get me a woman before I go back behind bars, do you? I'd take it as a powerful favor if you was to do that for me, Long."

"Jesus, Harry! And how does talking about hindsight remind you of women anyway?"

"Wasn't hindsight but foresight that did it," Baynard explained. "Foresight, foreskin. That's what reminded me."

"I'm not gonna go looking for a woman for you, Harry."

"Shit, I don't expect you t' line one up. Just stop someplace where there's whores an' chain me in a barn or something instead of inside a proper jail. That's all I'm asking. I can do the rest for myself, you better believe it."

Longarm shook his head. The man was incorrigible, plain and simple. He—"Whoa!"

"What the hell?" Harry muttered as he too drew rein.

The trail they were on ran beside a lively, chuckling, fast running little stream, which was probably why they hadn't heard anything to warn them of what lay ahead when they rounded a rock face and came out onto the south edge of a small glade set amid aspen and pine.

Over to the left, a hundred feet or so from the creek, there were two groups of armed men, both rigid with tension. The nearer group of—Longarm quickly counted—eight men were Ute Indians. The other bunch of five were white men, placer miners or so Longarm guessed from the rubber boots and muddy britches. Between these opposing groups there was something, a bundle of rags or blankets it looked like, lying on the ground in the shade of a small aspen tree.

Both groups were brandishing rifles and talking rapidly at each other, neither side appearing to listen to the other.

"Wait here, Harry. And don't go no place or you'll really piss me off, you hear?"

"I hear you," Harry said, his voice serious now. "Or you could give me my gun back. Them Injuns got our boys outnumbered."

"Nobody's gonna need a gun," Longarm said. He hoped that was the truth. "Stay here while I see what this is about."

Without looking back to make sure Harry complied with the order, Longarm reined his bay horse off the trail and bumped it into a lope to quickly close the gap between himself and the red and white strangers.

Heads in both groups turned at the sound of his approach.

Longarm pulled to a stop a few yards away from the men and sat there on the bay for a moment. Then he announced himself and showed his badge. "Stand easy there, all of you." He took a closer look at the Indians and added, "Short Leg Deer, is that you?"

"Yes, Long Arm, but I am now called Bear Killer."

"I thought I recognized you, Bear Killer," he said, acknowledging the new name. He had known Short Leg Deer as a teenage boy and had not seen him in four years or so. "Tell the others who I am, will you? And what in hell is going on here anyway?"

"These no account redskins are trying to stir up trouble, Long," one of the miners declared. "They're accusing us."

"Accusing you of what?" Longarm asked.

The miner pointed to the collection of rags on the ground. Longarm nudged the bay forward a few steps and to the right so he could get a better look at what lay there.

He grimaced when he saw.

At the near end of the haphazardly draped cloth he could see a hank of shiny black hair. Apparently someone had found and covered a body here. A silent and totally still form.

Longarm muttered a few curses and stepped off the bay. He had borrowed the horse from the army's Remount Service and did not trust it to stand ground so he tied it to the lower branches on a large aspen tree before he stepped between the red and the white men and knelt beside the body.

A pang of regret rushed through him when he pulled aside the multicolored cloth which turned out to be some torn clothing and several different blankets. The dead person was a girl. In life she had been pretty. Sixteen or seventeen years old, he guessed, with long glossy hair and small pale breasts.

She was naked now, her head lying at an impossible angle indicating a broken neck. Smears of dried, dark brown blood were visible on her upper thighs. The logical assumption was that she had been a virgin until the rape and that the killer broke her neck, either by accident in the course of the violation or deliberately once he was through with her.

"These bastard Injuns say we done this, Long," the

7

leader of the miners said. "We got better things to do than fuck Injuns. Though I got to say this one wasn't as ugly as most of them. I expect a man could get a hard-on for her if he was a mind to."

Longarm hastened to pull the blankets back over the dead girl, covering her nakedness. It was bad enough she had been raped. There was no need to compound the indignity by allowing strangers to stare at her now.

"She's one of yours?" Longarm asked Bear Killer.

The man nodded. "Blue Quail Singing," he said, then inclined his head in the direction of the miners. "We caught them with her."

"Caught us, my white hairy ass," the miners' spokesman snorted. "We was down here looking to cut some wood so we can build a sluice. You see we got saws and wedges and a maul over there. And we didn't know there was a dead body here till these lying bastards came and accused us of killing her. They're the ones knew where she was. I say it's probably one of them that killed her. Wasn't none of us, I can tell you that."

Bear Killer repeated that in the Ute tongue for his companions, and the Indians began to stir and tense up. They drifted slightly apart as if to prepare for a fight.

"You might mention to your friends," Longarm said, "that the first one of them that cocks his rifle is gonna get one of my bullets between the eyes. I'm not having a war break out here. And you know I can do what I say, Bear Killer. Tell them that too if you would, please."

"These men murdered my sister."

"Your clan or a blood sister?" Longarm asked.

"Clan."

Which made her closer to him than a blood sister would have been, Longarm knew. Not that he supposed it really mattered. "Whoever killed Blue Quail Singing will be brought to justice," Longarm said.

"White men do not give justice to Indians," Bear Killer said.

"I do," Longarm reminded him.

Bear Killer and his companions talked among themselves for a few minutes, then Bear Killer said, "Long Arm does not have the white man's disease of the lying tongue. Do you say to me that the guilty one will die?"

"I say to you that I will search for the guilty one. I say to you that when I find him I will take him before the court. It will be up to a judge if he then dies. I do not decide that."

"You could shoot him. I would shoot him for you."

"That is not our law, Bear Killer, and you know it. I told you what I will do. I will do it. I promise nothing more."

The Utes conversed among themselves again, Bear Killer arguing vigorously with a burly young Indian who wore his braids wrapped in gray fur ropes.

"We will wait. We give you until the moon is no more and the night goes black. If you have not yet found the man who did this, we will kill all the men in this village. Then we will know the guilty one is punished," Bear Killer said.

"I can't tell you how long it will take for me to find the one," Longarm said. "I have told you what I will do and I will do it."

"And I have told you what I will do," Bear Killer said calmly. "And I will do it." He spoke to the others, and as one the Utes turned and stalked away.

"Shit," Longarm said. After a moment he sighed and added, "Anybody know when the next dark o' the moon will be?"

Chapter 3

"Y'know, Long," Harry mused aloud as they rode slowly along the faint wagon track toward some nameless mining camp that lay at the head of a narrow gorge, "I can be dumb sometimes. Like grabbing me a mailbag by mistake. But I swear t' God I never stuck my foot in it as deep as you just done, making all those promises."

"I can't argue the point," Longarm conceded. "It's just that was all I could think of to avoid gunfire breaking out."

"What the hell were those Injuns doing up here anyhow? I thought they all liked it down on the prairie."

"Those are Utes, Harry. They're mostly mountain people. They'll go down onto the plains for the summer hunt, then come back up here to winter. They bring their meat in with them, then once the passes fill with snow they've got a sort of fortress up here that the other tribes can't get into. It makes for a peaceful life. Or anyway it did until we came along and changed everything with our roads and trains and such. The Utes still come up here but they aren't isolated now like they used to be."

"I thought the Utes had a reservation over to the west somewhere."

"They do. Ouray's people settled there and have been mostly peaceable since. Well, except for the odd massacre or outbreak. But they don't do that often. This band follows a chief named Iron Ax."

"You know them I take it."

"I know them."

"You trust them?"

"I trust everybody," Longarm said. "Even you. Just not very far."

"You talking about me or the Injuns?"

"Both." Longarm rose in his stirrups to peer upstream along the creek they were following. "I smell smoke. We must be about there."

"Yeah, or a bunch of them Utes snuck on ahead and burned the whole place down," Harry suggested.

"Don't even think it," Longarm told him. "It could happen."

"You think so?"

"I know damn good and well that it could. Iron Ax's people were part of the bunch that raided Pueblo back in . . . I don't remember the exact year, it was before I came out here . . . back before the war. Anyway, the folks who lived there took them for harmless. Then one Christmas Eve the Indians came to visit. The people opened their doors and invited the Ute warriors in for supper. What they got instead was massacred. Wiped out the whole community, all but one or two who managed to hide until they were gone. Men, women and children. Everybody dead. The way I understand it, that was the night Iron Ax got his name. He was still a raw kid, along on his first raid. Grabbed an ax off somebody's woodpile and started splitting skulls with it. Made him quite a hero."

"Jesus!" Harry blurted.

"He still has the ax," Longarm added. "Still keeps it sharp."

Harry began to look a mite pale. "I'm glad we're getting the hell outta this country while the getting is good."

"We aren't going anyplace," Longarm told him.

"The hell you say. I'm not staying around up here while there's Indians on the damn warpath."

"Nobody's on any warpath, Harry, and it's my job to see nobody starts out on one."

"What about me? I'm a prisoner. You're duty bound to protect my butt long as I'm in your custody."

"Harry, I will make you a solemn promise. Just like I done to those Indians. And just like with them, I will keep my word if it's humanly possible."

"What kinda promise?" Harry wanted to know.

"I will promise you that I won't ever deliberately let anybody, red or white, kill you before I can get you down to Denver for trial in a proper court of law."

"What if you can't keep me safe, Long? What then?"

"In that case, Harry, I will personally ask the judge to authorize payment for a real nice funeral for you." Longarm gigged his horse into a lope without waiting for Harry's response.

Longarm was not surprised that the camp had no name. It didn't deserve one.

The place was nothing more than a collection of shacks, cabins and tents thrown up in a meadow that bordered the stream. There was no store as such but there were two tent saloons, one at each end of the long, narrowly dispersed camp. Probably a man could buy things in the saloons other than rotgut whiskey. Tobacco, a few staples like rice and flour and salt, perhaps a woman.

He guessed the population would number several hundred or so, and right now in the middle of the day most of them were visible. They lined both banks of the stream and waded in the middle of it, gold pans in hand.

This camp was a placer dig and a fairly new one at that. Had to be new because as yet there was only one sluice box in sight. He could see a few rockers but only the one full-blown sluice.

The miners who had encountered Bear Killer and his companions had said they were looking to build a sluice, Longarm recalled. The appearance of the camp suggested they were telling the truth about that, regardless of what Bear Killer and the other Utes might believe. A good sluice that would process gravel from the stream bottom could instantly quadruple the output of a claim.

Longarm thought about that for a moment, then realized it was not really so. A sluice box or other device that would separate gold from gravel would not actually increase the output. There was only so much in the way of nuggets or dust available on a given claim, so once that was all extracted the digging might as well be abandoned and another located. The thing about the sluice box was that it let a team of partners gather the available gold that much quicker. But it would not create more gold.

Of course if Longarm ever came across a machine that would do that, well, he'd be rich as that fellow in . . . wherever the hell it was . . . that turned everything he touched into gold.

In any event, this camp was still growing. It would go into instant decline once the free gold in the creek played out. Either that or some lucky SOB would find the lode that this gold came from. Then that fellow would be rich. The camp would turn into a town.

And likely the place would get itself a name.

"What d'you want to bet there's no jail here," Longarm said over his shoulder to Harry.

"You got to turn me loose then."

"The hell you say. I'll just chain you to a tree or something."

"Bullshit, you will!"

"Bullshit I won't," Longarm shot back at him. "I'm not letting you go so don't start in about that."

"Then at the very least you gotta feed me."

"Yes, and myself too," Longarm agreed.

He drew up in front of the nearer of the two tent saloons.

Chapter 4

The saloon was empty except for a bartender who looked to be half asleep. He sat straddling a stool behind the crudely sawed plank that, placed on top of a pair of kegs, served as his bar.

Crates placed on their sides and piled between the bar and the wall provided shelving for a number of small items that were offered for sale. A keg placed on the ground—there was nothing fancy here, a floor for instance—presumably held liquor of some sort, and there was another crate beside it, this one standing upright, that held a collection of battered tin cups.

Bluebottle flies droned in and out with not so much as a bead curtain to stop their entry.

"Nice place you have here," Longarm said dryly as he and Harry entered.

"Yeah, I'll prob'ly remodel in a couple years though," the barkeep answered in a voice that was equally dry. "Soon as the mortgage is paid off."

Apart from his stock he couldn't have more than ten dollars invested in the place, Longarm figured. And that was only if he had to buy the tarpaulin new. If he'd bought it used, and it sure as hell looked used, the man likely was able to "build" his tent saloon for, oh, five or six dollars.

"Not much overrun with business, are you?" Longarm said.

"Got a keen eye on you there, neighbor," the barman

responded. "Never miss a thing." He sighed and shook his head. "You been spending too much time in cities, friend. Out here a man has to work to stay ahead. Pretty much every man jack in this camp is out there freezing his hands and feet off in the water, panning for those little flakes of gold dust."

The barkeep smiled. "Now come sundown, you see, when it's too dark to work, those old boys will come in here asking me to take their gold off them. And being an accommodating fellow, I will consent to do it."

"You aren't as dumb as you look, are you," Longarm said.

The barman's smile turned into a grin. "Nope. It's the way I comb my hair that makes me look stupid." He was as bald as a boiled egg. About the only hair on his head was in his eyebrows and ears and coming out of his nose.

Longarm laughed and leaned across the plank to offer his hand and introduce himself.

"Jerry Markley," the barkeep said in response, shaking Longarm's hand.

Harry piped up with an introduction of his own and added, "Excuse me if I don't offer t' shake hands." He held the manacles up for Markley to see.

"Another time," the bartender said.

"I expect we could use something to eat and a couple beers," Longarm said.

"I keep something in the pot. A little of this and a little of that. None of the meat will kill you, but I wouldn't advise you to ask what any of it is. As for the beer, I don't keep any. It's too difficult and too expensive to haul something as bulky as beer up here. Maybe when there's a proper road in, if the place lasts that long, but not now. What I do have is tobacco whiskey." His smile returned. "They tell me that after three or four drinks it starts to taste pretty good."

"You wouldn't know?"

"Not me. I don't drink hard spirits. No, sir."

"Coffee?" Longarm asked.

"I got coffee, yes."

15

"Then I expect we'll have that and a couple bowls of the stew."

"Speak for yourself," Harry said. "I'd like some of that whiskey. But treat it like the stew an' don't tell me what's in it," he said.

"Coming right up, gents."

Longarm looked around. There were no chairs or stools or even chunks of wood to sit on.

Markley saw and told him, "There's some rocks over by the creek where you can sit down if you like. Just remember to bring my china back."

His "china," when he served it, consisted of a pair of the tin cups, one with whiskey and the other containing coffee, and some crudely hollowed wooden trenchers filled with a thick and aromatic stew.

Markley's deprecating comments aside, the stew smelled delicious. And proved to taste every bit as good.

Longarm felt close to being human by the time he and Harry were done with their meal. They carried their empty "china" back inside the tent.

"How do you wash these?" Longarm asked.

"Throw the cups in the bucket there. The bowls go on the wood pile."

"Convenient," Longarm said.

"Waste not, want not," Markley told him.

Longarm tossed the trenchers onto a number of others beside the collapsible steel sheepherder's stove where the stew pot and coffee were bubbling.

"I don't suppose you could tell me a couple things," he asked Jerry Markley.

"Marshal, I will tell you many things," the bartender promised. "Some of them may even be true."

"I need to know where I can chain my prisoner so he won't get into too much trouble, and I need to know when the moon will next be full dark."

"You won't find any trees to chain your friend to. They've all been cut down for firewood or to build shanties, pretty much everything for a mile in any direction.

But we have a gracious plenty of rocks you could use. Pick any one you like. Nobody will mind.

"As for the moon, I got an almanac in my gear somewhere. I can dig that out for you."

"I'd be obliged," Longarm said.

He felt considerably less pleased with the situation though after Markley found his book and looked up the moon phases calculated for the month.

"Eight days," Markley said. "You have eight days until the moon is dark." He closed the book and put it away in a canvas pack that he kept inside one of the kegs that served to hold up one end of his plank bar. "Is it important?"

Longarm shuddered. Eight days to solve a murder or risk a breakout by Iron Ax's band of Utes. Eight lousy days. And one of them already nearly used up.

"Yeah," he said. "Yeah, I guess I'd say it's important."

Chapter 5

"I'd chain you in place, Harry. If I had a place. If I had a chain." Longarm stood beside the creek with one boot propped on top of a slanted chunk of rock. He had a pensive look about him as he pulled out a cheroot and clipped off the tip, then ducked his head and cupped his hands around a match to light it.

"The thing is," he went on, "I could prob'ly borrow enough chain and locks to chain you to some of these rocks along the water. But you know as good as me that at this time of year a stream can flood and come a torrent in a matter of minutes depending on the weather and the snowpack higher up. If that was to happen, Harry, you'd drown like a rat in a barrel, and what you done isn't enough to draw you a death sentence. I expect I won't risk one for you."

Longarm drew on the cheroot for a moment while he thought. Then, deciding, he nodded and turned his attention fully onto his prisoner. "Harry, I'm gonna put you in jail."

"I thought there wasn't a jail here."

"You're right. There isn't. So you and me are gonna make us one."

"I got to build a damn jail now, just so I can turn around and get locked up inside it?" Harry asked rather indignantly.

"Nope. We got no time for building, Harry. So what we're gonna do is, we're gonna define us a jail."

18

"We are gonna what?"

"Define. Like, you know, set boundaries. We're gonna say that this creek is one side of your jail. You can come to it. You can draw water from it even. But if you cross over it or step out into it, Harry, you are subject to being shot for jailbreak. Am I beginning to make myself clear?"

"Yeah. Well, sort of."

"Right. So this stream, it's one 'wall' of your jail. So to speak. The next wall . . . let me see. All right, look up yonder. You see that lean-to and the spit of dry land at the upstream end of the camp?"

"I see it."

"Good, because that's another wall. You can go all the way to it. Just don't take a step past it or you're in trouble."

Harry shook his head.

"See up the side of the canyon there? See that ledge? That's another wall, Harry. Don't go past it. And down that way . . . I'm gonna give you a lot of room downstream, Harry, because I'm gonna put you in charge of the horses. You can take them down that far to where there's some graze to be found. But you can't go on down the canyon into the trees, and you damn sure can't go out to the highway.

"The thing is, Harry, I got neither the time nor the patience to fuck around with you right now, so I'm gonna let you wander around inside those limits all you please. Just don't go beyond them or you will piss me off real bad. Are you understanding me, Harry? Are we clear on this?"

"I think . . . I think so."

"That's good, because no matter what happens with these miners and the Utes, in a few days I'll be done up here. What I want to do then is for you and me to ride down to Denver to turn you in. What I *don't* want to do is have to come looking for you all over again. If I have to find you again, Harry, things will go awful bad on you. On the way in. Inside the jail. In court. And in prison after. I guarantee it. You would not like the way it would

19

be if you make me come after you again for this same piddling little crime. On the other hand, if you cooperate and stay in jail for me, well, I'll make sure the judge knows you've done that."

"I understand," Harry said quickly.

Too quickly? Longarm thought that old Harry just might think he could run and get away with it. He might be working himself up to the attempt.

Not that there was anything Longarm could do about it if Harry did make a break for it. Now. A couple weeks from now would be a different story. And he'd meant every word he said there. One way or another, Harry would regret leaving if he decided to skedaddle, but Longarm would be just as willing to throw him some slack if he made like a properly confined prisoner here in . . . wherever the hell this was.

"I'll tell you what then," Longarm said. "Whyn't you take the horses on down and hobble them so they can graze until evening. I'll catch up with you then."

"You want I should strip the saddles and everything?"

"Yes, but not here. Make sure those saddles go wherever the horses are, just in case I got to go someplace in a hurry."

"He'll be ready for you if you need him," Harry said. "I'll make sure of it."

"That's fine."

"So, uh . . . what will you do next?"

Longarm grinned at him. "Truth is, I don't have the least idea."

Harry gathered up the horses and went in one direction while Longarm summoned his resolve and headed the opposite way.

"Sorry," the big man said. "You have it wrong. I can understand why they directed you to me, I suppose, but we don't have a mayor or any organized form of government here."

Longarm smiled. "Y'know, I've heard that same thing

20

said about Denver. For that matter, heard it said about the country was well."

"Or that you could wish that we didn't," the tall, burly miner said. "As for our little community, Marshal, we don't have a village government, but we do have a miners' court. I happen to be president of the court, such as it is."

"What sort of cases do you handle in your court?" Longarm asked.

"So far we've only had one. A man was brought before us charged with poaching on another man's claim. He was guilty."

"And the punishment?"

"We turned his poke over to the man he stole it from and banished him from the camp."

"That's all?"

"Yes. That was the sentence meted out."

"There was no other punishment?"

"I only concerned myself with the finding of fact and our verdict in response to it. If anything else happened to the man, on his way out of the canyon for instance, I wouldn't know about that."

"Sure you wouldn't," Longarm said, his tongue planted firmly in his cheek. Probably the dumb son of a bitch was beaten within an inch of his life or ridden out of camp on a rail while wearing tar and feathers. Or both. But the president of the court would not know anything about that. Officially.

Hell, he might well have thrown the first punch. But that would not have been in his capacity as president of the miners' court. Longarm had seen such groups at work before. For the most part they were conscientious and well-meaning. Certainly they were a cut above vigilance committees. But miners' courts too could degenerate into pettiness and self-interest. It sounded to him like that was not the case here. Human nature being what it was, that might well happen in the future, but for now both the camp and the court were young and sincere.

"I didn't catch your name," Longarm said.

"Oh. Sorry." The big man extended his hand to shake. "Charles Whelan," he said. "I'm a Vermonter."

"Good country, I've heard tell."

"Aye, but I doubt I'll ever go back. These mountains," Whelan paused and looked around them, at the craggy peaks and rugged mountain slopes, "they get into a man. I can go back to my shack after a night covered in mud and so tired I can scarcely manage to put one foot ahead of the other, yet I feel cleaner and freer here than I've ever known before. It is a good feeling."

"Yes, it is, isn't it."

"I wish I could help you find the killer of that girl, Marshal. I surely do. I have no idea who it could be, however."

"Something like this will not have been done by a large group," Longarm said. "That is, a group could do it, the girl having been an Indian and beneath human consideration the way some fools see things, but if it were done by a group it would not be a secret. The word would get out very quickly."

"They say a secret is safe with only one man," Whelan agreed.

"Have you had any other incidents involving anyone in the camp abusing women? Not necessarily rape, mind you. Any sort of rough treatment at all?"

"Marshal, I can answer that without equivocation. There have been no such incidents within the camp. I can guarantee it."

Longarm raised an eyebrow.

"We have no women here. None."

"Oh. Goodness. Even the whores haven't found you?"

Whelan grinned. "Not yet, but we keep hoping. If we're still here at the end of summer and none have shown up we shall probably send out for some. The prospect of spending a winter without female company would be quite daunting, don't you think?"

"I think so indeed. Although not having any women here . . . that makes things harder for me. Rape and murder aren't generally done just for a piece of ass, you know.

22

Those usually have to do with a man wanting to hurt or to make himself feel stronger and more important than he really is. This time," he shrugged, "I can't ignore the idea that this could prove an exception to that rule. I suppose that poor girl could have been killed just because she was carrying a warm place to put it."

"This is a harsh world out here, Marshal, and there are those who think that being far from city lights make them immune from common decency."

"Mr. Whelan, decency ain't all that common. Trust me. I'm in a position to know."

"Yes, I suppose you are at that."

"If you hear any whispers, will you let me know?" Longarm asked.

"Count on it."

"Thank you, sir." Longarm shook hands with the big Vermonter and turned back downstream. Behind him Whelan waded out into the icy water, the placer pan looking small in his massive hands. He was already wet almost to the waist and must have been numbed by the cold. But there was gold beneath this water, and the mountains would give up their treasure to only the hardy and the determined. There wasn't a man here, no matter how heavy his poke of gold dust, who Longarm envied.

Chapter 6

"No, sir. I don't remember any strangers coming nor going," the red-headed miner said. It was the same story Longarm had heard from everyone else he'd spoken with during the long afternoon.

"How about anyone from here pulling stakes in the past couple days?"

The fellow shook his head. "No, sir. But I can tell you this. Word is going around that those Injuns could be going on the warpath. We'll be having a camp meeting tonight. I wouldn't doubt but what some will vote to pull out. Might be some as wants to stay and fight for what we got here."

"What will you do?" Longarm asked him.

The man scratched the beard stubble on his cheeks and grinned. "Be more gold for me if everybody else goes. I expect I'll likely stay. Unless it gets to looking awfully bad."

"You say there's a meeting tonight?"

"Just after dark. You won't be able to miss it. There'll be a bonfire on the slope up yonder and a lot of drunks hollering and carrying on."

"All right, thanks. If you think of anything else, please let me know."

"Sure thing, Marshal. After all, you're the fella we're all counting on to keep those savages in line. And God help you."

"Thanks, neighbor. I appreciate that." Longarm turned

and had gone perhaps a dozen steps before the miner called out to him. Longarm stopped and turned back to face the fellow. "Yes?"

"You only interested in strangers coming in and out?"

"No, of course not. Anyone you know was on the road lately. I'd like to talk to him. See if maybe he saw anything suspicious."

"Guy came in three days ago with a wagon and trailer. He brought in rice, sugar, coffee, like that. Sold out in a jiffy too even though his prices were terrible high. He's no stranger though. Comes in every once in a while doing the same thing. Always makes out pretty good here, I think."

"Do you know his name?"

The man shook his head. "No, I don't think none of us made his acquaintance exactly. At least not that I know about. He's an old guy. Gray hair worn clubbed in back. Buckskins. Like he was pretending to be one of those old time mountain men."

Longarm asked, "Does he drive a wagon with a trailer on behind and six mules to pull it?"

"That's right. You know him?"

"I know him. His name is Joe Korn, and he isn't pretending to be anything. He really was a mountain man."

"No shit?"

"No shit," Longarm affirmed. "Trader Joe, they call him now. He sells stuff all through these central mountains. Can't stand to light in one spot and stay there, so him and his mules stay on the road."

"What's a man like that do in winter?"

"Goes south. Arizona, New Mexico, sometimes as far down as Chihuahua. He used to be quite a man. Come to that, friend, he still is."

"Think he could've killed that girl?"

"No, not Joe. He knows the Indians up here about as well as he knows the mountains. If he got horny he'd drive into a village and dicker with the headman. It wouldn't cost him more than a couple twists of tobacco

25

to get the loan of a girl for the night. He wouldn't need to rape nor kill."

"If you say so."

"Yes, but I thank you for telling me. Could be Joe saw something on his way in or else back out. Thanks."

Longarm headed back toward Jerry Markley's saloon. It was getting on toward dusk, and he was hungry again.

He wondered if it would be worthwhile to go chasing after Joe Korn on the off chance the old man might have seen something.

Three days ago Joe came up that road, the red-head said. That was probably before the girl was killed. The body hadn't had time to bloat. On the other hand the nights were mighty cold at this elevation, and she had been lying in the shade. That would slow the decomposition.

Someday, he hoped, maybe some smart SOB would figure out how to tell just how long a body was dead. That would sure as hell be a help to every peace officer in the land. As it was you could only take your best guess . . . and maybe be off by days.

As it was though it probably made no sense to go chasing around looking for Korn. Not with so little time remaining until Bear Killer demanded an answer. Dammit!

Longarm changed course and walked out toward the edge of the camp until he could attract Harry's attention and motion for him to bring the horses and come on in. He was sure to be hungry too.

It didn't so much matter if Harry wanted to dawdle, but Longarm wanted to be done with eating before that meeting got under way.

There were more miners in the camp than Longarm thought. He put the number in the crowd at something better than two hundred souls. They had brought firewood—roots and twigs, actually, for anything larger could be used for building purposes—and every man was expected to contribute his share before he chose a seat. As head of the miners' court Charles Whelan took charge.

When the entire population was present, including Longarm and Harry Baynard, Whelan called for silence. A low buzz of conversation continued, so Whelan a second time demanded silence. And a third. Finally, becoming pissed, the Vermonter pulled a cloth pouch from his pocket. The sausage shaped object looked like a typical gold pouch, but Whelan handled it like it was not especially heavy when certainly that much gold would have been.

"Quiet, I said," he repeated.

The miners continued to ignore him so Whelan tossed the little cloth sack into the four foot tall bonfire.

A horrendous explosion tore the fire apart and showered everyone nearby with ash and hot embers.

Blasting powder, Longarm realized. Whelan knew his audience. He'd come prepared. And his little attention-getter damn sure got their attention.

"Be quiet now and listen," the big man from Vermont said in an ordinary speaking voice. He had no need to speak up in order to be heard. They were indeed listening.

"Tom, put some more wood onto that fire for me before it goes out. Thank you. Vern, I want you to give an invocation before we start. The rest of you take your hats off and bow your heads. Vern, go ahead now, please."

A balding man with Burnside whiskers and a moustache so magnificent it made even Longarm's pale by comparison stood, clasped his hands together and asked the Lord for guidance for this company of sinners. While he was at it he also asked for some ladies of the night to come this way. Soon. Longarm did not know if that was an appropriate request to lay before that particular source, but no one in the crowd seemed to object to it.

"Thank you, Vern," Whelan said when the man was done praying. "I think."

There was some general stirring about as men dragged their caps back onto their heads, then Whelan got down to business.

"You all know why we are here. There is sentiment among some that this camp should be abandoned before

27

the mountain Indians go on a rampage and slaughter us all in retaliation for something we have not done. At least I do not know that any man among us did the killing in question. If any of you has information to the contrary, come to me, please. I will convey that information to Marshal Long. He does not need to ever know who told it to me. After all, the quickest way to defuse the threat of war would be to find the girl's killer. Does anyone have anything to say or a confession to make?"

No one did, but Whelan paused for a moment just in case the impossible might happen.

"No? Well, a word to me in private will remain confidential. Keep that in mind. All of you know Marshal Long, I hope. There he is. Marshal, please come a little closer to the fire so everyone can see you clearly. Thank you.

"The problem as we all know is that the Indians are demanding justice. I do not blame them. If one of our people were dead, we too would want the killer brought to bay and justice done."

"Aw, shit, Charlie," a voice interrupted, "she was just some Injun bitch. It ain't like it was a human got killed."

Whelan glared at the man who had spoken. "That is not a subject I intend to debate with you, Philip, but I can assure you the Indians do not regard her as having been without value, and that is the point. There are more than a thousand warriors out there." He pointed rather dramatically, and quite inaccurately, into the night that surrounded them. "What will you and I do if they decide to descend upon us to avenge their fallen sister?"

Longarm had no idea where Whelan had gotten his information about the thousand Utes. Hell, the entire Ute nation would have difficulty fielding that many warriors. Iron Ax's band might be able to call upon . . . at a guess he figured something on the order of forty to forty-five warriors. Maybe fewer. Enough to do considerable damage, of course, but nothing like the thundering horde Charles Whelan was suggesting.

He debated whether he should tell the miners that. He

did not want to embolden the whites, who might then become the ones to threaten Bear Killer and the others in the band. Longarm did not want that any more than he wanted a massacre of the white miners. But if the miners thought they were so thoroughly outnumbered, they were more likely to abandon the camp and take the killer with them. That would only put other unsuspecting travelers at risk, because Longarm had no doubt that Bear Killer and his clansmen would indeed wreak havoc if justice were not obtained for Blue Quail Singing.

Longarm stood quietly and listened for some time, until the tenor of discussion seemed to be heading toward a close. Then he added his two cents.

"You're scaring yourselves more than is reasonable," he told them, adding his estimate of the number of warriors available if it should come to war. "That's enough to worry about for sure. They could do plenty of damage. But they aren't gonna swoop in here an' slaughter every man in sight. That couldn't happen. So my advice is that you boys stay here where you are." He smiled and added, "Specially since any man that decides t' go will come under suspicion of murder. By me. And he'll play hell proving himself to me before I'd let him go down the mountain now. Do I make myself clear?"

"I believe that resolves the question before us," Charles Whelan declared. "From this moment on, no man will leave this camp without permission."

"Permission, my ass," a man in the crowd objected. "I got the right to come or go however I damn please."

"That's true," Longarm told him. "And I have the right to arrest any man here on suspicion of rape and murder. But you are right, neighbor. You have the right to pull up stakes and leave outta here any time you're of a mind to go, so you do whatever you think is best."

That was pure bluff and bullfeathers, of course. But it might keep at least some of his potential suspects close at hand. He needed them, dammit. He needed them here where he could talk to them. Someone among them surely would have seen or heard or be able to remember something that would point the way toward the killer of that girl.

He hoped.

"Sorry," he said now. "I don't mean to rain on your picnic, an' the truth is that I'm not gonna go arresting a man just because he's scared of maybe getting into a fight. But I'm really, really hoping every man who is innocent will choose to stay here. Please."

Longarm turned and walked down the hill toward the creek.

He had seven more days in which to find the girl's killer.

Chapter 7

"Dammit, Whelan, I'm stumped." In his exasperation Longarm flung three inches of perfectly good cheroot into the coals of the Vermont man's lunch fire. He regretted the impulse as soon as it was done, but by then of course it was too late.

"Doing no good?" Whelan asked sympathetically.

Longarm snorted. "Two hundred some men in this camp and I personally have spoken to each and every one of them. Or if not to them then to some member of their claim."

"Did you really expect someone to confess?"

"It ain't a confession you look for so much, though God knows I'd never turn one down. It's more . . . ," he had to pause for a moment to search for the words, "you learn to listen to the things a fella isn't saying. The things he's scared to say. The little give-away things. Inconsistencies. Slip-ups. In a word: lies." He shook his head. "I'm not hearing that here. I don't mean these boys are pure at heart an' innocent as a flock o' lambs. It's just that none of them seems at all nervous about anything I might wanna ask about that dead Indian girl. It's like . . . they're interested. Hell, of course they are. They got a stake in whether there's a breakout and maybe the camp has t' be abandoned. But none of them acts like he has anything to hide."

"So where do you go from here?" Whelan asked.

"Damn if I know, Charles. I only had eight days to

31

begin with. I've gone an' used up most of the third o' them." He sighed. "I expect what I really ought to do is something I couldn't do the other day when Bear Killer and his warriors were there. Been kinda avoiding it ever since too."

"How's that, Marshal?"

"Fact is, Charles, I don't know for certain sure how that girl died. The way she was layin' on the ground there it looked like she died from a broken neck. But that coulda come later. Or before. I mean, she coulda been stabbed or shot in addition to being raped an' beaten. It might help me if I can figure out what weapon t' look for. If nothing else it'll give me a direction I can use t' start over from."

"Will you have to go all the way out to wherever the Indians are camped?"

Longarm shook his head. "Indians don't generally like to have bodies laying around. Bear Killer prob'ly buried her that afternoon an' somewhere close by to where she was killed."

"Is there anything I can do to help?" the president of the miners' court asked.

"Yes," Longarm told him. "If you happen t' be a prayin' man, Charles, try some of that t' help me along."

Longarm hiked downstream along the creek, passing men who in the past few days had become amazingly familiar to him. There was Jesse, the farmer from North Carolina who looked like he didn't have a brain in his head . . . and probably didn't. Gary, the cow puncher who'd drifted up from Arizona and who very likely would soon choose the ass end of a cow again over the cold misery of gold panning. Douglas, bald and looking like a Connecticut school teacher but who carried a knife that was just short of being a sword and who had the reputation of using it if fucked with. People tended to avoid fucking with him, Longarm noticed.

He recognized each of them now and nodded in passing as he headed down to where Harry Baynard and the horses waited.

Harry pushed his hat off his face and sat upright when he heard Longarm approach. He blinked and rubbed sleep out of his eyes. "What's up, boss?"

"Not you, I see."

"Just a little daydreaming. You know what I mean?"

"About?"

Harry grinned. "Pussy. What else is worth daydreaming about?"

"Aren't you getting a little old for that?"

The grin grew bigger. "Marshal, I figure I'm gonna be horny right up until three days after I'm dead. Beyond that we'll just have to see. D'you want the horses?"

"Just my own, Harry. You'd better stay here. After all, you're in jail. An' I don't wanna be thinking about watching you. Besides, I won't be gone but an hour or so. You can sidle along and see what you can hear. You never know. You might come up with something useful."

"All right. I'll clean the mule shit outta my ears and flap them a few times."

"Yeah, that ought to do it." Longarm picked up his blanket and brushed it free of grass stems and gravel, then spread it on the bay's back followed by the saddle. He slipped the headstall onto the horse and buckled it, then removed the hobbles and tied them in place behind his cantle.

"Sure you don't want me to come along?"

"No, Harry, and I'll tell you why. We get off down this canyon we're apt to run into a damn grizzly bear. If we do, an' if it's a female, you're apt to go chasing after her waving a hard-on and shouting 'Powder River, let 'er buck.'"

"Female, hell. It's been so long I might take after a boar grizzly too." Harry laughed and grabbed his crotch, thrusting his skinny hips at an imaginary grizzly bear.

Longarm shook his head. "The world is gonna be a safer place once I get you locked away behind bars, Harry." But he was smiling when he said it.

He swung onto the bay horse and put it into a quick jog down the canyon.

33

Chapter 8

The meadow where the girl died was farther than Longarm remembered but not so far that a man on foot couldn't
reach it in less than an hour. The bay horse carried Longarm there in half that time.

He spent little time at the crime scene itself. There
would have been no point after all the stumbling around
and smoking and spitting by both red men and white. One
thing Longarm did notice was that there was nothing obvious about the place as an ambush site. There were no
rocks to hide in or dense brush for concealment. It was
just a grassy spot at the edge of an aspen grove, reason
enough to draw the attention of someone who wanted to
cut some wood but otherwise unexceptional so far as he
could tell. The place certainly did not suggest it would
lend itself to hiding in wait for deliberate murder or rape.

He sat there on the bay for a few moments, looking
around and trying to get the feel of the place. Then he
began working up the hillside in a broad, fan-like sweep-
ing pattern.

It used to be that Indian burials stood out at the very
top of whatever hill or prominence that was available, but
they no longer did that, the graves being too likely to be
seen and looted by souvenir hunters. Nowadays the burial
platforms were more likely to be laid into the branches of
a sturdy tree or erected inside some thick cover to keep
them from being so obvious. It took him the better part
of an hour to find this one.

The platform, built of aspen saplings lashed together with strips of bark, was hidden inside a thicket of young aspen growth. The construction materials had been cut here, taken from the very center of the thicket. The flat, rickety platform was tall enough that it would be fully exposed to air and sunlight but low enough that there was a screen of leaves and branches on all sides. The uprights were the trunks of young trees that had been growing there and remained rooted in the thin, rocky soil. The platform was perhaps seven feet off the ground, the girl's body covered by a blanket.

Longarm dismounted and took a few minutes to finish the cheroot he'd been smoking when he got there, then dug around in his saddlebags for the small can of neat's-foot oil that he carried there for use on his saddle and boots. There were other things that would work better for what he had in mind, but the neat's-foot oil was the smelliest article he had with him and would just have to do.

He shook out a bandanna and tied that around his face like a dust shield or highwayman's mask, then dabbed some of the aromatic neat's-foot oil onto the cloth just below his nose. The smell was strong but not unpleasant. Stronger would have been even better.

Once that was done he mounted again and forced the bay into the whippy aspen branches until it stood next to the burial platform on the uphill side. By standing in his stirrups Longarm was able to comfortably reach the body that lay there.

The girl had been wrapped in a blanket and tied down to discourage the ravens and other carrion eaters. He could see where something had been pecking at the covering but so far they had not succeeded in getting through to the dead flesh underneath. Eventually, of course, they would. Blanket and corpse alike would decompose, and all traces of meat and sinew would be consumed. The bones would fall apart and in time so would the lashings that held the platform together. In a matter of years there would be no trace of the girl whose mortal remains lay here.

But that would be in the fullness of time. For the moment . . .

Longarm used his knife to cut away the cord that held the blanket down, then peeled the thick wool back.

Someone had gone to the trouble of dressing Blue Quail Singing in readiness for her last journey. Her blouse was ripped at the throat and along one sleeve. Longarm assumed the murderer did that, but he supposed it was also possible the damage occurred when Bear Killer and the others were trying to put her clothing back on her.

She was not as bloated and smelly as he'd feared. The chilly nights likely accounted for that. Even so he was glad for the mask and the scent on it that helped cover the stink of rotting human flesh.

Longarm did not especially like doing what had to be done, but waiting around fretting about it was not going to accomplish a hell of a lot. He took a deep breath and began feeling around in the girl's hair, searching her skull for any indication of breakage there.

He cut her blouse open—he damn sure was not going to wrestle her out of it again—and examined the pale, mottled flesh for bullet or stab wounds. He rolled her onto her side so he could look at her back. It was dark from the blood that had pooled there but was otherwise undamaged. He could see no indication of bullet holes or knife cuts.

He let the body back down again and picked up her left hand. The first and middle fingernails were broken and dirty. He used the tip of his knife to scrape underneath them a little. It was hard to tell after so much time had gone by, but that could have been skin he found there. There was a faint, reddish tinge to the material. Blood? He couldn't be sure but it seemed possible.

Probably the girl had been right-handed. He stood a little taller and reached across the body for the right hand so he could repeat his examination of her nails. He hadn't quite grasped the dead girl's hand when the bay fidgeted, causing him to lose his balance for a moment. He dropped onto his saddle and grabbed for the reins to settle the animal.

He heard the sudden zing and crackle as if the world's largest bumblebee was tearing through the aspen leaves, and a moment later there was the flat, dull report of a rifle shot.

"Oh, shit," Longarm mumbled as he bent low over the bay's neck and spurred the horse uphill, in the direction from which the gunshot came.

Chapter 9

It took the horse several precious moments of crashing and thrashing through the whippy, clinging aspen branches before he broke out into the open again.

Longarm caught a glimpse of movement at the crest of the hill. Something dark. A head? He thought so but could not be sure. Whatever it was, whoever it was, was moving fast from right to left and quickly disappeared.

Longarm reined the bay around some jagged rocks and straight through a tangle of low, fan-shaped juniper as he gave chase.

By the time he reached the top of the hill the rifleman was gone.

The question of the moment was twofold. One, had that all too brief flicker of movement toward his left been genuine? Or was it a feint meant to draw him off the scent? And two, was the son of a bitch setting up in hiding for another try at him?

All right, there was a third question. Why?

Longarm hadn't learned a damn thing from examining the body. It didn't look like there was anything *to* learn there. So why did someone shoot at him just now?

If he was getting too close to somebody he certainly did not know it. For that matter did not believe it. He was as completely in the dark about this now as he had been the first moment he saw those groups of men gathered on opposite sides of the body and rode over to see what the problem was.

So why the hell did the guy shoot at him just now?

While he was pondering those questions, Longarm was very cautiously easing down off the top of the hill toward where he had seen that movement. He thought back. He hadn't been especially conscious of it at the time, but in addition to seeing something—a head or a dark hat, he suspected—he heard the clatter of hoofs on hard ground. So the guy had been shooting from horseback. Which might well explain why he missed at such short range. It could not have been more than sixty or seventy yards. Slightly downhill, which always makes the shot more difficult, but even so at that distance Longarm should have been in the bag. A horse fidgeting beneath him could make the shot more difficult, of course. And the bullet may well have deflected off the aspen branches it had to pass through. Even so . . .

There!

Longarm spent a few moments peering away downhill and to his left, in the direction where he thought the shooter escaped, then stepped down off the bay to briefly examine a series of scrapes in the gravel. It took a good bit of weight and movement to disturb the hard surface of the ground here. A man traveling on foot will do so without leaving any sign of his passage. A bear, a cat, even the small, sharp hoofs of a deer will leave no imprint unless the ground is wet and muddy. But a running horse can do it.

It looked like this one really was leading off to the left. Away from the no-name mining camp.

Longarm made a mental note to himself to ask Harry who left the camp after Longarm did.

But for now he was more interested in seeing if he could trail the son of a bitch. Right now the bastard had left himself outside the protection of the herd. Back there he was one of several hundred. Out here if Longarm encountered him he would know who the shooter was. Who, presumably, the murderer was too for Longarm could think of no reason why anyone other than the murdering rapist would want to keep Longarm from learning more about the girl's death.

Given a choice he would . . .

A wink of flame and a puff of smoke at the edge of his vision snapped Longarm's attention toward a spot some five hundred yards distant.

A good two or three seconds later he heard a slug spang off a rock on his right. The bullet went whining into the distance without coming closer than thirty, forty yards of Longarm.

A warning shot? Longarm frowned. So the SOB was out there. Watching. Waiting. Ready to take closer aim the next time?

Longarm considered himself duly warned.

On the other hand he was not one to back off of a situation just because somebody else did not like what he was doing.

Fuck this guy and the horse he rode in on. On second thought, he would leave that to poor, horny Harry. Longarm would settle for running the bastard down and putting some handcuffs on him and some questions to him.

Longarm kneed the bay into a canter. He headed straight for the spot where that second shot came from.

"Well, hell," Longarm muttered aloud.

So. Things were not always what they seemed. That was not, he knew, an original observation. But it damn sure was a true one.

In this case, learning a few more facts blew the shit out of his expectation that it was the murderer he was chasing and who shot at him in order to protect himself.

It looked instead like the reason for those gunshots had been to run him off from the body all right but not in order to protect the identity of the murderer. Rather it had been an effort to protect the peace and privacy of Blue Quail Singing.

The trail Longarm was following led straight to a cluster of tepees set in a small valley north of the burial site, and the man Longarm was trailing was the big, sulky Ute

40

with his hair wrapped in squirrel fur who had been with the group Longarm first saw standing over the dead girl. He recognized the fellow when the Indian came out into the open and rode into the village. At that point Longarm was about seventy-five yards behind him.

Longarm too rode into the middle of the village but he ignored the warrior with the gray fur braid wraps, heading instead for the lodge that stood at the center of the village.

A scalp pole was planted in front of that tepee. And not all the scalp locks displayed there were made of black hair. One was blond and another a light, reddish brown. Longarm had never asked but those scalps probably came from the Pueblo massacre. He knew Iron Ax had participated in that Christmas slaughter. Now of course Iron Ax claimed to be thoroughly reformed. And indeed he had always been both fair and friendly when Longarm dealt with him in the past.

Longarm dismounted and handed his reins to a young woman who hurried out of a nearby lodge and came running.

Longarm stood for a moment facing Iron Ax's tall and gaudily decorated tepee. Soon the old warrior stepped outside, fumbling to fasten the thong that held his breechclout around his hips. Longarm wondered what he'd disrupted in there. A little afternoon dingle dipping perhaps. There was gray in Iron Ax's hair but that didn't necessarily mean there was no sap in his tree.

"Long Arm," the chief of the band said by way of greeting.

"Iron Ax," Longarm responded. "It is good to see you again."

Iron Ax grunted. "Welcome to my lodge, Long Arm. Bear Killer told me you were here. I have been expecting you. Come in. Eat with me."

"Thank you, old friend. I will be honored to share your meal." He would also be in deep shit if he didn't, Longarm knew. To refuse the offer would insult Iron Ax. Not a good idea.

Longarm gave no more heed to his horse nor to the

Winchester carbine in the saddle scabbard. Nothing on the horse would be disturbed. Not that a Ute would not steal from him. Pretty much any one of them would be delighted to rob him blind and then laugh when they bragged to him about it afterward. But that would not happen while he was a guest in their village.

Longarm ducked low to pass through the open flap at the tepee entrance, then passed carefully around the fire to the honored spot beside Iron Ax.

A pot of aromatic stew simmered over the fire. Sitting cross-legged on a pile of buffalo robes at the back of the lodge was an extraordinarily pretty girl of fifteen or so. The laces of her doeskin dress were undone and from the way she was sitting Longarm could see all too clearly that she was not wearing anything under it.

An older and rather homely wife squatted off to the side.

Longarm had no difficulty figuring out which one of the females Iron Ax had been playing with when Longarm's arrival put a halt to the pre-dinner fun.

"Sit, Long Arm. Eat. We will talk later."

"Yes. Thank you."

The stew—he could tell from the bones that the meat consisted of ground squirrels, the little burrowing varmints that most whites referred to as prairie dogs even though they weren't—was as tasty as it smelled.

Chapter 10

The social amenities were properly observed. Iron Ax ate with his honored guest, both of them gorging in silence until their bellies ached. They belched and scratched their crotches and passed wind. They smoked, the taste sharp and biting and unpleasant—kinnikinnick instead of tobacco, which was probably a none too subtle suggestion that Longarm come up with a gift of tobacco—then belched and farted some more. By that time it was fully dark outside, and a council fire had been lighted on the open ground before Iron Ax's scalp pole.

With Iron Ax leading the way, Longarm went out and took a seat on an antelope skin laid out immediately to the right of the chief's softer and more comfortable buffalo robe.

The night was already chilly and getting quickly colder, and Longarm wished he'd thought to fetch his coat. It was rolled up and tied behind his saddle. Wherever the hell that was. He knew better than to go wandering off looking for it.

Younger warriors, Bear Killer among them, began drifting along to the circle around the fire, each of them bringing a robe or wicker seatback. Longarm recognized the few who had been there the day Blue Quail Singing was found. The others were mostly strangers to him although several faces seemed familiar from the last time he had visited with Iron Ax's band.

Iron Ax was in no great hurry to begin the proceedings.

He said something over his shoulder, and his aging wife quickly came forward with a blanket to drape around his shoulders. The young girl from the chief's lodge dashed back inside the tepee and soon emerged with another blanket that she arranged carefully over Longarm's back and shoulders. The heavy woolen blanket felt good against the growing cold of the night.

He hadn't particularly noticed until then, but apparently the whole village had gathered, young and old alike, to watch from just outside the ring of flickering, dancing fire light. Bright eyes gleamed and even though there must have been two dozen small children among them, Longarm did not hear a whisper or a whimper out of them. All remained ghostly silent and properly respectful, waiting to see what the men and this odd white stranger had to say.

Eventually Iron Ax opened the council discussion by producing a long pipe, much more ornate than the one they'd shared after supper, and lighting it from the flames of the ceremonial fire.

Iron Ax puffed a little, spoke a little, puffed some more. Longarm was fairly sure he wasn't missing anything by not knowing the language. When Iron Ax decided he'd spoken enough for the moment he puffed on the pipe again and passed it to Longarm.

Longarm very solemnly smoked for a good four or five minutes—tobacco this time not kinnikinnick—his expression closed and serious. After a bit he blew smoke in the four prime directions, held the pipe up to the sky and mumbled some very carefully incomprehensible mumbo jumbo beneath his breath. The idea wasn't really to say anything; it was to be seen as taking this whole thing quite seriously. And he could do that.

Finished, he passed the pipe on to the dark-skinned, elderly warrior beside him.

And so it went, all the way around the ring until everyone had had an opportunity to speak.

It was a good thing they'd all already eaten because by the time the pipe returned to Iron Ax's hands they had to have been at it for several hours. Longarm was deeply grateful for the blanket over his shoulders because by then the night air was crisp and cold and carried the scent of snow despite the lateness of the season.

No one seemed to actually give any reports to the chief—unless the information was conveyed during the pipe-smoking comments—but when Iron Ax finally put the pipe away and got down to business he already had a good grasp on the events that brought Longarm to his doorstep . . . well, sort of. Flapstep? To his lodge then.

"Our brother Long Arm is a welcome guest," Iron Ax assured Longarm. Or maybe reminded the warriors. Long-arm couldn't swear to which. "Long Arm has always been a friend to The Real People. Long Arm's heart is good and his tongue is straight. The Real People have known this many years now. Long Arm has no need to fear any member of this tribe. This is so. Yes."

Again Longarm wouldn't have placed any bets on whether he was the target of the comments or if the chief wanted to remind some of his more hot-blooded warriors.

"A shot was fired this day. This is true."

Longarm nodded agreement but did not speak. It would have been rude of him to interrupt.

"No shot was aimed at our brother Long Arm. The man who fired this shot did not mean to harm. He meant only for the one who visited the death place to know he should not take from the one who was no longer there. Long Arm is our brother. No man here would say otherwise. No one fired a bullet at our brother. No man will. This Long Arm should know. This is true. Waugh!"

Iron Ax clamped his jaw closed and stared into the fire.

Me next? Longarm wondered. He waited for a bit, the silence not at all uncomfortable as there was never a rush at a council fire, but they seemed to be waiting for him to speak.

"I am honored to be called the brother of Iron Ax and his people," he said eventually. He wished he had a drink. Or a cigar. Or a drink and a cigar. That sort of thing would have to come later though.

"I am pleased to know the truth of what this day saw. I have no hardness in my heart for one who would guard his sister who is no more. I went there to know more about the things that took place on the day she was taken from her people. I have promised to find the one who killed her. This I will do no matter how long the trail I must follow. This I will do even if it takes me years. I will not forget. I have said what I will do. That promise will not be forgotten."

He decided that was enough for the moment. He shut up and tried to look solemn and dignified, which is not something a white man can easily do when he is sitting cross-legged on an antelope skin with a trade blanket wrapped around him.

After a couple minutes the warrior with the squirrel fur in his hair spoke. If the fellow had any English he did not choose to show it. He spoke in the guttural, choppy cadences of the Ute tongue.

The others listened—there was never a rush to speak at a council—and after more silence there were more comments. In Ute. No one offered to translate. Longarm supposed—hoped—if there was anything he needed to know he would be tipped to it afterward either by Iron Ax or Bear Killer.

Along about midnight, after most of the children had melted away into the darkness and the fire was being allowed to die down, the pipe was brought out again. Longarm assumed, correctly as it turned out, that the council was ending.

About damn time too. Maybe the Indians were accustomed to sitting like this for extended periods, but Longarm's legs had gone to sleep several hours back and hadn't been heard from since. When he was finally able to extend them from the cramped position he'd been in for so long they itched and tingled until he thought he couldn't stand it, and he knew better than to try to stand on them right away.

He was the last one to get up from the fire. Only because he couldn't get up any quicker. Iron Ax had already gone back into his lodge, and the other men were dispersing to their own tepees.

Longarm wasn't sure if he should go looking for his horse and gear or exactly what. That problem was solved when the young girl from Iron Ax's lodge appeared at his side. He thought at first she was there to collect the blanket he'd been wearing. Instead she'd come to collect him.

"Come," she said, her accent thick but the English more than passably understandable.

She smiled and tugged at his shirt sleeve, leading him in the direction of Iron Ax's lodge and the promise of warmth there.

Longarm had no objection to being led around by a pretty girl. That was something he didn't generally mind anyway. He smiled back at her and followed.

Chapter 11

Iron Ax was already snoring, his old wife at his side. The woman was not asleep. Longarm could see the gleam of her eyes in the faint, red light given off by the coals of the lodge fire. She said nothing though and did not move although she seemed not to mind that Longarm knew she was awake for she made no effort to hood her eyes or draw the lids nearly closed.

The girl led Longarm to a newly laid bed on the side of the lodge. It was tall and fluffy and smelled of fresh pine boughs. Several tawny lion skins were laid over the pine clusters, and a heavy buffalo robe was partially folded back to indicate what would serve as the top covering. A leather sack about the size of a cottontail rabbit and filled almost to bursting was laid there to serve as a pillow.

There was, he noticed, no bed made for the girl.

She took the blanket off his shoulders, folded it and laid it aside, then began unfastening his buttons and buckles.

Indians generally sleep naked, Longarm knew, so the girl's attentions did not necessarily mean anything beyond the fact that she was getting him ready for bed.

Once he was standing there wearing nothing but a blush the girl whispered something in the Ute language, her eyes wide when she saw the size of his pecker, which was, he would have conceded, showing off despite his wishes to the contrary. Hell, this girl wasn't old enough to be making the beast with two backs. Or anyway shouldn't have been. What Iron Ax did with her was his business, not Longarm's.

She contrived to turn him so his pecker was where the old woman could see too. The girl said something else, and Longarm couldn't be sure, but he thought he heard a low chuckle from Iron Ax's bed. The damn girl wasn't making this easy for him.

Just as matter-of-fact as if it were the most natural thing possible—and come to think of it, it probably was so far as she was concerned—she slipped out of her clothes too and knelt on the bed to hold the buffalo robe ready for him to crawl under. Once he was there she joined him, snuggling in close beside him with her face against his throat. Her breath was warm on his skin.

Her nipples went past warm. They burned into his skin, warm and hard with arousal.

Longarm swallowed and fought off an impulse to take her.

She was pretty enough, Lord knew. Young and slim, with a shapely body. Conical tits and a flat belly. She was a little long waisted, with legs slightly too short for her and thighs that were perhaps a little too heavy. Give her ten years and a dozen kids and she would have an ass like a washtub. But that would be then. This was now. And now she was almighty pretty.

Her hand crept between their bodies, and her fingers encircled his cock.

Longarm pushed her hand away and shook his head. Fifteen years old, fourteen maybe . . . a grown man just doesn't go around fucking children.

She said something in her own language, paused and thought for a moment then asked, "No want?"

"Yes want," he admitted. "Too young. You are too young."

"Twenny year too young?" she asked.

"Twenty?"

"Twenny," she repeated.

"You can't be."

She smiled. And took hold of his cock again.

Longarm groaned. And reached for her.

She acted like she'd never been kissed before. Come to think of it, he realized, maybe she hadn't been. She'd been fucked but quite possibly never kissed.

That was all right. He didn't mind teaching her.

Her breasts were firm little mounds, the nipples tiny and hard, like a pair of dark raisins perched on little tea saucers. Longarm licked them for a while. The girl, getting into the spirit of the game, licked his in turn, and Longarm was sure he could feel his toes curl. Damn, that felt good.

She teased his balls for a while, then became impatient with all the white man's foreplay and rolled onto her back, grabbing his cock and tugging on it. She wasn't exactly subtle, but he did not hold that against her.

Longarm rolled on top of her, and she spread her legs wide to admit him. When he entered her she gasped from the size of it even though she was already wet and ready to receive him.

She wrapped herself around him with her legs and her arms alike and clung to him, thrusting her hips up to meet each downward thrust of Longarm's body.

Her breath became very quickly ragged and quick, and he could feel the lips of her pussy contract tight around him each time he drove into her.

She said something into his ear and whimpered a little as her slender body was wracked with wave after wave of spasms.

Feeling her release was enough to send Longarm over the edge too, and he battered her belly with his own in a series of frantic thrusts until his seed shot hot and deep into the girl's body. He gasped, emptying himself into her, then collapsed on top of her, she hanging onto him and taking his weight onto herself.

From several feet away Longarm heard the old woman say something, and the girl answered with a laugh and a hug around Longarm's neck.

For just a minute there he had purely forgotten that

there was a spectator with them in the lodge. Not that he was complaining.

He kissed the girl and reached between them to stroke her breasts and tweak her nipples. Then, his cock still lying wet and limp inside her, he began to grow hard again.

"D'you know what the word *seconds* means? No?" He grinned. "Here. Let me teach you."

Chapter 12

Longarm woke to the feel of the girl's hands on him and a faint, gray glimmer of impending daylight above the smoke flaps in old Iron Ax's lodge.

"Can you say 'fourths'?" he asked.

"Fors."

"Close enough." He kissed her and let benevolent nature take its course. A little while later he pushed the buffalo robe back, exposing his skin to the morning chill. The cold was invigorating after his deep sleep and delightful wake-up. Longarm yawned and sat upright.

"Good morning, yes, Long Arm." Iron Ax and his older wife were already awake too, the woman kneeling beside last night's coals, busy stirring up fresh fire there, while Iron Ax perched like a pile of dark tanned and deeply wrinkled leather on the edge of his pallet. "Your night was good, yes?"

"My night was very good, yes. Thank you."

The old man nodded solemnly, his face impassive. But Longarm thought he detected a hint of twinkle in the chief's dark eyes. He obviously had been awake and watching while Longarm was rutting on top of Iron Ax's younger wife.

None of the Utes seemed to mind this, so Longarm saw no reason why he should mind it either.

And the girl was really very good. Tight and active.

Poor Harry, Longarm thought. If only he'd known

what he was missing. He likely would've keeled over from the force of sheer jealousy.

Longarm leaned over onto one cheek and ripped off a real rip-snorter of a fart, then nodded his thanks to Iron Ax. He stood, pulled on his trousers and followed Iron Ax outside and on to the edge of camp so they could take care of their morning evacuations. Half the men in the band were similarly occupied. The women apparently did their business on the other side of the camp.

By the time Longarm and Iron Ax returned to the chief's lodge, the women had breakfast ready.

Longarm was amused to note that, now that the needs of the honored guest were all met, the younger wife gave her attention to Iron Ax while it was the older woman who attended to Longarm. He smiled inwardly, grateful as hell that it was the young one who'd come into his bed last night.

"Iron Ax, it is true that we are friends, yes?"

"This is a true thing, Long Arm."

"May I ask my friend a question?"

Iron Ax nodded.

"I would know the name of your wife if I may," Longarm said.

"My wife she is Autumn Three Seeds."

That, Longarm dimly remembered, was the name of the old wife, not the young one.

Again he was pretty sure he saw a twinkle in Iron Ax's eyes although the old chief's expression remained stonily impassive. The old bastard knew good and well what Longarm wanted to know, and he was just perverse enough that he wasn't going to say.

No harm done, of course. Longarm smiled and nodded his acceptance of the chief's wishes.

When Longarm walked outside again after breakfast his horse, already saddled, stood there, a small boy holding onto its reins.

Longarm opened his saddlebags and brought out all the tobacco and matches he had with him. He went back into Iron Ax's lodge and presented the items to his host, then returned to the bay horse and mounted. Iron Ax followed him outside.

"Iron Ax, my friend."

"Yes, Long Arm?"

"Tell your young men I will now return to the place where your sister's spirit left the earth to fly up. I will look so I know for sure the cause of her death. If any warrior among your people wishes to shoot at me, let him do it now and save us all some trouble."

"No one of my people will shoot at you, Long Arm. No warrior here will follow you."

Longarm nodded. "I thank you for your hospitality, Iron Ax. You are a true friend. The Great Father in Washington will know of your friendship."

The dancing light returned to Iron Ax's eyes. "He will know every thing of your visit, Long Arm?"

Longarm grinned. "Every part of it that's important, friend."

Iron Ax chuckled, then turned and went back inside his lodge.

The young wife, whose name Longarm still did not know, stood waiting there for him. She was fingering the strings that held her dress closed and was smiling a welcome to her husband and master.

The old bastard didn't have it too awful bad here, Longarm thought. Savage or no, he did have a few comforts.

Longarm was smiling as he headed back toward the ridge where Blue Quail Singing was laid out in the bright sunshine and bone dry mountain air.

Chapter 13

There was no body!

Sometime during the night some son of a bitch had stolen Blue Quail Singing's body. The flimsy platform was empty when Longarm reached it. Even the covering robe had been taken.

Longarm cussed and snarled, but that accomplished just what he expected it to, which was nothing. Well, nothing except to allow him to vent his spleen a little.

Damn it all anyway though.

Who the hell would take a body? And why?

The answers to those questions seemed plain enough on the surface of things. Only the murderer was apt to want the body hidden so as to avoid closer inspection. But why *now,* dammit? The dead girl lay here for days, undisturbed except by the magpies, until Longarm came along yesterday.

Now all of a sudden she was gone. Carried off to . . . where?

He tied his horse well away from the burial scaffold and examined first his own horse's hoofprints so he would recognize them again—he knew a deputy, a good one nowadays, who when he was new to the game once found a trail and tracked himself all the way back to the county seat he came from—then Longarm walked back to the platform and looked for sign.

Unfortunately the ground was too hard to take much of a track to begin with and it had been pretty thoroughly churned up anyway by the Indians who buried the girl there, then again by Longarm when he first visited the site and finally was disturbed again by whoever it was who took the body.

Longarm shook his head in frustration, but there was little more he could do here. If he knew where the body was taken . . .

But he didn't. And he wasn't very likely to either. He couldn't track whoever stole it. Not with this mess to work from. Nor was he likely to find it any other way.

The murderer had an entire mountain range to hide a body in, and Longarm could spend the next eight or ten years searching for Blue Quail Singing and still probably not find her mortal remains. The body could be stuffed into any crack or crevice, buried deep or simply covered over with rocks. It could be, and in fact probably was, miles away by now, in any direction at all.

Of course he'd already gotten a fairly good look at the girl. There were no bullet holes in her. The skull was intact. He knew that much from yesterday, and the first time he saw her he'd noted there was blood on her thighs suggesting that she was raped. Her neck had been broken and so was the presumptive cause of death.

But, dammit, he did not really know that, did he? Not without finishing his examination.

He sighed and reached for a cheroot. And then remembered too damned late that he'd given everything to Iron Ax and all his matches too.

Fine though this day had started out to be, it was not going particularly well now. And Longarm was running out of time to solve the murder.

For a moment Longarm considered getting Harry and hightailing it down to Colorado City so he could wire a request for assistance from the army. The presence of a troop of cavalry would put a halt to any danger that the Utes might elect to start a war over this.

But would the army be willing—or for that matter be able—to send in the cavalry in time to avoid bloodshed?

Probably not, he answered his own question. It would

take too much time for him to get down to a telegraph key. More time for his message to be considered by the U.S. Army's entire damn chain of command. Still more time for orders to be issued and logistics worked out and a force to be assembled. Plus there would be the travel time involved from wherever the troops were billeted in order to get them up here.

No, that was not a realistic option. The army could get here, sure. They just could not do it soon enough to thwart a breakout.

They could clean up afterward, but they could not keep it from happening in the first place. In order for that to be done, Longarm was going to have to do it himself. Somehow.

He was not yet desperate but he was damn sure dejected when he returned to the bay horse and settled into his saddle.

He followed the slope down to the creek and turned upstream toward the nameless mining camp. He hadn't yet reached the limits of Harry Baynard's "jail" when the excitable thief came running to meet him shouting something that Longarm could not make out until Harry came close.

"Thank goodness you finally came back," Harry said, panting and grabbing hold of Longarm's stirrup strap.

"What's the matter now?"

"There's . . . there's . . . ," Harry paused to gulp some air, "there's been a murder, that's what."

"Another one?"

"Y-yes. 'Nuther one."

"Shit!" Longarm prodded the bay into a lope, leaving Harry behind, standing doubled over with his hands on his knees and his head hanging while he tried to recover his breath.

Chapter 14

The big Vermonter Charles Whelan met Longarm outside Jerry Markley's saloon and crooked his finger, beckoning Longarm to follow him. Whelan led the way on foot, traveling upstream to the edge of the town.

A cluster of men was gathered there, surrounding a figure lying stretched out on the gravel of the creek bank. More were streaming down off the hill or trudging along the creek to join the throng. Pretty soon the whole camp would be there with the body.

Longarm dismounted and pushed through them so he could see who the dead man was.

He recognized the corpse although it took him a moment to bring the man's name back to mind. Longarm had spoken with him but not for very long. He hadn't seemed particularly bright. "Fargo, right?"

"That's him," someone said. "Fordyce Emmanuel Fargo."

Longarm gave the fellow a questioning look.

"Hey, I didn't know him all that well, but he used to say his name . . . the whole thing, just like that . . . whenever he got drunk."

"We've all heard him do that, Marshal."

Ford was—had been, rather—a wizened little fellow who seldom bathed and washed his clothes even less often. One of his peculiarities—there were others—was that instead of removing a garment when he got a new one, he just wore the new one over top of the old. He looked something like a walking ragbag and smelled like something you might find floating in a gutter. Longarm had not pursued his conversation with Fargo to any depth the one time he'd spoken with the man, although he might have lasted a little longer had he been standing upwind at the time.

"His clothes are damp. Anyone know why?" Longarm asked.

"He was in the crick when we found him."

"Facedown?" Longarm was thinking it entirely possible that Fargo was drunk, fell and drowned by accident.

"Faceup," came the answer.

Giving in to the inevitable, Longarm knelt beside the body and fingered the back of Fargo's head. There were no lumps or depressions to suggest he'd hit his head by accident. Or been whacked on it by someone else.

Fargo's spade beard covered the upper half of his chest. Longarm had to lift the greasy hair and comb his hands through it in order to get down to where he could see skin. "Looks like he might've been strangled. There's some bruises. I don't think it's what killed him though," he added, feeling the Adam's apple and hard cartilage of the throat. "His windpipe wasn't crushed."

"D'you think a knife wound coulda killed him?" a man in the crowd asked. Barney something. Longarm couldn't remember Barney's last name.

"Yes, Barney, I would say a knife could kill most anybody. Why d'you ask?"

"Cause when we dragged him outta the water he was bleedin' from the chest an' belly, that's why."

Feeling more than a little chagrined, Longarm tried unbuttoning the many layers of Fargo's clothing. After a few moments he said the hell with that and used his knife to slit the shirts and underthings open up the front.

His hands felt dirty, as if he might have lice on them from touching Fargo's beard and clothes. Come to think of it, maybe he did. He went over to the creek and washed as best he could before returning to the body.

Using the tip of his knife blade to shove the ragged

shirts apart, he got a look at Fargo's torso. The dead flesh had the yellowish color and waxy texture of a corpse taken from a watery grave before there was time for decomposition to set in.

Standing starkly plain against the pale flesh were four, no, five—he almost missed that one down by the belly button—stab wounds. There was no sign of blood on them now, that having been washed away.

"I thought you said there was blood when you pulled him out?" Longarm asked.

"That's right."

"Then how come I don't see any now?"

"We kinda . . . it was messy. You know? And some of the boys is a little squeamish."

"What'd you do, wash him off?"

"Not exactly. We, uh, we kinda dunked him a couple times. You know. To wash the mess off. Then we drug him the rest o' the way onto the bank."

Longarm supposed it hadn't really mattered. Blood or no blood to verify the fact, any one of at least three of those stab wounds could have killed him.

"What's your considered opinion here, Marshal?"

"I'd say the man is dead," Longarm told them.

The one who had just spoken looked at Whelan and said, "Lucky we got a professional here, isn't it, Charlie? I tell you, he don't hardly miss a thing."

Longarm grinned at him, and the fellow smiled back.

"You ain't touchy, I can say that for you."

"Hell, William, I can't argue with the simple truth," Longarm said. "So now let me ask you boys to do the rest of my work here too. Does anybody know who did this? Or why?"

"Can't tell you for certain sure about the 'why' part, Marshal, but it's pretty sure we know who."

"And maybe why," another man added.

"Go on. I'm not contradicting you. Not yet."

"Ford was drinking last night."

"Shit," somebody else cut in, "Ford was drinking every night."

The speaker shrugged, then continued, "Him and Earl Shiver tied it on pretty tight. Singing. Declaring they was partners for life. Share and share alike. That sorta shit."

"That sounds innocent enough," Longarm said.

"So it was, I s'pose, but then Ford got to needling Earl about him being such a horny son of a bitch, alla time thinking about pussy. Which he was. That Earl, he claimed he had a dong a foot long. Not that I ever looked to see, mind you, but he was alla time bragging about his damn dick."

"And moaning how it needed a workout," another man said.

"So last night Ford got to telling Earl that he . . . Ford, I mean . . . bet Earl was the one that tore off a chunk of that red meat. The Injun girl that turned up dead is what I took that to mean though I never heard Ford come right out and say that.

"Anyway Earl, he got pretty upset about that. Which struck Ford funny, so he repeated it. An' repeated it some more, like drunks will do.

"Then Earl got really pissed and told Ford to shut up, that somebody might overhear. Which we pretty much all of us did, of course. Ford talked loud when he was drunk, and last night he was even louder than usual. Earl didn't like that. He didn't want nobody pointing a finger his way. I think he was scared you, or somebody, would turn him over to those damn Injuns."

"Is he the one who did the Indian girl?" Longarm asked.

"Damn if I know. You, Billy? Tom? Leroy?"

If any of the miners knew if Earl Shiver was Blue Quail Singing's murderer they were not willing to say so now.

"Did anyone actually see Earl knife Fargo?"

No one had.

"But they was arguing plenty fierce when they left off drinking and headed up the crick here."

"Where does Earl live?" Longarm asked.

"Up yonder about a quarter mile, but you won't find him there."

"No?"

"I just come past there, Marshal. Earl's gone. Took his mule and all his gear, even stripped the canvas off that he was using for a roof. He walked away and left his claim behind."

"Ran is more like it," somebody else injected.

"Running for his life," another said.

Longarm shook his head. Murderers were so fucking stupid. "Earl should've thought of all that before he stuck a knife between Ford Fargo's ribs."

"You going after him, Marshal?"

"What do you think?"

"But what about them Injuns? They could come down on us soon as your back is turned."

"No, I'll send word to them where I've gone. And why." He looked around. "Harry. I want you to deliver a message for me."

"Me? Jeez, Long, I'm not carrying no note to a bunch of damn Indians."

"Sure you are, Harry. Except you won't be taking a note exactly. Nobody in that camp can read. So I want you to memorize what I want said and tell that to Bear Killer and Iron Ax."

"Iron Ax? Jesus God, Long, Iron Ax is a murderer his own self."

"So is Bear Killer if you want to look at it that way, but both of them know you're riding with me. They don't have to know why. They won't lift your scalp." Longarm hesitated just for a moment and with a wink and a sly smile said, "Prob'ly."

"Long!"

"I tell you what, Harry. You tell Iron Ax that Long Arm would appreciate it if he was to treat you as an honored guest. Say that an' you won't regret going." He was thinking about that second wife of Iron Ax's, wishing he had time to deliver the message himself, actually.

"Now come along. We got to get your horse and gear.

And listen close while I tell you where to find Iron Ax's camp and what I want you to say when you get there."

Harry did not look like a happy man, but like a man walking to the gallows for his own hanging he dutifully followed Longarm back to where he'd left his gear.

Chapter 15

Ford Fargo had been dead for at least twelve hours, Long-arm figured, regardless of the miners' claims that he was bleeding when they pulled the body out of the water. Dead men, of course, do not bleed, and Fargo was dead long before he was found.

What Longarm suspected was that congealed blood had pooled near the wounds despite the influence of the water—in fact the icy creek water might have contributed to the almost instant coagulation—then was washed away when the body was removed from the water. What the miners observed would have been that and not, as they believed, fresh bleeding.

In any event, Longarm's point was that Fargo was killed sometime during the night. It was now the middle of the following day, and Earl Shiver had had that long in order to make his escape.

There were, as he recalled, three hundred sixty points on a compass. Shiver could have run in the direction of any one of them.

The question was . . . which one and only one had he taken.

Tracking the man was not an option. It simply could not be done. A man would have to be deliberately trying if he wanted to leave any sort of trail across the hard, rocky, gravel-strewn ground here. Shiver was on foot according to the miners, accompanied by a pack mule. The mule might, just might leave a scrape or mark on the ground when it passed but nowhere except perhaps on the damp fringes of the creek bed would either man or beast leave an actual footprint.

Longarm knew he would need more than tracking skills if he wanted to find Earl Shiver and bring the man to justice. He hated having to delay the start of his pursuit but better a slow and deliberate chase in the right direction than a full gallop down the wrong trail.

He rode upstream to the shack where Earl Shiver had lived and spent a few minutes there familiarizing himself with the sharp and rather pointed hoofprints of Shiver's mule, then approached the man's nearest neighbors. Well, the nearest living ones anyway; Fargo had occupied the placer claim closest to Shiver's.

"Sure, Marshal. I'd say I know Earl about as good as anybody around here. We've shared many a pipe an' a good many pints too," said a middle-aged gent with streaks of gray in his beard and around his ears. The neighbor's name was Thomas Viele. He'd been knee deep in the cold water when Longarm stopped to talk with him.

Longarm dismounted and gave the bay a slack rein so it could crop at the few sprigs of grass underfoot.

Viele waded onto the bank, water dripping off his legs and arms. He had a pan full of gravel that he set carefully aside before giving his full attention to Longarm. "What d'you want to know about the man?"

"You heard what happened last night, I suppose," Longarm said.

Viele nodded. "It's a terrible thing, the taking of a man's life."

"I'll be going after Shiver for the murder of Ford Fargo," Longarm said. "I suppose you know that too."

"Yes, of course. It's the right thing t' do. I like Earl well enough, understand, but wrong is wrong, and what he done to Fordyce can't be allowed t' stand."

"No, sir, it can't. What I need from you, Thomas, is any information you have about Shiver. You, uh, didn't happen to see him leave, did you?"

"Nope. Last night I sat outside for a spell after supper.

65

Smoked a pipe and watched the stars for a bit until it got too cold. Then I come inside and went to bed. I never saw when Earl came back. Heard his mule squeal a couple times. That could've been when he was packing up getting ready to pull out, but I don't know that for sure. Don't know which way he went neither, which is what I suppose you'd most like t' know."

"Yes, sir, I surely would."

"Marshal, I'd be pleased t' help you if I could, but like I said, I never saw nor heard anything that'd help."

"What about Shiver as a man?" Longarm asked.

"I don't know what it is you're asking."

"Where did Shiver come from? Do you know that?"

"Now that much I can tell you, for we talked a fair amount, Earl and me. He was from Georgia. Savannah originally. Then he got the gold fever and went to Dahlonega. Learned a little about gold and came out here three, four years back. Like all of us he believed he'd hit the mother lode." Viele gave Longarm a sad smile. "Like all of us he hasn't found it. But we keep on looking, don't we? Break our backs lifting gravel, ruin our joints with the rheumatiz standing in freezing cold water day after day, live hand-to-mouth 'cause we got no wage to count on. I'll tell you a truth, Marshal, if I didn't love the thrill of it all s' damn much, looking for a surface vein to follow or a pigeon egg free nugget, if I didn't have those things to look for and think I have as good a chance of finding as any-damn-body, Marshal, without those things in the back of my mind I expect that I couldn't hardly stand this life chasing gold."

Longarm laughed. Then asked, "How would you judge Shiver as a prospector then? Not a miner, mind you, but a prospector out looking for it?"

"All on his own, you mean?"

Longarm nodded.

"Earl's no woodsman. He grew up in the city. I'd say he's the sort who will follow the strikes that others make, but he wouldn't be one for going out on his own to look for placer gold. And if the truth be told I don't think he would know how to recognize hard rock ore even if he stumbled across some."

"Would you say he's a dangerous man?"

"Fargo damn sure woulda said so, wouldn't he?" Viele countered. "But to answer your question, Marshal, I suppose any man will be dangerous if you press him."

"Shiver own any guns that you know of?"

"I know he has a pistol. I've seen it. He carries it in his pocket sometimes. And he's a good shot with it. I've seen him knock jays out of the trees, but I doubt he's ever killed a man or anything like that. He certainly never mentioned anything like that when we was talking."

"Mr. Viele, you've been a tremendous help to me. Thank you."

"I have?" Viele asked in a mildly disbelieving voice.

"Oh, yes. You've told me where I should look for your friend Earl. That's more than I could've asked for."

"Well, I'll be damned."

Longarm shook the man's hand, then stepped back into the saddle. He reined the horse downstream and headed back through the camp with no name and on toward the road he and Harry were following before they stumbled into this mess.

He was all the way out of the nameless drainage when he realized he had forgotten to replace the tobacco and matches that he'd given to Iron Ax. He scowled and hoped Earl Shiver's lead was not insurmountable, damn him.

Chapter 16

Longarm pushed the horse. Hard. A horse can be replaced; a human life cannot. And his concern here went much deeper than Ford Fargo and Earl Shiver. Back up in those mountains there were scores of white miners and dozens of Indian warriors, and if Longarm could not find justice for the killer of Blue Quail Singing there was going to be a helluva lot more blood spilled than was shed already.

Nightfall found him on the rough, winding road that linked the South Park mining camps with Colorado City, Manitou and the upstart new town that catered to wealthy nobs from back east Colorado Springs.

With any kind of luck, Longarm thought, sheer force of habit would prompt Shiver to stop and make camp rather than travel in the dark. Longarm figured he could pick up time on the man, perhaps even jump ahead of him, by continuing down as hard as he could press the tired horse.

He might even be lucky enough to stumble over Shiver's campsite. But he was not going to count on that. Not damn likely.

The moon would not rise until ten or eleven if he remembered correctly. Until then all he could do was give the horse its head and ride hard.

The road trended sharply downhill, rising and falling in places but steadily falling overall. That was not an unalloyed blessing. Running downhill requires less energy than moving on the flat or uphill, but it is hell on the legs, the knee joints in particular, plus momentum and stony, uneven footing vastly increase the dangers of a fall.

Twice Longarm thought he was going to end up trapped underneath the horse. Frequently it stumbled, which was only to be expected, but twice it lost its balance and thrashed its head in frantic efforts to recover.

Both times it managed to regain its equilibrium and avoid disaster. Longarm hadn't given the animal credit for its abilities before. Now he came to admire it. It had heart by the bucketful. A man could not ask better than that in any animal.

The first rose-hued hints of dawn streaked the eastern sky to light Longarm's way down the steep incline that descended into the slender canyon that protected the town of Manitou and the springs that were still held sacred by the Indian tribes.

The bay horse was exhausted. It had every right to be, Longarm thought. It had given him one hell of a ride in the past twenty-four hours, spending most of that time in motion, from Iron Ax's camp the previous dawn and now all the way down into the gateway to the plains.

A limping, painful walk was the best the bay could manage. But it never once offered to quit under him, and he did not at all doubt that if he put the spurs to it now it would run until its great heart burst.

He reined the animal to a halt outside a small café that showed lamplight in its windows. The horse stood with its head down, nostrils flared as it sucked wind, flanks trembling with fatigue.

Longarm patted its neck and rubbed its poll when he dismounted. He did not ordinarily bother with such gestures, but this horse had earned some gratitude. He tied the reins to a rail—probably unnecessarily since it was not likely the horse would be moving another step unless it had to—and went inside, taking off his hat as he stepped through the doorway and entered a room that smelled of coffee and frying bacon. His mouth began to water at the scents of civilized cooking.

After being out so long it felt a little odd to him to be standing under a roof now. He hadn't been inside a proper building in several weeks. Thanks to that dang Harry Baynard.

Still, if it weren't for him being up there with Harry there probably would already be a state of war between Iron Ax's Utes and the placer miners. So it was not an entirely bad thing that he'd been there.

"Good morning, sir. What would you like today?" The waitress was a young woman, Longarm guessed in her early twenties, with blond hair done up in a tight bun. She wore an apron that at this early hour was clean and still stiff from the influences of starch and a sadiron. She was not pretty but she had a welcoming smile.

"I'm afraid all I have time for right now, miss, is a question."

"Very well. I shall help you if I can."

Longarm suspected that there were a number of ways she could help if she were inclined to do so, but he didn't have any time for that. Unfortunately. The face was not all that much, but she had an outstanding set of tits underneath the bib of that apron.

"I need t' know where I can find a stable, miss."

"We have a shed out back. You're welcome to use that if you like."

"That's nice of you, miss, and I thank you for the offer, but what I need is a public livery. I've gone and wore my horse out pretty thoroughly. I need to have somebody see to him and rent me another."

"I see. Very well then." She had dimples when she smiled, Longarm noticed. "You go down this street right here, down past the springs and then . . ."

Longarm was perishing for a cup of coffee, and some breakfast wouldn't have been hard to take either, but his needs could wait a little longer. The bay horse deserved better than to suffer any further due to his selfishness.

On the other hand it wouldn't hurt his feelings any if he found reason to come back this way when he had a little time on his hands. He smiled regretfully down at the waitress, then turned and stepped back out onto the board sidewalk.

"Come along, little fellow. Let's you and me find you a place to rest up."

Chapter 17

"This horse is in need of some extra good care," Longarm said when the bearded and rheumy-eyed hostler came yawning down from the loft. "He gave me everything he had this last day and night. I figure he deserves some pampering."

"Yeah, sure." The man used a fingernail—not a very clean one either—to probe for some scrap of something caught between two of his few remaining teeth.

"He's hot and bad tired," Longarm went on. "I want him watered . . . just a quart t' begin with though, no more . . . and given a thorough rubdown. Wash him off. Clean his feet. Then he can have free choice hay and a little more water. An' when that's done, not before, I wanted him grained. Give him a good hot feed mix. Lots of corn in it and bright oats. No mold nor dust. Got all that?"

"Sure, mister, I got it. That'll be twenty five cents."

"Mister, you haven't been listening. The kind of care I want this horse to have, you aren't gonna give for no quarter of a dollar. I want you to do him right, d'you hear me? Right. It's worth a dollar to me."

The livery man gave the bay a sneering look and said, "Mister, there's no damn horse worth a dollar a day for board."

Longarm paused. Then shook his head. "Thanks for warning me."

"What the hell is that s'posed to mean?"

"It means I wouldn't trust you to swamp a saloon floor nor empty the spittoons, much less to take care of a horse that's got more pride and decency in him than you'll ever in your life have." Longarm turned away and began to lead the bay away.

"Listen t' me, you son of a bitch. Why, you . . ."

It was as far as the hostler got. It wasn't only the horse that was tired. Longarm hadn't had any sleep in that time either, and his body too had been tested by the day and night of travel.

Before the livery man could finish his sentence he was staring into Longarm's cold, marble-hard eyes from very close range. Longarm had a fist bunched in the man's shirt at the throat and was lifting him onto tiptoes.

They stood like that, nose-to-nose, for several long moments before in a chillingly low voice Longarm asked, "What was it you was saying about me now?"

"N-n-nothing," the livery man sputtered. "I didn't mean . . . that is, I . . . n-nothing. Sir."

"I didn't think so, you miserable fucking weasel."

"Yes, sir, I . . . uh . . . yes, sir."

Longarm growled under his breath and let go of the man's shirt. He managed to rein in an impulse to give the SOB a shove. A rancid manure pile, much too long in place, was temptingly close behind him. Longarm felt downright proud of himself that he didn't send the asshole backpedaling into it.

Longarm led the horse outside into the morning sunlight and back up the street.

"You," he barked a couple minutes later.

"Me, sir?"

"You, sir."

The boy blinked. But then it was very likely that never before in his life had anyone called him "sir." Particularly anyone outside his own family and a total stranger at that. He looked to be twelve or thirteen years old.

"Are you on your way to school, son?"

"No, sir. School's not in session now."

"Do you have a job? Anything important to do today?"

The boy shook his head. He had a pug nose and freckles.

"Would you like a job?"

"Doing what, sir?"

"D'you know how to take good care of a horse?"

"That one?"

"Uh huh. This one."

"He looks tired."

"He is. And I want him to have special care because of it."

"I'd take care of him for you, mister. Good care too."

"I believe you, son, but here's what I need done for him." Longarm went through his list of demands and the order in which he wanted them done. "Can you handle that?"

"Yes, sir, I sure can. In fact I think I oughta walk him over to the creek and let him stand hock deep in the water to cool his joints. If it's all right with you, that is."

"I like that idea."

"The only thing is, mister, I don't have the hay and the grain you want for him."

"Do you know where you can get those things?"

"Oh, sure. I just, well . . ."

"You don't have any money to buy them, is that it?"

The boy grinned. "Yes, sir, I expect that it is."

"I'll tell you what then." Longarm dug into his pockets and brought out a tiny coin, considerably smaller than a dime, and handed it to the kid.

The boy's eyes went wide at the sight of the two-and-a-half-dollar gold quarter eagle.

"Buy the feed out of that, can you?"

"Sure, but what you want won't cost but maybe fifteen cents or so."

"I know that."

"You don't even know me."

"You look trustworthy to me." Longarm smiled. "Though from the way you talk I'm beginning to think you're trying to palaver your way right out of the job. And by the way, whatever is left over after you take care of what the horse needs is your pay for the job. If you still want the work, that is."

"Yes, *sir!*" The kid grabbed the bay's reins from Longarm's hand, his grin wider than ever. "My name is Will Grampion, sir, and I live right over there in that house with the flowerpots on the porch. We have a shed out back. That's where I'll keep the horse. You can check up on me any time, sir. I'll do a good job for you. Honest I will."

"I believe you, Will." Longarm stuck his hand out to shake with the boy, then introduced himself.

"I won't let you down, Mr. Long. I promise."

"I know you won't. Now if you'll excuse me, I need to go catch that trolley that I see coming."

A horse-drawn trolley ran on tracks from Colorado Springs through Colorado City to a terminus at Manitou. Now that he was back to the civilized world Longarm figured he was better off using that for transportation than trying to look after a horse anyway. If he did need a mount he could always rent another until the bay was thoroughly recovered from the workout he'd given it on the way down here.

Chapter 18

Now that he was here, Longarm's problem was that he didn't know if he was ahead of Earl Shiver or still trailing behind the murderer. If he had to guess he would tend to think he was ahead of the miner, that he'd passed the sleeping fugitive sometime during the night. But he did not know that for certain sure, dammit. Nor did he know where Shiver would go once he came down out of the pass. If he fled by way of the pass at all.

Longarm had a fair degree of confidence that Shiver would come this way. It was the shortest route to civilization. And if a man wants to hide he is a far sight better off trying to do it in a crowd than off by himself where he would stand out like a block of coal on a freshly fallen field of snow.

No, Longarm was betting Shiver came this way. Manitou here was the first town he would come to once he broke out of the confinement of the pass.

Would he stop here to get liquored up in relief at the thought that he still had his freedom? Or would he be smart enough to bypass Manitou for the much wilder gin mills and whorehouses—and the much larger transient population—of Colorado City. Strangers are far less noticeable in Colorado City than in Manitou.

On the other hand, Shiver might not know any of this.

In any event Colorado City seemed the better bet between the two, Longarm decided after mulling it over in silence.

Manitou was small and relatively quiet. Strangers would stand out more here. So would any loud revelry. A man could do things in Colorado City without drawing the least lick of attention to himself when those same things would land him in the pokey in Manitou. Anything short of an actual shooting probably wouldn't even be noticed down in Colorado City.

And there was no question at all in Longarm's mind that Shiver might be heading for Colorado Springs. That hoity-toity community didn't even allow saloons inside its established town limits. Plenty of churches but no booze. No booze, that is, out where it could be seen. Never mind what-all might take place behind closed doors there. Longarm had no illusions about that and frankly did not care. His interest at the moment lay with Earl Shiver, Iron Ax and those endangered miners who remained up in the Park.

Colorado City it would be then.

Longarm left the bay horse in young Will Grampion's care and walked over to flag down the trolley.

The driver slowed his car in response to Longarm's wave, applying the brake and at the same time easing back on the horses' lines. The heavy trolley was still rolling when Longarm grabbed the handrail and hopped onto the lowest step.

"Colorado City?" the driver asked as Longarm eyed the posted list of fares and dropped a coin into the box on the dashboard.

"How'd you guess that?"

"That belly gun. Men going heeled don't gener'ly ride to Colorado Springs. And they mostly dress better'n you too."

"I see." Longarm leaned against one of the vertical poles that allowed people to hold on where there was standing room in the car. "I don't suppose you've seen anything this morning of a gent just down from the mountains. Middlin' sized man wearing britches with the lower legs rubberized. Probably a checkered wool shirt. Green, I think. Carrying a bundle?"

Shiver could have gotten rid of his mule, for once he hit the towns the animal would only be a hindrance to him. It was entirely possible he would be riding the trolley now. Or that he would take a train to get even further away. Denver, Pueblo. Once he hit the main line there was no end to the places the man could flee.

"What for do you want to know?" the driver countered Longarm's question.

"I'm looking for him."

"Hell, mister, I ain't stupid. If you wasn't looking for him you wouldn't be asking me about him. What I'm asking you is, *why* d'you want to find this mining man? That is what he does, isn't it? Pants like those mean the man's a placer miner. Got no gold in the creeks around here, which means he's down from the diggings up South Park way. Now you think he's down here. Which is all well an' good as far as it goes, but I'll ask you again, exactly why is it you want to find this gent in a green shirt?"

"I'm a deputy United States marshal, and this fellow is suspected of murder. Worse than that, one of his murders could set off an Indian outbreak up there. I need to produce him to show the Utes they will receive the justice any man is entitled to."

"I see. You're a deputy marshal?"

Longarm nodded.

"And you say there's gonna be an outbreak if you don't find this fellow."

"That's right."

"Know what I have to say about all that? Firstly, I don't care if you call in the army and they kill off every stinking Injun in this state. Hell, in this whole country. In fact, I hope you do. Secondly, Marshal, as a lawman I would have to say that you and every other cocksucking lawdog can go fuck yourselfs."

The trolley driver did not utter another sound the entire couple miles to Colorado City.

Chapter 19

At nine thirty on a weekday morning the saloons of Colorado City were doing a bang-up business. Every one was open and every one seemed to be doing at least some trade. The free lunch spreads were especially popular as the gents—working men, judging by their clothes—came in for beer and breakfast.

Longarm envied them. Sort of. They looked and acted like their concerns were simple ones. Something to drink. A place to stick their peckers. That seemed to be about the size of it.

No need to worry. No need to think. Lift a box and put it onto a wagon. Lift the next box and take it off. At day's end collect your pay. The day's biggest decision would be whether to buy a bottle or a woman.

Half of them probably couldn't read. The other half probably didn't. They looked and acted like they hadn't a serious concern in the world. And yet Longarm knew that was not at all so. These men had feelings and disappointments, love affairs gone awry, ambitions still to reach for or yesteryear's ambitions shattered and destroyed.

He was just in a shitty mood after a night of hard travel, no damned food and responsibility for the lives of several hundred men, both white and red, hanging over him.

This was, what? The fifth day? Three more to go. If

he did not find Blue Quail Singing's killer by that time there would be hell to pay.

Yeah, there were times when he thought it would be easier to get a job loading freight or skinning mules. But this did not seem an opportune moment to go looking for that work.

His brief chat with the streetcar conductor was a reminder that Colorado City was the sort of place where killers might be more warmly welcomed than lawdogs. If only because anyone you met could well be wanted for something.

Accordingly he decided to keep his mouth shut and do his looking for Earl Shiver without advertising who he was after. Nor, for that matter, that he was looking for someone to begin with.

Starting at one end of the town's main street, which ran parallel to the same creek that flowed out of the pass above Manitou, Longarm ambled along from one saloon to another. He paused only briefly to glance into each. Failing to see Shiver, he backed out and went on to the next joint.

"Hi, sweetie. Want a little something to start your day off right?" He was greeted by a painted and powdered old whore at a saloon called—he had to glance up at the sign over the door—The Magpie.

Cow pie was more like it. The place smelled of sour beer and old sweat. Or maybe it was the bawd that smelled so bad. She looked like she should have retired twenty years back. When she grinned at him he saw she had no teeth. None that he could spot anyhow.

She cackled. "That's right, honey. I don't got a tooth in my head. You ever get blowed by a woman with no teeth? Best damn thing you'll ever feel, I guarantee it."

"No thanks." He managed a smile. "I'm looking for a friend o' mine and don't have time t' tarry."

"For you, pretty man, only twenny cents. What d'you say? Fifteen then? Won't take you but a minute. Step around back in the alley there, you don't even have to take your britches down. Just slip a couple buttons. Ten cents? I'll swallow your jizz, mister. You can watch me do that. Just a dime, eh?"

Longarm felt like he had vermin crawling in the seams of his clothing. He began to itch. "Sorry, mama. Not today."

"You son of a bitch."

He hurried down the sidewalk to the next saloon.

Earl Shiver was not in Colorado City.

No, that wasn't necessarily right, was it. Shiver was not standing at the bar of any of the saloons in Colorado City. Longarm could state that with some confidence. But Ford Fargo's murderer could be snoring in any one of a hundred flops or proper hotel rooms in the town or he could be shacked up with some whore. Longarm could have passed within a dozen feet of the SOB this morning and not known it.

He could also still be somewhere up there in the pass, making his way slow and easy down to civilization while Longarm half killed a good horse trying to get here.

That was the thing. Longarm just couldn't know.

The only thing he could know for sure at this point was that he was having a really shitty day. His feet hurt from all the walking. His eyes burned from lack of sleep. His belly was rumbling and complaining from being empty so long. And he was running out of time to stop Bear Killer and his warriors from starting a full-scale uprising.

Damn it all anyhow.

Longarm stepped off the sidewalk and went out into the middle of the street to flag down an up-bound streetcar, this one driven, thank goodness, by a different driver.

"Manitou," he said as he wearily climbed the steel steps. The driver nodded to the coin box, and Longarm dropped a nickel in.

Twenty five minutes later he got off at the end of the line.

He stepped off the car but he could quite happily have

fallen off it and just curled up on the ground and slept right there where he landed. He was that damned tired.

And still there was no sign of the man who murdered both Ford Fargo and Blue Quail Singing.

Chapter 20

Longarm let out a long, sorrowful sigh as he climbed onto the board sidewalk and stopped there for a moment to lean against the porch roof support. He wanted a cheroot but would have to buy some before he could indulge that particular desire. What he could manage first was a good meal. Hot grub goes far to put the lead back into a man's pencil.

The café where that pretty girl worked was only a half block away. He figured to go there first, then come back down the block to the mercantile that lay in the other direction, a cigar store Indian standing outside doing the advertising for the place.

Coffee first and food and then . . . dammit, he couldn't spare the time for sleep. Not now. Earl Shiver could be coming down the pass this very minute and if Longarm was chasing shadows in his dreams he couldn't be keeping an eye out for his fugitive.

So tired his feet were dragging, Longarm walked up to the café and let himself in.

The girl's dimples showed when she smiled. "Change your mind about having that meal, did you?"

"I did for a fact, miss. Can I ask you a question?"

"If it's about what time I get off work, the answer is 'no.'"

"No, miss. What I want t' know is if I can still get some breakfast even though it's lunchtime."

Her expression changed to a pout but only as a tease.

She quickly laughed. "To tell you the truth, I was sort of hoping you would go ahead and ask me anyway."

Longarm smiled. "That's a date. But not until I'm done with the work that's before me. Could be a few days."

"I'm not going anywhere," she said.

"Even if you do I'll track you down an' find you again."

"You do know how to turn a girl's head, don't you." He heard the clatter of pots in the kitchen, and several townspeople came inside too. The girl's coquettish expression changed and she became brisk and businesslike. "I am sure I can get my father to fix you a breakfast if that is what you would like."

"Thanks. In that case I reckon I'll have biscuits and 'bout a gallon of gravy to pour on 'em. Mess of eggs. Maybe a piece of meat to set them eggs on."

"We have fresh pork chops," she suggested. "Just butchered this morning."

"Perfect. I ain't had pig meat in I can't tell you how long."

"Coffee now?"

"Please." He chose a seat that allowed him to watch outside through the front window. If Shiver came down the pass Longarm did not intend for the man to pass by unnoticed.

The girl hurried off, came back a moment later with a steaming hot cup of coffee and then whisked away again to take the lunch orders from the other customers.

Longarm's belly was groaning full when he emerged from the café a half hour or so later. That little ol' gal's pa could cook, no question about it. On his way out he looked back at the girl—her name was Emily and she was cute as a bug—and gave her a wink to remind her of the promise he'd made then headed back down the street to buy matches and some cheroots. Now that his other needs, well some of them anyway, were tended to he wanted a smoke to make it all set right.

Still needed sleep though. Lordy, he was tired. If he

lay down now he would probably sleep for a day and a half.

He stifled a yawn behind a closed fist as he reached the door to the mercantile.

Longarm heard a flurry of boot soles on hard-packed earth and others on the boards of the sidewalk. Damn, he *really* must have been worn out. It took him a good half second to respond. And that was much too long.

He felt something strike him low in the back, somewhere in the vicinity of his kidneys, and some other hard object slashed down onto his right shoulder.

Longarm spun, lashing out blindly with a clubbed fist. He felt the blow make contract with something bony—a face, he thought—and heard what sounded like the crunch of breaking cartilage.

There were . . . he could not tell. Four of them. Five. Hell, there could have been a dozen of the bastards for all he could see.

He felt woozy and unsteady on his legs.

Something impacted the back of his head. His Stetson absorbed some of the blow but there was plenty of it left, enough to stagger him. He struggled to keep from going to his knees.

While Longarm was occupied with that, one of the half-seen sons of bitches got in another whack over the top of his head. It sounded like a ripe melon falling onto flagstones.

Longarm wondered without much concern whether his noggin split open as nicely as a melon would. And if his brains came busting out all wet and red like a melon's guts.

He knew there was something wrong with that thought, but he could not identify where the error was. Actually he could not identify much of anything just at that moment. He heard more impacts. It sounded to him like somebody was kicking his ribs and belly and back.

Funny that he was listening to this but could not feel any of it except in a detached and very distant sort of way. Yet he could hear it quite clearly.

Funny. Yeah. But not very.

Then he realized that there was some sort of fog that was clouding his vision. The fog grew darker and thicker and pretty soon he could not see anything at all.

He heard something strike his head. And again.

And then he could not hear anything more.

Nothing at all.

Chapter 21

"Where am I?" It took Longarm a moment to identify the low, rasping whisper as his own voice.

"Hush. Don't fash yourself."

"Where . . . ?" He struggled to get up, but a pair of soft hands held him down. Small though those hands were he hadn't strength enough to overcome them.

"You are in my house. In my son's room to be precise."

"Who . . . ?"

"My name is Morticia Grampion if it matters."

"Di' you say . . . ?"

She laughed, a delicate and slightly furry sound, the sort of sound a cat would make if cats could laugh. "No, Mr. Long, I did *not* say that I am a mortician and no, you are not dying. Although God knows that's a wonder considering how badly you were beaten. By tomorrow morning you should be as colorful as a circus clown. You can call me Tish, by the way. It is ever so much easier to say, even when you have all your wits about you. Which I think you do not have at the moment."

She turned away, dipped a once white cloth into an enameled basin and rinsed it, then applied the cool water to his face again. The damp, chill touch felt marvelous.

"Gram . . . Gram . . ."

"Grampion," she prompted.

"Yeah. I heard that . . . before."

"Of course you have." Her voice was as cheerful as a

sparrow's. "My son Will is taking care of your horse."
She added, her voice a trifle disapproving, "At an outrageous price, I might add."

"You don' approve?"

"Will is quite thrilled, but I don't want him to think money is so easily come by."

"Folks don' seem to have much tro . . ." He paused and held himself rigid for a moment as a lance of sudden pain stabbed through him. "Don't have much trouble learning that lesson, missus."

"It is miss actually, not missus. When Will's father learned he would become a daddy his feet became suddenly very itchy."

"There's some take things that way," Longarm said.

"So I have learned."

"How'd I—"

"Get here?"

He nodded.

"Will saw the fight. He ran and brought the men out of the barber shop. They chased away your assailants. Then Will had them bring you here."

"Thank you."

"I thought you were dying."

Longarm tried a grin. He wasn't sure how well he managed that from Tish Grampion's viewpoint, but he gave it a shot. "You want me t' leave since I ain't gonna die on you?"

She gave him a startled look and must have seen the grin. She smiled. "No, but thank you for the offer. If I decide to take you up on it I shall let you know."

Longarm nodded. Then winced again. Movement was most definitely not a good idea right now.

Longarm sighed and let himself go limp. He'd learned a long time ago that the best way to fight pain was simply to accept it and welcome it into himself rather than trying to fend it off.

He lay quiet, breathing slowly and deeply as if asleep while Tish continued to bathe his wounds. When she got down to his chest and belly he discovered that he was naked underneath the sheet she'd spread over him. The wet cloth was cool there but not as refreshing as it had been on his face and neck.

It occurred to him about then that Tish Grampion was a very handsome woman. She had dark auburn hair done up in a tight bun, green eyes and high cheekbones. She had a long, patrician neck and a firm chin. There were, rather incongruously, a spray of freckles across the bridge of her nose. Two tendrils of the dark red hair had escaped from the bun and drooped down over her left eye.

She was a big woman, he saw, but not fat. Just built to a larger scale than most. Her waist would likely tape out as big around as Longarm's or even larger, but on her it was just fine due to the size of her chest and her butt. Proportion, Longarm thought. All a matter of proportion.

"You are not asleep," Tish said, "and I can see you sneaking looks at me."

"I'm only about half awake an' I wasn't sneaking nothing," Longarm protested.

"As you please."

"Since you ask, yes, what I see there is pleasing, thank you."

"I bore a child out of wedlock, Mr. Long. It does not necessarily follow that I am either cheap nor easy."

"No, ma'am. I never said anything like that, an' if I implied it then I apologize."

"Very well." She sniffed and turned her head away. After a moment she looked at him again. "No, I suppose you neither said nor implied anything, and I am the one who should apologize. I've just become . . . sensitive to the assumptions men sometimes make."

"I understand," he said.

"Do you?"

"I think so. I try."

She smiled. "That should be quite good enough, shouldn't it." She looked at the sheet that lay over top of him and began to laugh. "I don't know that all of you agrees with your gentlemanly attitude, Mr. Long."

He realized, rather belatedly, that his pecker, as it

sometimes did, had a mind of its own. The damn thing was standing tall.

"That don't mean I think you're easy, Miss Grampion. It means I think you're a fine looking woman. Sorry."

"Don't be. The compliment is unquestionably sincere."

Tish gave him an impish look. And lifted the edge of the sheet to peer underneath. "Oh, my."

Longarm felt his erection begin to subside under her scrutiny.

"I think," she said, "that we should stop the bathing now."

"Yes'm, that might be a good idea."

She moved as if to drop the sheet, then picked up the edge and took another peek, this time clucking and shaking her head. "Goodness gracious sakes alive," she said, her voice barely containing the laughter that threatened to bubble out.

Longarm laughed heartily. Then clamped his jaws hard closed as the jostling of the laughter sent another wave of pain jolting through him.

"Is there anything else I can do for you, Mr. Long?"

"Other'n the obvious, you mean?"

"Other than the obvious, yes." She did not sound at all offended.

"No, I . . . yes, come to think of it there is. I think I had some money in my pockets when that ruckus got started."

"Yes, it is all over here on the bedside table."

"If Will isn't busy could he run an errand for me?"

"Yes, but you mustn't pay him any more. You've been too generous with him as it is."

"You won't mind if I smoke in your house, Miss Gra— I mean Tish?"

"Not at all."

"Or had a wee drop of the demon rum perhaps?"

"Make it whiskey and I might be persuaded to join you. After Will is in bed and won't know, that is."

"Then I reckon whiskey it shall be. Rye suit you?"

"To a T, Mr. Long." She plucked a ten dollar eagle off

the nightstand and said, "Would you mind if I do the shopping for you instead of Will?"

"Not at all. But I tell you what. Now that we know each other good enough that you've given me a bath, how about you call me Longarm instead of Mister. That Mister stuff always makes me feel old."

"Longarm it shall be then," she said. "Now if you will excuse me, I will go fetch the tools of debauchery." She tucked the sheet high under his chin and plumped the pillow behind his neck. "I'll tell Will to stay close by. If you need anything just call out. One of us shall come immediately."

"Thanks."

Tish Grampion turned away. By that time Longarm was already wondering just how quickly he could get shut of this bed and return to the very serious business of finding Earl Shiver and bringing the son of a bitch to justice.

Chapter 22

"Sir?"

Longarm opened one eye. The other seemed to be glued shut. After a moment it popped open too. The boy was standing at the foot of the bed. He seemed rather excited about something. "Something wrong, Will?"

"No, sir. Not really. Mr. Long, sir, before she left she went an' called you Longarm. Whyfor would she do that?"

"Because it's my name, son. Well, my nickname. My proper handle is Custis Long, just like I told you. But my friends all call me Longarm, an' I'd be pleased if you would call me that too now."

"Thank you, sir, but . . . I mean . . . Mama didn't know anything about that name, but I do. Are you telling me you're really him? Really and truly cross-your-heart-hope-to-die him?"

Longarm smiled. It didn't hurt too terribly much this time, and he suspected he'd been able to sleep a little since he last knew what was going on around him. "Can I leave off the part about hoping to die, Will?"

"Oh, I . . . but you really are him?"

"If you mean am I the deputy U.S. marshal called Longarm, yes. I am. Not that I know of any other carrying the name."

"Oh, gosh. Wait till I tell everybody. Longarm. Deputy Marshal Longarm, right here in my own house, laying in my own bed. Oh, gosh. I never expected to meet anybody famous. Wow."

"Not famous, son. Famous should be somebody important. Like the president or a hero or an author or something. I think what you could say I am is notorious."

"Notorious," Will repeated, mouthing the word. "How d'you spell that?"

Longarm told him.

"What's it mean?"

"Ask your mama. She'll understand the difference between notorious and famous."

"But you're a hero, so you oughta be famous, oughtn't you?" the boy persisted.

"I'm no hero, that's for sure. If you want a hero, read up some on John Paul Jones or Thomas Paine. Nathan Hale or Dan'l Boone. Now they were heroes. *And* they were famous."

"Well you're the famousest person I ever hope t' meet, sir." He grinned and amended that. "Uh, Longarm, I mean."

"How's the horse, son?" Longarm asked, wanting to change the subject to something more comfortable.

"He's doing pretty good. Needs a couple days of rest, but he'll be all right, I think. I've cooled his feet in the creek twice now and rubbed him down afterward both times."

"There's something else I need to ask you, Will."

"It's about those men, ain't it, Longarm?"

"Yes, it is, Will. Your mom said you saw them. Do you know who they were?"

"Oh, sure. They're a bunch of good-for-nothings. There was Fats Randisi an' Long Haired Jim Reasoner and Paul Newcomb and some guy named Sherman. I don't know what the rest of his name is. The others mostly call him Sherm. Newcomb, he's the one who works over at the livery stable. I think you seen him this morning."

"So that's what it was about," he said. "I was wondering. I shamed Newcomb this morning. I shouldn't have done it really. I overreacted to something he said, and the

93

only excuse I have is that I was tired and worried and out of sorts. But I wouldn't say he had any right to come jumping me from behind with a bunch of friends neither." Longarm sighed.

"Are you gonna shoot those fellas, Longarm?" Will sounded rather eager to find a front row seat if the great Longarm was going gunning for a gang of local toughs.

"No, Will, I don't expect that I have cause to gun them down. Not even to arrest them for they've broke no federal laws worth worrying about. But if I get the chance I reckon I would like to have another word with this Newcomb fella anyway for he was the ringleader." Longarm smiled. "You don't have to look quite so disappointed to hear that, Will."

"Yes, sir. Uh, mama said I should sorta keep an eye on you. Is there anything you want?"

"Yeah. I could use the thunder mug. Pull it over here beside the bed if you would, then you can go look to the horse again. I'll be all right."

"Yes, sir." The boy fetched the article in question, then let himself out and pulled the door closed.

Nice kid, Longarm thought. He idly wondered if Paul Newcomb had been a nice kid once. Then . . . nah. Probably not, he decided.

He got something of a rude awakening when he tried to maneuver himself off the side of the bed.

His body was one huge ball of pure agony that had managed to splinter off into a thousand little spikes of sharp pain. It was all he could do to keep from crying out loud and very nearly more than he could manage to get done what he had to do.

It was pretty clear that he was not going to jump out of bed right away and get to looking for Earl Shiver. Critical though time was becoming there is only so much a man can do. And right now he'd reached his limit for one day.

94

Chapter 23

Longarm woke to a nightmare. Or a bad dream at the very least. He was surrounded. Hemmed in on all sides. There was no place to run. Even if he was in any shape for running, which he most emphatically was not.

They lined up around him like so many pickets on a garden fence. They were staring at him. Every one of them. Huge eyes. Tightly pinched mouths. All of them. Silently observing. Accusing? Accusing him of what, dammit?

They had dirty faces and tangled hair and freckles and . . . freckles? What the fuck kind of cutthroats had freckles, for Pete's sake?

Longarm blinked and struggled to get his wits about him. There were some who might have claimed that would be an all day job and then still fall short of the mark—Billy Vail's clerk Henry came immediately to mind—but he got himself together as well as could be expected after being thumped on the head a few too many times lately.

"Will?"

"Here, sir."

Longarm rolled his head to one side. He raised an eyebrow.

"I, uh, did we wake you? I told everybody not to make no noise. Not a peep or we'd all get thrown out. That's what I tol' them."

" 'Them' being . . . ?"

Will grinned. "These is my friends, Longarm."

"All of them, I take it," he said dryly.

"Yeah, well, it's pretty much everybody. 'Cept for Poudre Pete. He had to go down to Fountain to visit his gramma for a couple weeks. And Big Jory. We couldn't none of us find him. But this is every other kid in Manitou, yeah."

"Boy kid, you mean."

"Well we wouldn't want no dang ol' girls around."

"No, I'm sure you wouldn't," Longarm offered without further comment. Hell, if he'd told them they wouldn't believe him. Not at this age.

They were all—he gazed around the bed, which was completely rimmed with wide-eyed little boys—they were all eight, ten, no more than twelve years old, he judged. At that age girls all had cooties. Funny how the little sons of bitches—that's cooties, that is—all magically jumped ship and disappeared once a boy got to thirteen or thereabouts. These little boys weren't to that stage quite yet.

He smiled a little, remembering. At this age these boys would be hiding under the covers pulling the pud. But they wouldn't have the least idea about why, not apart from the fact that it just plain felt good.

They'd grow out of that too, of course.

"Tell me, Will, is there some particular reason you called this meeting?"

It was not Will but a wide-eyed kid who couldn't have been much more than three feet tall who spoke up. "Sir? Sir? Will told us you're a deputy U.S. marshal, the one they call Longarm. Is that true, mister? Is it really?"

"Yes, it is, son. Will didn't lie about that."

"You got proof?" a slightly older kid demanded, earning him some obvious annoyance by a number of the other boys and a menacingly dark look from Will, who after all was the one whose word was being doubted.

"Yes, as a matter of fact, I do. Will, hand me my coat, will you, please? I think your mom . . . come to think of it I got no idea what she did with it."

"I know. I know where it is. She took everything off to clean it up. It was pretty messy after, well, you know."

"Yeah. I seem t' recall how that might could be."

Will dashed out of the room but was back half a minute later carrying not just the coat, which had been brushed and hung on one of those wooden gadgets like they hang ladies' dresses from in the shops, but all of Longarm's things.

He got through the door with all of it clutched tightly against his chest but dropped one of Longarm's boots. Inside the bedroom though, which Longarm figured should count as an official success in the complete retrieval, that sort of thing being important to little boys.

"The coat is all I need right now. You can put the other stuff on the chair over there. Thanks."

He found his wallet and opened it to display the badge. "Would that be good enough proof for you?" he asked the skeptic.

The boy pursed his mouth and whistled soundlessly. "Wow. You really are him."

"Will told you that already, didn't he?"

"Yeah. Jeez."

"Here. Take a good look, then pass it around so everybody can see." He doubted he could have pleased them any more if he'd just offered to give each and every one of them a hundred dollars in gold. The wallet made its way very slowly around the bed, each of the kids examining the badge like they were trying to memorize it, each of them wanting to touch the embossed face of the metal, each of them close to peeing themselves over the thrill of holding a real life, sure enough, guaran-damn-teed U.S. deputy marshal's badge in his very own hand.

Shit, Longarm thought, any time he got to feeling down about himself or his job all he'd need to do would be to gather up a bunch of kids and let them play with his badge for a couple minutes. If that didn't perk him up then nothing would.

"Marshal? Sir?"

"Yes?" This one was a pudgy kid with red hair and impossibly blue eyes.

"Could we see your gun? Maybe?"

Longarm couldn't see where there would be any harm in that. He nodded to Will, who fetched the heavy gunbelt off the chair and handed it to Longarm, taking pains to touch only the leather and not the big Colt itself.

Longarm slid the .45 out and weighed it in his hand for a moment, then flicked the loading gate open and tilted the muzzle up. He brought the hammer back to half cock and slowly spun the cylinder so that one by one the squat, heavy, brass and lead cartridges dropped out into his waiting palm.

Once he was sure the revolver was empty he spun the cylinder again to double check, then closed the loading gate and let the hammer down. He turned the Colt around and offered it grip first to Will Grampion.

"D'you mean I can hold it?"

"It's empty."

"Yes, sir, but . . . honest?"

Apparently a real for-sure deputy's Colt revolver was even more exciting than a real for-sure U.S. deputy's badge had been. Will took the Colt like it was as fragile as bone china and looked like he wasn't daring to breathe while he held it.

Eventually the .45 too made its way around the bunch, traveling lovingly from hand to hand . . . and threatening to cause warfare to break out as each boy showed himself reluctant to let go of the precious object so it could move along to the next one.

When all of them had handled the Colt—and it did take a little while to accomplish that—Longarm tucked the now returned wallet under his pillow, reloaded the Colt and slid it back into the holster where it belonged. Ordinarily he would have draped the gunbelt over the bedpost but he did not wanted the loaded firearm hanging there in easy reach of a room full of kids so this time he wrapped the belt around the holster and stuffed that underneath his pillow along with the wallet.

"Gosh, Longarm, thanks," Will said, initiating a loud yammer of gratitude from the boys.

Longarm suspected there would be some bragging going on once the ones who'd missed out returned to town.

"Fellas, we best be going now. My mom oughta be back soon. We got to be out o' here before she gets home."

"It's been a pleasure t' meet you fellows," he told the boys as Will shooed them out of the bedroom. Will paused at the door. "Is there anything you need, Longarm? Anything I can bring you?"

"I'm fine now, thanks."

"Thank you, sir. Really." Will stepped back and pulled the door closed behind him.

Once the boy was gone Longarm began to smile. Kids. God love 'em.

Chapter 24

Longarm was not accustomed to sleeping during the day and once night arrived he found himself wide awake. Even the influence of Tish Grampion's chicken and dumplings—long on the broth and light on the dumplings as befit a meal for an invalid—failed to put any weight on his eyelids.

He had nothing to read and no bedside lamp to read by even if he had prepared himself with a copy of the *Police Gazette* or the good old *Rocky Mountain News*. And he sure as hell did not feel like getting up and going anywhere. That hostler Newcomb and his plug-ugly pals had done a bang-up job on him, damn them. And he did mean "bang" up.

About all Longarm could do at the moment was lie propped up against his pillow and heal. And listen.

He heard Will and his mother in the kitchen having their dinner after the lady first came in and fed Longarm his. The two of them chatted a little about the events of the day, but as far as Longarm could tell, young Will somehow forgot to mention inviting the entire townload of boys in for tea this afternoon. Not that Longarm blamed him. A kid with any gumption whatsoever soon learns that it isn't a lie to keep your mouth shut, particularly about things that mothers might not approve of.

The two of them ate and then he could hear the clatter of dishes being washed and an occasional word that suggested Will was doing the drying while his mom washed.

The back door opened and closed a couple times, then opened and slammed. Trash being taken out, Longarm figured, or the two residents making their last trips out to the backhouse. Soon after that the light that had been showing underneath the door to his room—Will's room—disappeared and the place went silent.

Pale moonlight filtered in past the flour sack curtains hung at the window. From out on the street Longarm could hear an occasional shout or the clop of hoofs as big drays rumbled past. He closed his eyes and tried to interest himself in sleep but just couldn't do it. He was wide awake now. And bored.

The boredom was swept instantly away when he felt a chill seep into his chest. Something in the house wasn't right. He did not know what. But something wasn't right.

Longarm reached for the gunbelt that should be hanging beside his head, realized his error and felt beneath the pillow instead. He slid the dark and deadly .45 out of the leather and held it on his chest, pulling the sheet up to cover it.

Not that he was expecting trouble. Had no reason to do that. But God knew who or what could hear about him being here and think he was a threat to them. Shiver, Newcomb or some asshole fugitive he never heard of could decide this was a good time for a preemptive strike, now that Deputy Marshal Custis Long was lying hurt and abed.

Longarm shifted position a little so he could better see the window. Then he waited.

Ten minutes passed. Fifteen. He pushed the sheet down and wiped his palm on the bedding, then renewed his grip on the Colt and pulled the sheet up over it again.

Any SOB that tried to come in that window . . .

It was the door that pushed open, not the window.

He heard a very faint creak of metal on metal as the hinges softly protested, then he could see the movement.

The door swung open only a matter of inches and then a pale figure slipped silently into the room and carefully pushed the door closed again. Longarm heard a faint grating noise and realized it was the sound of a locking bolt being slowly slid closed. He figured he could wait for whoever was there to make the first move, or Longarm himself could . . .

With a snarl he threw the sheet back and sat upright, Colt in hand, unmindful of the fierce lance of pain that shot through his back and abdomen.

"Freeze, fucker!"

The person at the door did not freeze.

She gave out a weak little yelp of stark terror and fainted dead away.

Chapter 25

"Oh, good grief!" Longarm tried to jump out of bed. *Not* a good idea. He let out an involuntary gasp as the pain struck him, and he collapsed onto the hardwood floor. Which did absolutely nothing to ease the hurting.

Unable to run or even walk to Tish Grampion's side, he crawled.

He scuttled across the floor on hands and knees until he reached her side. By then she was coming around and beginning to stir.

"Did you . . . did I . . . did you shoot me?"

"No, but I sure as hell might've. What are you doing sneaking in here in the middle of the night?"

"I came to check on you, to see if you were sleeping soundly."

He sniffed. "You put on some sort o' lavender scent so you could come an' look at me sleeping?"

"I didn't . . ."

" 'Course you did. You weren't using any of that stuff before supper, an' you haven't gone out anyplace since nor had company in."

The light was too poor for him to be sure but he thought she blushed. "Only a little," she said.

"You didn't answer my question," he accused.

Tish ignored it this second time too and came to her feet—which, unlike Longarm, she was able to do quite easily now that she was conscious again—then leaned over him to help him into a more or less upright position.

Off the floor anyway, even if he was bent over like some grumpy old codger who needed a cane and an ear trumpet.

She draped his arm over her shoulders and helped support him back into bed. She covered him with the sheet, plumped a pillow and put it behind his head.

"Are you comfortable?"

"Yes, I s'pose so."

"Good." Then she hauled off and slapped him a good one across the face.

"Hey!"

"That's for frightening me half to death in my own home."

"I'm sorry," he said.

"Are you?"

"Yes, dammit, I said so didn't I?"

"Well . . . all right. In that case I suppose I can forgive you."

"Then maybe you'll get around to telling me why you came in," he said.

Tish only shrugged.

"If I didn't know better, I'd think . . ." He stopped there.

"Think what?"

Longarm shook his head. "Never mind. Reckon I wouldn't think anything like that after all."

"It's all right if you do," she said. "You would be right, you know."

"Think you know what I was thinking, do you?"

"Of course I do. The same thing any man would come up with given the circumstances."

"You say I'd be right if I thought that?"

She nodded. "I want you to understand though that I don't do this with every Tom and hairy Dick that comes around. I have a hard enough time trying to raise Will and maintain a decent reputation without that."

"Then why me?" he asked.

"Apart from the fact that you're handsome?" She giggled. "And hung like a horse?"

"I can't argue with those observations, but do tell me. Why, apart from those things?"

"You are . . . how can I put this without hurting your feelings? You are safe," she said. "By that I mean you aren't likely to go around town beating your chest and telling all your pals how you tore a piece off the little cunt who got herself knocked up by that fancy man a while back; reckon she's at it again, boys, so y'all line up and let's everybody take a crack at her."

"No, I, uh, I wouldn't be saying anything like that," he agreed.

"Exactly. If only because you don't have any pals in Manitou. Though you do seem to have some enemies. They would be happy to believe me if I went around complaining that you were telling lies on me."

"Uh huh."

"As for the rest of it," she smiled and pushed the sheet back away from him, "as for the rest of it, you *are* quite a nice looking man." She laughed. "And then there's the part about you being hung like a horse."

She reached over and took hold of the member in question, which as if it had a mind of its own began demonstrating the truth of her last comment.

Chapter 26

"Oh . . . mmm . . . am I . . . mmm . . . hurting you?"

Longarm reclaimed his lips from hers and shook his head. "No, you're fine."

Actually she wasn't hurting him. Not enough to worry about anyhow. What she was doing was suffocating him. He couldn't hardly breathe for the kisses Tish was plastering all over his face.

"Mmm . . . you taste . . . like a . . . mmm . . . a man."

"Hell, I'd hope so."

Tish laughed lightly and kissed him some more. She was draped across his torso, covering him from the waist up.

She was naked and she was a damned fine looking female as he had ample opportunity to observe now.

"I want . . . want you," she whispered in a husky voice.

Longarm didn't bother. He did however reach down and take a handful of soft, heavy tit and give it a squeeze. Tish responded with a renewed assault on his mouth.

After a few moments she disengaged and began licking his throat and his chest. She stopped at his left nipple and suckled it, alternately licking and sucking, creating a roaring need in his loins as his senses were brought to an acute level so that the faintest touch of her tongue or lip was enough to send an electric jolt through his body and down into his cock and his balls.

Longarm groaned aloud. The sound encouraged Tish. She licked her way across his chest to the right nipple and repeated the performance there. His right nipple was even more sensitive than the left, and he was not sure he could bear any more of her attentions without spraying the bed and both parties in it with a gush of hot semen.

He cupped the back of her head and pushed gently to ease her away from that overly sensitive nipple. Tish obviously thought he meant something else by the gesture. Obediently she dipped her head lower, finding the tip of his throbbing cock and drawing it into her mouth. Longarm steeled himself, making a determined effort not to become too aroused too soon.

"Let me taste it. Please."

"You're sure?"

"Yes. Please. I haven't . . . it has been so long. So awfully, awfully long."

Longarm nodded and stroked her face and the side of her head, smoothing her hair back behind her ear and watching with pleasure as Tish took him into her mouth.

Lordy, he thought. How is it that a woman is always her most beautiful to a man when she has his cock in her mouth.

He realized after he posed the question that it was self-answering. But it was nonetheless true. Custis Long hadn't yet encountered any woman who failed to meet that measure.

He groaned again when she pushed herself onto him so that his shaft probed deep into her throat.

"You sure . . . you want to?"

He felt her bob her head to answer in the affirmative.

That was all he needed. He let go of the iron control he'd taken over his body. Gave in to the wonderfully sensitive wet heat that engulfed him and let the come flow.

Tish gurgled and squealed and bucked like he was choking her, but she hung in there for every powerful spurt and the slower flow that came afterward, sucking him dry and swallowing everything she took in.

What felt wonderfully good to begin with soon became too much to bear, the pleasure turning into a subtle pain that could be borne only briefly.

He pulled her off him.

Tish looked up at him. She gave him an impish grin and licked her lips with a wildly exaggerated sweep of her tongue.

Longarm chuckled. "Well, you said you wanted to taste it."

"You didn't tell me it'd come in a quart measure," she said with mock seriousness.

"Don't exaggerate, woman. It couldn't've been more than a pint, pint and a half tops."

Tish laughed and tossed her head to throw her hair back off her face. She was flushed and bright eyed and at that moment very pretty. "Is there more where that came from?"

"I dunno. Take a look."

Which she did, examining his cock and his balls with her eyes, her fingertips and her tongue. Closely examining.

Longarm responded quickly, coming again to rigid attention under Tish's scrutiny.

"It really is a lovely thing, you know," she said.

"It used t' be little," he said with a straight face. "I dunno what you went an' done to it t' make it like this."

"Liar." She slapped his chest. But she looked pleased, taking the quip as the compliment he intended. "If I hurt you," she said, "let me know, and we can do something else."

She knelt at his side and kissed him again, thoroughly and for a considerable length of time. Then, slowly, she eased herself down onto the bed at his side. Lay snuggled tight against him and then without breaking off the kisses lifted up and moved on top of Longarm's body.

"Are you all ri—"

"Hush, woman. Pay attention t' business."

"Yes, sir, Marshal, sir."

Longarm smiled and kissed her. Tish seemed to like kissing about as much as any girl he'd ever come across.

She tipped her butt high above him and then very carefully, very gently lowered herself, one hand between their bodies to find his cock and guide him inside the hot, dripping wet depths of her body.

"Let me," she said. "Just let go and let me do this, please."

The feel of her was overwhelming. Exquisite. He pressed his head back against the pillow and closed his eyes.

Tish began to move, slowly at first, making broad circles with her hips, each churning motion carrying him deep inside her and then sliding out again almost—but never quite—all the way.

"You're good," he whispered.

"Shh. Hush now."

He hushed.

Tish's gyrations became quicker, her hips describing smaller circles and her breath coming faster and faster. The edge was already off Longarm's need, which probably was one of the chief reasons why she'd wanted to take him in her mouth to begin with, so she could take her time and allow her own senses to build. And build. And explode.

Tish's body stiffened, and she cried out loud. Loud enough that Longarm was reminded they were not alone in the house. He hoped the boy did not hear and come to see if Longarm needed anything.

Tish herself seemed unaware, lost in the power of her climax. The muscles that surrounded her vagina rippled and contracted, squeezing Longarm's cock and driving him over the edge so that his climax followed close behind hers.

"Oh! Oh, dear. Oh, my."

Longarm laughed and kissed her. "Oh, yes," he said.

Tish's body lost its rigidity, and she collapsed onto him. Her weight hurt actually, but it was not more than he could bear. And he wanted her to hold onto the pleasure of this moment for as long as possible.

It seemed a very long time before she finally roused herself and rolled off him to cuddle again tight against his side.

"Thank you," she whispered.

Longarm kissed her temple, which was what he could reach at the moment. "I thought I was the one supposed t' be saying that."

"Oh, no. It's definitely me for I am the one it meant so very much to. Thank you, dear Longarm. Thank you very much."

Her fingers circled and tugged idly through the hair on his chest and after a few moments the movement ceased.

He glanced down at her face, so soft and pretty in repose, her eyelashes dark and curly against the roundness of her cheek. She had dropped off to sleep.

Longarm smiled and held his arm protectively around the sleeping woman.

Chapter 27

"Longarm? Sir? Have you seen my mom this morning?"

Longarm groaned and struggled to sit upright. The effort was hampered by Tish's presence on the narrow bed, which was intended to be used by one person at a time. "I . . . just a minute, Will. I can't get to the door right now." He reached down under the edge of the bed and rattled the lid of the thunder mug, intimating but not exactly saying that he was occupied with it at the moment.

Tish came awake too, her eyes wide. Longarm held a finger to his lips to silence her. "Give me a minute, Will."

"Yes, sir."

Longarm helped Tish raise herself over top of him to reach the side of the bed. She grabbed up her nightdress and pulled it on. She leaned down and planted a quick kiss on Longarm, then tiptoed to the window and lifted the sash.

She looked like she was laughing when she snuck out of her own house, probably to go around to the outhouse and then come back inside through the kitchen door nice and loud so Will would know where she was.

"Have you seen her, sir?" Will called through the closed and fortunately bolted bedroom door.

"No, Will. Sorry." Well, not at that instant maybe. To that small extent it was not a lie. After all, Tish had already left.

Further inquiry was stopped when Longarm—and presumably Will as well—heard the screen door on the back porch slam shut. Longarm breathed a little easier. He did not want to shatter any of the boy's illusions, especially those involving his mother.

Now that he was sitting up, Longarm found that he wasn't feeling half as battered and sore as he'd been last night. Apparently Tish's medicine worked better than anything a doctor might have prescribed.

Oh, he was still plenty sore. And his bruises were turning interesting shades of purple. But he could move now without screaming or passing out. Seemed like a helluva improvement.

Experimentally he planted his feet on the floor and stood upright. His belly hurt and he was shaky on his feet, but he figured he could manage. Sort of. The really good news was that there was no blood in his urine when he opened the thunder mug, genuinely this time, and took a morning piss. His kidneys had taken a pretty good pounding but it looked like there was no serious damage there.

The blows to his head he didn't worry about. He'd long ago decided he couldn't be hurt by being hit in the head. Too hard-headed. And Longarm himself was not the only person to hold that opinion.

The bending and pulling required for him to get dressed hurt like hell, but he managed to get everything— even his socks and boots, which were the hardest to do— tugged, tucked and presentable. Eventually.

It felt good to be upright and mobile again. Moving around seemed to lubricate the muscles and warm them up, enough to allow him some degree of comfort the more he did. Once he was dressed and the big Colt retrieved from beneath the pillow he unbolted the bedroom door and stepped out into the narrow passage at the rear of the small house.

He could smell coal smoke and hear the clatter of pots and dishes in the kitchen.

Tish had a fire roaring in the stove and a pot of water ready to make coffee as soon as the cooking surface became hot. Will was busy distributing plates and silverware. Longarm gathered that he was invited to breakfast, which suited him just fine. Tish was stirring something in a large bowl. That something looked suspiciously like pancake batter, and Custis Long was not a man who liked to pass up a stack of hotcakes.

The lady of the house gave him a secretive and knowing little smile when Longarm joined them. It seemed she had no regrets about last night. Longarm himself damn sure had none. The woman was a pleasure. And that could be taken in any of the several possible meanings.

"Good morning, Will. Ma'am."

"Good morning, Mr. Long." The soft smile returned, and for a moment Longarm was remembering the tastes of her and the way those lips looked when held tight around him. Her lips, her nipples, her body. In his undoubtedly prejudiced opinion a thoroughly lovely woman, Miss Morticia Grampion.

"If you're still feeling bad, Longarm, I can bring your breakfast in to you," Will offered. He sounded like he'd been planning on doing that, probably so he could brag to his pals about the time he and the famous U.S. deputy spent together.

Longarm squeezed Will's shoulder and said, "Thanks, but I can get around on my own now, I think." He smiled. "Thanks to you and your mom."

The boy seemed pleased.

"Don't keep our guest standing there, son. Show him where to sit and get a cup down for him. But don't pour the coffee. It hasn't boiled yet. I'll tell you when."

"Yes, ma'am."

Longarm winked at the boy and sat in the place that was indicated.

He was enjoying this pleasantly domestic scene, but truthfully his thoughts were on Earl Shiver and where to find the son of a bitch.

113

Chapter 28

Shiver had had more than enough time to reach any of the foothill towns by now. He had to have come out of the pass, probably while Longarm was lying immobile after the . . . he couldn't call it a fight since he hadn't managed to do any fighting, damn them . . . after the beating he'd taken.

Unless Earl Shiver was a complete idiot he was somewhere in the vicinity this very minute.

Of course it is also true that most murderers indeed *are* complete idiots. They are willing to act but don't take time to think. And in general the fuckers are so stupid that they believe they can get away with it.

So far as Shiver was concerned, he already lost out on that score. He was known. He would be found. He would be brought to account for what he did to Ford Fargo. That, as far as Longarm was concerned, was a given, not worth worrying or even thinking about.

Longarm's worry now was not with Earl Shiver but with Iron Ax's band of Utes and all the people they might harm if they held to their promise and cut the wolf loose.

This was—he had to think back for a moment to try and work it out—this would be the sixth day. Two days to go. Well, three after this one was done. But it would take a full day for him to get back up the pass and on through the mountains to where the Utes were encamped.

No, Earl Shiver did not matter at this point. He was a walking dead man, soon to hang or be gunned down.

But Bear Killer mattered. Iron Ax mattered. And the memory of Blue Quail Singing certainly mattered.

"Are you all right?"

"What . . . oh." He smiled. "I'm fine, thank you."

"You looked so far away."

"Reckon I likely was at that. Thinking." The smile turned into a grin. "It's something as comes hard to me, y'see."

"That, sir, is a line of blarney if ever I heard one."

"No, ma'am, never. I never say anything but the truth. I swear to it."

She laughed and turned to her son. "Will, I think you should be careful what you believe of what this man says."

"Oh no, mama. Longarm is a deputy marshal. He wouldn't tell a lie. Not never. Would you, Longarm?"

Longarm ruffled the kid's already unruly hair. "I might pull your leg, son, and I been known to be flat-out wrong a time or two, but I wouldn't ever tell you a serious lie. An' that much you *can* believe."

Will gave his mother an "I told you so" look.

"Get Mr. Long a cup of coffee," Tish said. "It should be ready now."

The boy hurried to comply, filling a cup overly full and then having to carry it from the stove to the table one tiny baby step at a time, his concentration focused on the nearly overflowing rim of the china mug, the tip of his tongue visible at the corner of his mouth as if that would somehow keep the dark, steaming coffee in there where it belonged.

"The hotcakes will be ready in a minute too. Will, get down that jug of molasses if you please. And the crock of butter." She smiled. "I hope you two are hungry because I made a double batch of hotcakes, and I don't want to see any leftovers when you are done."

That, Longarm figured, was a request he and the boy would do their level best to honor.

• • •

The man could believe he'd gotten away scot free and be bellied up to some bar right there in plain sight. Or he as easily could figure somebody would be looking for him and go into hiding for a week or a month or even longer. Longarm did not know enough about Earl Shiver to make any reasonable guesses about what the man might do now that he was out of the mountains. Which he surely was.

He could be hiding anywhere.

What would be harder for him would be to hide that mule. Of course there would be literally hundreds of back-yard sheds and stables where a horse of mule could be quartered. Longarm's bay was in one behind the Grampion place right now, and Shiver's mule could be in any other. If—and it was a very big *if*—if the man could get the owner's permission to use the shed.

Even so it would be easier to walk through the back alleys and look for a mule than it would be for him to peep into every bedroom window in Manitou and Colorado City.

That, he thought with a bit of amusement, could be mighty entertaining. But it could also get a fellow hanged or his head blown off.

What he reckoned he would do today would be to keep on looking for the man but look even closer for the mule.

Chapter 29

Longarm was not entirely sure he wanted to do this. He still felt like shit. His back hurt, his face hurt, his arms hurt and his legs hurt. About the only parts of him that did not hurt were his ears, his hair and his pecker.

He considered it a blessing that that asshole hostler Paul Newcomb and his friends hadn't thought to damage those too or he wouldn't have had such a very pleasant night of it in Tish Grampion's company.

Now, though, it was back to business. And the first logical place to look for Earl Shiver's mule would be here at the Manitou livery stable as that would be the first place Shiver would have come to where he could leave the mule while he himself stayed out of sight.

The truth was that, entering the livery, Longarm would prefer that Newcomb was someplace else this morning. But Longarm would do whatever needed to be done. *Whatever* needed to be done!

Years of habit made him lightly touch the butt of his Colt as he entered the barn. The gesture was so automatic and ingrained that Longarm was not aware that he had done so and if asked would have denied it.

He headed down the wide aisle between the twin rows of stalls, the passage built large enough in both width and height to accommodate a full-sized freight wagon or Concord-style coach. There were an even dozen stalls, six to either side. Four were empty and one held a collection of lop-eared, bleating goats. Eight, no, nine of them milling about in the one stall. All does, Longarm saw, although none of them seemed to be lactating at the moment and none of them looked like they were carrying kids.

The other stalls held horses housed one animal per stall. All of those were light bodied animals, either saddle horses or small pulling stock suitable for lightweight buggies, spring carts or the like. There were no mules.

Longarm slid the double doors open at the back just far enough for him to walk through and went outside to see what was being held in the corrals behind the livery barn.

There he found mostly draft horses, those huge and bulky creatures that could weigh more than a ton apiece and could pull damn near anything that didn't have roots planted deep in the earth.

Longarm always thought there was something magnificent about the big horses, the Percherons and Clydesdales and—the rarest of pulling horses but perhaps the most beautiful—the Shires with their glossy black coats and brilliant white stockings and face markings.

Longarm ignored the big horses save for the few moments he spent simply admiring them. His full attention was drawn to some mules who stood in a tightly compact group in the southwest corner of the back corral.

There were five of them, he saw. He walked past the very large first corral and approached the second, slipping the latch on the gate and letting himself inside with the mules and a handful of rather nondescript horses that he guessed were the animals the Manitou livery owned and kept for hire either as saddlers or light draft stock.

The horses were of no interest, and he passed them by. When he approached the mules their big ears twisted and flapped, and one very leggy gray mule walled its eyes and sneaked around to the far side of the group.

Four of the mules, Longarm saw, were tall, very well built beasts, each of them almost identical in size although they varied as to color and markings. One sort of marking that all four shared, he noticed as he came close, were harness marks. And all of those had identical placement.

The four, he concluded, were part of the same hitch. A four-up that would draw a wagon or coach and work always as a single team. None of those was of interest to him.

The fifth mule though could well belong to Earl Shiver. Longarm waved his hat and yipped, sending the tall gray into a panic. The other three members of the team bolted along with their timid hitch-mate, moving immediately and as one. They spun about and dashed into the next corner of the corral, standing there shoulder-to-shoulder with their rumps facing outward.

It would, Longarm thought, be mighty dangerous to walk up to those old boys from behind right now. It was probably a very good thing that he had no interest in them.

The one mule that was left behind was small enough to be a placer miner's companion.

Longarm wished he had paid attention to Shiver's mule when he had the chance earlier in the week. Hell, he didn't even remember ever seeing it at all, much less getting a good enough look to remember it now. His interest at the time was on the men in the no-name camp, not in their transportation.

This mule was friendly enough. With the others gone it turned to Longarm for company, coming to him with its muzzle extended, looking for a handout.

"Sorry, old fellow. I don't have anything for you," The best Longarm could manage was to scratch it in the hollow under the chin where it could not reach for itself and to rub its poll and fuzzy ears. "Wish you could tell me who you belong to," he said.

The mule did the next best thing. It turned its head to nip at a flying critter that was buzzing around its near hock. That exposed the animal's off shoulder, which showed harness markings that suggested the animal was used on a regular basis to pull something. A delivery wagon perhaps or something of that nature.

Whatever use this smallish mule was put to, it was not a miner's pack animal. The flattened hair and sometimes calluses caused by pulling harness are very different from the marks that can be left behind by a pack saddle.

"Shit," Longarm mumbled.

He scratched the friendly little mule for a moment longer, then reached into his pocket for a cheroot.

He cussed again. He kept forgetting, dammit, that he didn't have any smokes. He had given away everything he had to Iron Ax, and he hadn't had a proper smoke since.

Yesterday he'd been on his way inside the mercantile when Newcomb and chums attacked him from behind.

This morning he was thinking about mules, not cheroots, and had come the exact opposite direction from the mercantile when he walked out of the Grampion house.

He expected he'd just have to correct that oversight now.

Longarm gave the mule one last pat and headed for the street, carefully latching the corral gate behind him and then walking swiftly toward the back door of the livery barn that he'd left standing a little bit open.

Cheroots and matches, he was thinking. And then he by damn was going to find Earl Shiver's mule and let it lead him to its owner.

With any sort of luck there was still time for him to put Shiver in irons and take him up the mountain so Iron Ax and Bear Killer and the rest of the men of the band could see that Long Arm keeps his word and that justice would be done.

Even for the murder of a red-skinned girl.

Chapter 30

Longarm felt a crushing blow on the back of his head. The sound of something striking him was dull and hollow . . . proof enough that it was his skull that was hit.

The result, however, was anything but a joke. He dropped to his knees, stunned by the force of the blow.

Acting to save himself purely on reflex Longarm continued his fall, stretching out full length on the straw that littered the sour smelling barn floor and rolling quickly to his right. He came up short against the front of one of the stalls.

Looming over him and seeming as tall as a California sequoia, Paul Newcomb raised the ax handle high overhead for another chopping blow. The first had been softened and partially deflected by Longarm's Stetson. It looked to Longarm like the man meant to kill him this time.

Newcomb made an abrupt but unfinished attempt to hit downward at his intended victim, then stopped.

Longarm lay close against the wooden wall, and Newcomb was trying to hit downward at an angle that would have only bounced off the boards instead of contacting Longarm's head with full force.

Newcomb took half a step backward to give himself more room to swing the potentially lethal club and shifted his hands so he could swing from the side.

Had Longarm lain there accepting the blow it could well have killed him. As it was, Newcomb's change of position gave Longarm time enough to swivel sideways on his hip and lash out with his feet.

His boots caught Newcomb at ankle level and spilled the thin, wiry hostler onto the barn floor at Longarm's side.

"You son of a bitch," Longarm snarled. "You ain't got a bunch of helpers with you this time."

"Fuck you, mister," Newcomb spat back.

Longarm rolled toward the liveryman and grabbed him by the throat, fully intending to throttle him if he could.

Newcomb went pale and jerked backward, tearing himself away from Longarm's grip, weakened by the pounding he'd taken yesterday and now again this morning.

The man scrambled on hands and knees to recover the ax handle that he'd dropped when he fell. Longarm threw himself forward and tackled Newcomb from behind, sending both of them crashing back onto the floor, Longarm half on top of the wildly squirming Newcomb.

Newcomb's searching fingers came up inches short of the ax handle. Longarm raised his fist and with an overhand sweep of his arm clubbed Newcomb on the spine between his shoulder blades. Newcomb wheezed and cried out but the blow did not deter him. He tried again to reach the ax handle.

Longarm crawled up Newcomb's back, digging in with hands, boots and knees until he straddled the man's shoulders. Longarm was a head taller and probably thirty pounds heavier than Paul Newcomb, but Newcomb had power in his seemingly scrawny limbs. He wriggled violently from side to side, then bucked Longarm off like the deputy was nothing more than a cat on a mule's back.

Longarm flew in one direction. Newcomb rolled in the other.

The ax handle lay a good five feet away, and Longarm lunged for it, stretching out and throwing himself full length onto the floor with his hand extended.

His fingers wrapped tight around the hard, hickory shaft, and he swept it to meet Newcomb as the hostler too tried to grab the ax handle.

The slender club struck Newcomb in the face. Blood splattered and teeth crunched. Newcomb cried out and rolled away with both arms wrapped tight to his face.

Longarm raised the ax handle and held it poised to deliver a killing blow to the unprotected back of Newcomb's head.

Just in time he regained control of himself.

No. No, dammit, he was not going to do it. Not while the man was lying there facedown, out of fight at least for this moment.

Shaky but more or less intact, Longarm rose to his knees and took a moment to lean his hand against the front partition of one of the stalls. Then he came upright. Slowly, using the ax handle to lean on as if it were a cane. His knees were watery and he was trembling with the after-effects of the powerful surge of juices that had rushed through his body.

It was over now.

He leaned against the stall and dropped the ax handle over the top of the stall and into the loose straw inside.

His head was pounding and his breath came in short gulps, but he was alive. He was all right. He brushed himself off, hoping the only thing he'd rolled in was the bedding straw that had been spread over the floor of the center aisle. He didn't have time to have his clothes cleaned, dammit, but if he'd been wallowing around in horse piss and road apples he wouldn't have very much choice about it.

A few yards distant, Paul Newcomb shook his head, droplets of congealing blood flying off his chin and cheeks, and managed to reach his knees and then his feet.

Doubled over and not once looking back at Longarm, Newcomb staggered blindly toward the tack room that served him as office and living quarters too.

Good riddance, Longarm thought.

At least now he knew Earl Shiver's mule was not being boarded here. He could not think of one good reason why he should come back to this barn again. Not one.

Longarm removed his Stetson and pushed the crown,

even flatter than usual and wildly dented at the back, back into place. He ran a hand over his hair and put the hat back on. His scalp was damn well tender there, and he still hurt like hell from yesterday's brawl. Damn these bastards anyway.

He glanced back toward the tack room. The door was closed and there was no sign of Newcomb. That, Longarm thought, was just as well. He started back out onto the street. He still needed to find Shiver. Or at the very least needed to find the man's mule as that might give him some idea of where to look for the mule's owner.

Longarm was thinking about that, about the job he was trying to do, when he heard the faint screech of hinges and a moment later the distinctively metallic *clack* of a firearm being cocked.

Instinctively Longarm whirled and dropped into a crouch, the big Colt already in his fist by the time he completed the move, his finger already beginning to squeeze the double-action pull that would discharge the .45.

Paul Newcomb stood in the open doorway, a cocked revolver rising to take aim where Longarm's unprotected back had been just a moment earlier.

Longarm's Colt roared before Newcomb could get the shot off.

A lance of flame spat toward Newcomb's chest, a lance that was tipped with hot lead. The bullet struck Newcomb just below the throat. His head was thrown backward, and he stumbled back a step. Righted himself and hung there for a moment as if suspended by unseen wires, his eyes wide with surprise.

Then the light of life left them and his eyes became flat, empty planes where there had once been the spark of humanity.

Paul Newcomb dropped to his knees and then toppled face forward into the dirt and gravel outside his own livery barn.

"You dumb fuck," Longarm muttered angrily. "You just couldn't leave it alone, could you."

Longarm felt as old as the hills around him as he dipped his hand into his coat pocket and extracted a fat brass .45 cartridge. He flipped the loading gate open, shucked out the empty shell casing and slid the fresh cartridge into the cylinder in its place.

"Damn you. Damn you anyhow," he whispered.

Down the street he could see people beginning to run toward the livery now that the shooting seemed to be over.

He hoped there was a local lawman among them so he could get this shit reported and done with.

Chapter 31

Longarm retrieved his badge and firearm—well, the Colt; he hadn't gotten around to mentioning that he might be carrying something else—from the broad and otherwise empty top of the town marshal's desk.

"Is that everything?" he asked.

Marshal Tom McLanahan nodded. "I have your sworn statement, Deputy. We'll hold a coroner's inquest as soon as we can get a panel together. This afternoon probably. I doubt they will need anything from you but if so I presume we can call on you?"

It was Longarm's turn to nod. "If I'm still here. Under the circumstances I'd rather not be. I'd much prefer t' be on my way up that pass with a prisoner in tow."

"I agree. We may feel ourselves secure down here, immune from Indian depredations. But the Utes . . . some of the other tribes as well . . . still come to bathe in the mineral springs and to worship whatever their concept of God is. They think the springs holy, you know."

"I'd heard that, yes."

"I suppose that is where the town's name comes from. Anyway, the Indians do come down here sometimes just to visit the springs, and of course they pass through twice a year when they go out onto the plains to hunt at the start of summer and again each fall when they go back to their mountain retreat, wherever that is."

"Not far enough away for comfort," Longarm told him.

"My point is that we are as anxious as you to avert

another outbreak, Long," the local lawman said. "As it is we have the occasional murder. A band of young bucks will catch a lone traveler, never more than two, and slaughter them for scalps and booty and whatever glory they find in such a terrible business."

"Yes, sir."

"I'll ask around about this Earl Shiver of yours, but really you are more likely to find him in Colorado City than here. Manitou is a law abiding community."

Longarm had to raise an eyebrow in response to that one.

The town marshal saw and correctly interpreted the federal man's skepticism. "Yes, well, with an exception every now and then of course."

"Of course." Longarm began to turn toward the door, then stopped again. "Did Newcomb have family or the sort o' close friends who might want to even the score for him? Say, by shooting me in the back while I'm busy looking for my boy Shiver?"

"I wouldn't think so. The man had no family here, and his friends were of the drinking pal sort like the ones who jumped you yesterday. I doubt their loyalty would extend beyond the grave." McLanahan chuckled. "Of course I have been known to be wrong before now."

"Very reassuring of you, Marshal, thanks."

"I will, um, drop a hint into a few ears today if you like. Something gentle. On the order of, 'I'm watching you, so fuck up and I'll beat you into mash and feed you to the hogs.' "

"I appreciate a gentle nature," Longarm said with a straight face. "Always have."

The town marshal smiled at him. "If I learn anything about your man, Long, I'll let you know."

"Thank you, marshal, an' if I find him I may want t' stop by here and borrow some leg irons. To show off for the Indians, if you see what I mean."

"I hope I have the opportunity to make that loan, Long."

"My friends call me Longarm. I'd take it well if you cared t' do the same."

"Then Longarm and Tom it shall be," McLanahan said.

Longarm liked him. The town of Manitou was getting its money's worth with that man, he thought. Longarm touched the brim of his Stetson in a silent salute and walked outside onto the covered sidewalk.

As soon as he was out of the marshal's office his facial expression changed to one of haggard strain and his shoulders sagged.

He'd been holding himself rigid and erect in there, trying to make out that he was just fine, but the truth was that between yesterday's injuries and that fight this morning he felt like he could keel over and collapse any old time at all.

He had good powers of recuperation, always did have, but this was pushing things just a little bit too far.

Longarm dragged the bulbous Ingersol out of his pocket and examined it for the time. He was hoping for lunchtime. After all, he'd been inside the marshal's office for quite a while.

It was . . . not quite late enough.

Close enough, he decided. Close e-damn-nuff.

He was weary. He was hurting. He just plain needed a little longer to let his body catch up with the demands he was placing on it.

After a moment's reflection, Longarm headed not up the street toward the café with its cute waitress but down, toward the Grampion house.

He would see if he could beg a noontime bite from Tish.

Chapter 32

Morticia Grampion won the argument by the simple expedient of ignoring the opposition. In this case, Longarm's opposition.

He wanted to have a quick meal and then get away to Colorado City in search of Earl Shiver. Tish wanted him to take a few minutes to rest and recuperate, then have a light lunch and then finally walk down to the trolley stop for the ride to Colorado City.

In addition to ignoring Longarm's comments and complaints, Tish went about the self assigned tasks of taking care of him . . . on her own terms.

She called Will in from the shed, where he was busy giving Longarm's bay its second rubdown of the day, and sent him on an errand. All the way to Colorado Springs.

"Mind me now, son. I want you to ride to the end of the line. You remember Abel Davidson's greengrocery, don't you?"

"Yes'm."

"I want you to go there and get me a handful of watercress. Tell Mr. Davidson what you need. Ask him to pick out the freshest he has. Can you do that?"

Will gave his mother a dirty look. Who was she kidding, asking if he could do something that simple.

"Tell Mr. Davidson I'll be by to settle the bill with him real soon."

"Okay."

"Wait a second, Will," Longarm said. He dug into his

pocket and came up with a half dollar that he handed to the boy. "This will pay your fare and for the . . . what-chamacallit your mom needs."

"Yes, sir, but I still have change from that quarter eagle you already gave me."

"I know, but this is extra work you're doing. Now take that and go on."

"Yes, sir." The boy gave his mother a hug, then stood awkwardly in front of Longarm for a moment as if un-decided just what he should do. It was clear that he wanted to hug his hero but was not sure if the gesture would be welcomed or if it might be seen as being baby-sissy.

Longarm settled Will's dilemma by extending his hand to shake. The boy pumped Longarm's hand gratefully, then snatched his cap off a peg beside the door and went dashing out to do what his mom said.

"There," Tish said with satisfaction once Will was off and away. "That should keep him out from underfoot for a couple hours."

"You don't need the, uh, whatever that was?"

Tish smiled. "Oh, I will use it. He would think it strange if I didn't. But no, I wouldn't say that I actually need it."

She crossed the kitchen to the chair where Longarm was sitting. Tish walked around behind him and began rubbing the back of his neck. It felt good, he realized. Better than he would have thought. She ran her hands over his shoulders and upper back and began to squeeze as well as rub. Then she kneaded the corded muscles of his neck and ran the balls of her thumbs over his temples.

"You're tense," she said.

"No, not really."

"I can feel it," she insisted. "Relax. Let down and let me do this. You'll feel better." She bent down and kissed him lightly. "I promise."

Indeed, he felt much better after a few minutes of her light massage. He admitted as much.

"Good. Now we'll go to the next step." She began to

unfasten the buttons on his vest and then his shirt.

"Look, I don't have time to—"

"Hush." She stopped his protests with another kiss, this one longer and deeper. It was, Longarm discovered, rather difficult to utter a complaint when he had a tongue in his mouth that was not his own.

"But I can't—"

"Didn't I tell you to be quiet? Now please shut up and let me make you feel better."

She led him into the bedroom, her own room this time not the one he'd borrowed from her son, both of them shedding clothes along the way. By the time she pressed him down onto the bed both were naked.

He liked the way Tish Grampion looked without clothing. Never mind that she was old enough to have a half-grown son. She was one of those women who looked better with their clothes off than on.

"Where does it hurt?" she whispered to him. "Here? Here? Maybe here?" She used her tongue to indicate where she meant. Actually his nipples did not hurt. They were one of the few body parts that didn't. But Tish licking them felt so damn good that he wasn't about to tell her she should quit. "Or here?"

She unpinned her hair and shook it out, then dragged the cool, silky ends of it across Longarm's chest and belly, then surrounded his erection in hair so that it spilled down onto his balls as well. "Does it hurt here?"

"You might wanna kiss it an' make it well," Longarm suggested.

Tish laughed. Then kissed it and made it well.

"Still hurts," Longarm insisted.

"Perhaps more drastic measures are called for."

Tish dipped her head lower, engulfing him in the wet depths of her mouth. He began to tremble.

She pulled back far enough that she could speak. "Just lie still. Let me. I'll do all the work, dear."

Longarm shut up and lay perfectly still while Tish gently, deeply took all of his hurt and tension away.

Within moments he trembled, then exploded into her

mouth with great, gushing spurts of hot fluid.

She stopped moving and suckled gently there. Only when she was satisfied there was no more to be had did she allow him to slip from between her lips. "Feel better?" she asked.

"Yeah. Reckon I damn sure do." He moved as if to rise, but Tish laid a hand on his chest to stop him.

"Not yet," she said.

She used the tip of her tongue to arouse him again, then straddled his waist and lifted herself over him. Using one hand to guide his entry, Tish lowered herself onto Longarm.

This time she offered no objection when he began to move within her. She smiled. And before long his relaxation was complete.

Tish sighed. Still smiling, she got off of him and found a cloth, which she used to wipe his cock with tender care. Then she bent down and kissed him, first gave a light peck to the tip of his cock, then repeated the kiss on his lips. "Feel better?"

"Mmm." He smiled sleepily.

Tish kissed his eyelids. "Rest a little. I'll make us some lunch and call you to the table when it's ready."

"Mmm." Longarm doubted he had ever been so relaxed. And if he still had aches and pains from the recent pummelings he'd taken he could no longer remember just where they were supposed to be.

The lady's medicine was strong, he decided.

Those were the last thoughts he had before he drifted into slumber.

Chapter 33

He fell asleep. He fell fucking asleep. He could not *believe* that.

A hundred people, *two* hundred people, could die if he did not do his job and find Earl Shiver in time to avert a disaster with the mountain tribes. So what did Deputy United States Marshal Custis Long do?

Why, he had a little nooky and then went to sleep, that's what he did.

Longarm was disgusted with himself when he woke up. Thoroughly pissed off. What right did he have to be down here taking life easy when people were in danger those few miles away. Lordy, he didn't deserve to wear a badge. He probably ought to be fired and his name stricken from the rolls. Jesus!

He leaped off the bed.

Well, he tried to jump up anyway.

Sharp jolts of pain stopped that little exercise. He would have to admit that he cried out just the least little bit when the fiery lances of pain struck.

Moving more slowly and with great care, Longarm collected his clothes from the bedside chair where everything mysteriously appeared all brushed and folded and tidy even though he distinctly remembered getting mighty damned dirty wallowing around on the barn floor with Paul Newcomb that morning.

Women! he thought. And smiled.

He could hear Tish out in the kitchen humming a

133

happy tune as she did something there. Something that had the whole house filled with a mighty fine aroma of cooking meat and . . . he paused and sniffed the air . . . baking. Uh huh. She had something baking in the oven too.

Longarm finished dressing, feeling perhaps a little less stiff although no less sore by the time he was done, and stamped the floor a couple times to get his feet settled comfortably into the black stovepipe cavalry boots that he favored. He was buckling his gunbelt into place as he walked out of Tish's bedroom into the kitchen.

It was a damned good thing he hadn't decided to joke with her and leave his pecker flopping out of his fly or something because Will and two of his pals were there bent over some sugary sweets and jabbering merrily the way little boys will do.

If any of the three of them thought anything unusual about the idea that Longarm would emerge from Will's mother's bedroom none of them said anything about it. For that matter they didn't look like it was something they gave any particular thought to. Could be she had told them some story to prepare for the possibility, Longarm figured. Or it just as easily could be that they just didn't give a damn.

Will jumped up and ran to greet Longarm. The boy seemed excited. "We heard all about it," he said breathlessly.

Longarm frowned. " 'Bout what?"

"You know what. We heard about that danged old Mr. Newcomb at the livery. We heard he tried to shoot you, but you was too quick for him."

"*Were* too quick, not *was*," Tish corrected from her position beside the stove.

"Yeah, right, you was . . . were . . . too quick for him."

"Is that what you heard?" Longarm said.

"We heard he called you out. Right there in the street. We heard you was . . . were . . . you were walking by not doing nothing," he glanced at his mother, "not doing anything . . . and he come outside an' called you out. There

134

you was, the two of you, ten paces apart. Newcomb, he had his gun already in his hand when he hollered at you. They say you never hesitated, not for an instant. They say you was so quick you drawed and fired before that ol' Newcomb could get his shot off."

"That's what they say, is it?" Longarm marveled.

"It sure is, Longarm. That's what all the fellas are saying. That's the truth of what happened, ain't it?"

"Except for none of it being so, it's real close to the truth, Will," Longarm said with a grin.

"But it really did happen that way, didn't it? Didn't it?"

"I'm not gonna give you boys a blow by blow account of a man dying, Will. I just won't do that. I will admit that Mr. Newcomb tried to kill me. An' I reckon I would have to admit that I was able to keep him from doin' it. But that's about as far as it goes, all right? I don't want to talk about it. Not right now."

"Tonight maybe?"

"We'll see."

"Could I have the empty shells from where you shot him?"

"I don't keep those things around."

"Are they still in your gun? Could you look please?" one of Will's buddies asked. He had been with the pack of kids in the bedroom last night, but Longarm could not recall the boy's name now.

Longarm shook his head. "I don't walk around with empty chambers," he said. "A sensible man always reloads right away after he's had to fire because he never knows when he'll have to shoot again."

The boys looked at each other like Longarm had just expounded on the meaning of life.

"Could we go look for them?" the other boy asked.

Longarm shrugged. "There's only one empty cartridge. I'd suppose it's still inside the barn if nobody has picked it up by now."

"We could look for it," Will said, "an' then we could

go over to Mr. Silas's barber shop. He ought to be done laying Mr. Newcomb out by now."

Without another word or a backward glance the boys went thundering outside into the afternoon sunlight.

Longarm watched them go, then shook his head. Kids!

Tish was laughing. But then she had a little boy. Probably she understood them. Or if not understood then at least had become somewhat immune to their bloodthirsty enthusiasms.

Had he himself ever been that way, Longarm wondered? Uh . . . probably. Not that he could remember it. But he supposed he must have been very much the same when he was that age.

"Hungry?"

"I could eat a horse," he assured her. "Hair, harness, shoes and all."

"Hopefully this will be a little more nourishing than that," she said.

"You shouldn't have let me sleep so long."

"But you looked so cute, sleeping like that."

"Cute?" he roared.

Tish only laughed. "Hush now. Your lunch is ready."

Longarm wasn't sure if he should swat her ass or what. He settled for kissing her. And accepting the plate that she handed him.

He did, he had to admit, feel one hell of a lot better now than when he'd walked in here an hour or two ago. A hell of a lot better.

Chapter 34

It was late when Longarm got done making his rounds of the Colorado City saloons. He could scarcely believe how many of them there were. And every one of them doing business. Some better than others, of course, but no one seemed able to go broke by opening a watering hole down here.

As squeaky clean as Colorado Springs was, with no saloons at all permitted within the town limits, and as ordinary as Manitou was, Colorado City was a veritable Sodom to match Pueblo's Gomorrah.

People must flock in from miles around just to belly up to a bar here. Or if not for miles and miles then at least from Colorado Springs.

Longarm kind of suspected that Colorado City's business came largely from the holier-than-thou crowd in the next town over so that just like in any self-respecting whorehouse, the man who was your friend and neighbor at home would not even be recognized over here.

Human nature, Longarm thought with a shake of his head. Lord love 'em.

He dragged the Ingersol out of his pocket and checked the time, then grunted. He really would prefer to keep on looking for Shiver, but the last trolley was scheduled to leave Colorado City in ten minutes. If he missed that ride he would have to walk the several miles back to Manitou.

And the truth was that he simply did not feel up to that

sort of exertion after all the punishment he'd absorbed lately.

Dammit!

So far he hadn't gotten a sniff of either Earl Shiver or the man's mule. And he had looked for both just as diligently as he knew how. Looked for Shiver inside the saloons and looked for the mule behind them and inside Colorado City's several public liveries.

There were a few privately owned barns and stables that he hadn't managed to look inside. But not very many. Earlier in the afternoon, while he had daylight to work with, he'd traveled through the back alleys of the town, peeking inside every woodshed and lean-to he passed.

He had found some interesting things, including rats, chickens, rabbits, pigeons and a helluva lot of barn swallows.

And he'd found one pimple-faced kid of fourteen or so rutting between the fat legs of the family maid. That was behind a tall and obviously very expensive house built on a hillside overlooking the creek that Manitou and Colorado City shared. Handsome place. Ugly maid. Even uglier kid.

He reckoned that what they said was true. There were some things you just plain couldn't buy. Looks, for instance. Health would be another.

Earl Shiver's whereabouts seemed to be a third, dammit.

Now, barely in time to take the last car back to Manitou, Longarm came out of yet another saloon and made his way down the dark street toward the depot. His mood was such that he very nearly hoped some stupid son of a bitch would try to rob him tonight.

He had two more days to find Shiver and drag the man back up the pass to display before Iron Ax and his people.

Two days. And at least a day and a half of that would be required just to make the trip. The distance was not so terribly great—it wasn't next door either, but in terms of miles to be traveled he did not think it would be all that much—but there was some serious climbing to do along the way, and there is little that will wear down a horse quicker than a steep uphill grade.

It was a shame there was no railroad that would make that climb for him. Oh, there were two of them built and operating into the high country of central Colorado. One of them came up from the south. The other came down from the north. And neither one of those sons of bitches was anywhere close to here where Longarm needed them.

No, dammit, he had to find Shiver by daybreak tomorrow or run the likelihood of missing that deadline set by Bear Killer and the boys.

The truth was that he would gladly keep on searching right through the night.

But . . . where?

Longarm already looked into—and behind—every saloon in town. Got a look into every shed or stable he found. And conducted about as complete a search as he knew how to make.

He'd found . . . nothing. Not a damn thing.

He was tired. He hurt in every bone, muscle and sinew of his body. His head ached something ferocious. The only cigars he'd found in the saloons were cheap rum crooks that tasted like they were made of dried horseshit . . . and maybe they were.

This morning he'd had to kill a man for no good reason except that the son of a bitch wouldn't have it any other way. And now it looked like a whole bunch of white miners and red Indians too were going to die just because he couldn't find that asshole Earl Shiver.

No, sir, Longarm's humor had been better than this a time or two in the past.

So when he stepped off that train in Manitou in the middle of the damn night he had not been drinking of the milk of human kindness and he was damn sure not in the mood for the reception committee that he found waiting for him.

Chapter 35

There were three of them. Presumably they were the same three who'd jumped him the day before. Lordy, had it been that recent ago? It felt like a month past. His back, belly and ribs, on the other hand, felt like maybe they were still kicking him.

"What's this?" Longarm asked. "You come back to see if you can do it again? If so you boys really fucked up. This time I can see you coming."

"You killed a friend of ours this morning," one of the men accused. Longarm had no idea which one he was. They'd never gotten around to formal introductions.

"I didn't know he was that good a friend," Longarm said.

"Nah, he wasn't really. But then how much of an excuse does a man need to stomp shit outta a stinking damn deppity marshal."

Longarm smiled. "Now you did me a favor right there, boys. You acknowledge knowing that I'm an officer of the law. Thank you."

"What the hell difference does that make?"

"It means that yesterday a good lawyer could've pleaded that you didn't know that I'm a deputy marshal. This time I know that you do. And *that* means that this time you are guilty of interfering with an officer in the performance of his duties. I expect that'd be good for twelve to eighteen months behind bars. It also means that if you lay a hand on me this time you will be guilty of assault on a federal officer. That one goes at the rate of five to ten years. Any single one of you wants to show a weapon? Any weapon? That doubles the sentence, an' you could be looking at as much as twenty years."

"The hell you say."

"Check it out, bub. Ask your lawyer."

"We don't need no damn lawyer."

"Hell, we don't need any of your shit neither," another of the trio snarled.

"There won't be charges against anybody if you don't file none," the first one said. He took a half step to one side. The man he was crowding over against took two so that the three were spread apart an arm's length or so from one to the other.

"What makes you think I wouldn't file charges against you?" Longarm asked mildly.

"This." The one who spoke yanked a revolver out from under his coat.

He looked smug. Until he realized that somehow, without him ever noticing it happen, Longarm had drawn his belly gun too, and now the muzzle of the big Colt was pointed toward his midsection.

"No, I . . ."

Longarm's .45 lighted the street with the fire that erupted in a fan shaped sheet from the muzzle and through the gap between the cylinder and barrel.

The first one who'd touched his pistol doubled over, hammered hard in the gut by Longarm's slug.

The man on his right, to Longarm's left, dropped to one knee and tried to take aim. In his excitement he jerked his trigger too soon and put a bullet into the street about halfway between his boots and Longarm's.

Acting with calm, deliberate speed, Longarm shot that man in the face. His head snapped back hard enough to break bone, and a spray of blood and brains made a halo in the light of the street lamp behind him. The blood looked black and shiny in the harsh light of the gas globe.

"No, no, no, I give . . . I give, mister . . . for God's sake don't shoot me." The third man dropped a little nickel-plated breaktop revolver in the dirt and held both hands as high as he could reach. He glanced down to see where his gun landed and with the toe of his shoe kicked it aside. "Don't hurt me, mister, I ain't armed."

What with his frustration, his pain and his anger it was all Longarm could do to stop himself short of blowing a .45 slug through that one's chest too.

"Move, shitface, and you die. D'you understand me?"

"Y-y-yessir."

"Good. Now hold still. You," Longarm said in a louder voice. "You with the hole in your belly. Drop your gun and step away from it. Do it. Now!"

The man Longarm shot first was still more or less upright. He was bent over at the waist, one hand clutched tight to his stomach and the other hanging down at his side with his revolver still dangling loose in his fingers.

"Drop . . . the gun . . . and step . . . aside," Longarm said with slow, deliberate care. "Do it *now!*"

"Mister, he don't hear you. He ain't paying no mind to you right now."

"That's fine," Longarm said, "but if he doesn't pull his head out of his ass and drop that piece this instant I'm gonna put a chunk of lead through the top of his skull."

The man made no effort to move, neither to drop the gun nor to raise it.

Longarm cocked his Colt—the heavy Thunderer was a double-action revolver so it was not strictly necessary for him to cock it before he fired, but doing so gave a crisper and lighter trigger pull and allowed for greater accuracy than just pulling back on the trigger—and began to raise it to take aim into the crown of the wounded man's cap.

"Do it, Fats, he's gonna shoot again, drop it," his pal screamed.

The wounded man, who seemed to be the one Will Grampion said was Fats Randisi, dropped his pistol. It landed muzzle down in the dirt and, being already cocked and ready, discharged into the ground at the impact.

The revolver leaped crazily into the air and skittered

away to one side when it accidentally discharged like that.

Randisi watched it go with an odd, detached look, then put both hands tight to his belly and dropped to his knees.

"Whoever is listening," Longarm called out in a loud, strong voice, "fetch me a doctor and the town marshal right away." In a much quieter voice he added, "But you don't hafta be real quick with the doc if you don't want to. Considerin' where this bastard is shot the doctor will just be going through the motions anyhow."

"Don't . . . you son of a bitch . . . don't be saying that," Randisi gasped.

"Careful, Fats. Keep it up an' you'll make me mad. Do that an' I might decide to hurt you."

"Very fuckin' funny."

"I certainly thought so."

"How can you act like nothing's happened?" the other living one squawked.

"Why, nothing much has happened," Longarm said. "Not t' me anyhow. As for your friend, you saw where he's shot as plain as I did. He's a dead man. Just hasn't quite finished dying yet."

"You're one cold son of a bitch," the man accused.

"Under the circumstances I kinda thought it was justified. Which one are you?" Longarm asked, shifting the subject.

"Huh?"

"You. What's your name?"

"My name?"

"What? Are the questions too hard for you? Yes, dammit, what's your name?"

"R-reasoner," the fellow stammered.

"And this one is Randisi, which means that dead one over there must be Sherman, is that right?"

"Yessir. Kid Sherman."

Longarm snorted. "Kid Sherman? You gotta be kidding me then. That guy hasn't qualified to be called 'kid' anydamn-thing for a good forty years."

"Jesus, Deputy, I didn't name him. I'm just telling you what the man is called. Uh, was called, I mean."

"Fine. Tell me, d'you have long hair?"

"Do I have what?"

"Aren't you Long Haired Jim Reasoner?"

"I'm called that, yeah. But I ain't wanted for anything. Honest."

"Then all you got to do is serve your time for this little dust-up and you'll be a free man again, Mr. Reasoner."

"I can't . . . listen, I can't be going behind bars. You know? I just can't. We can . . . we can work something out, can't we? You and me? Huh?"

"Let me tell you what your choices are, Mr. Reasoner. You can stand trial for assaulting a federal officer and do your time for that. Or you can see if you can pick your gun up and shoot me before I shoot you. Take your pick."

"Oh, Jesus, Long. Don't do this to me."

"Now the way I see it, Jim, this is something you've done to your own self. Ah. Looky here. I believe the town marshal is coming up the street. Make up your mind, Reasoner. Either put your hands behind your back or grab for that popgun. What? No guts? Fine. Hold 'em where the marshal can put the manacles on you, mister. And you. Fats. You're bleeding all over the damn street. Stop that, will you? You're making a mess."

Longarm waited until Marshal McLanahan was there to snap the handcuffs onto Reasoner, then shucked the empties out of his Colt and reloaded.

He felt so tired he was not sure he could put one foot in front of another to make it back to the Grampion house.

And he *still* hadn't found that bastard Earl Shiver, dammit.

Chapter 36

Longarm overslept the following morning. Tish had already abandoned the bed they'd shared through the night—or what was left of the night when Longarm finally got there—and was in the kitchen talking with Will.

As far as Longarm knew she hadn't bothered to say anything to her son about her and Longarm's sleeping arrangements. But she was open and honest about it. Longarm liked that about her, and it was obvious that Will felt no ill will about his hero sleeping with his mother.

Longarm thought his body was fixing to break in half when he levered his way into a sitting position and swung his legs off the side of the bed. He hurt in places he never knew he had.

And he still hadn't found that son of a bitch Earl Shiver.

Right now Longarm and Shiver should be high-tailing it up the pass into the mountains to find Iron Ax and stop a war.

Instead he was limping out to the backhouse for his morning shit while Tish Grampion made biscuits and gravy for him.

Not that he intended to turn down the biscuits and gravy or the coffee that went with them. But Lordy, he did feel terrible about not being able to get hold of Shiver. The man was here. He had to be here. But *where*?

Longarm washed at the basin set on the back stoop,

then came inside and dried his hands on Tish's dish towel. The freshly boiled coffee smelled better than ambrosia. Well, he'd never smelled any actual ambrosia and was not entirely sure just what the stuff was. But it was supposed to be the best of the best, and this coffee smelled even better than ambrosia would. Longarm was certain sure about that.

"Good morning." Tish gave him a kiss to go with the greeting and went back to stirring the sausage gravy she was making in an oversized iron skillet.

"Good morning yourself." Longarm stepped up behind her and gave her a little hug while she worked, then poured himself a cup of that coffee and carried it to the table where Will was poring over the adventures to be found on the pages of a dime novel. Longarm took a look at the yellow cover. This one was about Texas Jack Omohundro. There really was a Texas Jack. Longarm had met him. Longarm was also pretty damn sure the Texas Jack he knew had never done half . . . make that a quarter . . . hell, make it any . . . of the marvelous feats attributed to him in that book.

Longarm had no opinion of how good the man was as a scout and a buffalo hunter. Maybe he was every bit as good as he claimed, unlikely though that might be. But Longarm knew damn good and well that Texas Jack was no quick draw artist with a six-gun because Longarm had seen the awkward, long-barreled Smith & Wesson that Texas Jack carried. And more to the point he carried the thing stuffed down inside a fancy holster that probably required a key and a note from your mother to get the gun out of.

Not that Longarm intended to step on any of Will's fantasies though. Whoever wrote those dime novels always made out that the heroes, unrealistic as they were, believed in decency and fair play, and that was something that was good for a boy to learn. Men too. If those idiots last night lived by any code of decency and common sense they would still be with their families instead of being dead, dying or on their way to jail, as the individual case might be.

"Mama said there was another big shoot-out last night," Will said, looking up from his book.

"Mm hmm, reckon there was. But I wouldn't call it all that big."

"Tell me about it, please?"

Longarm figured the boy was going to hear it anyway so he might as well hear the truth as some exaggerated fantasy like was in those yellow-cover dime novels. He gave Will the bare bones of the situation while he drank that first wonderful cup of coffee, then reached for that first wonderful smoke of the day.

"Wow, Longarm. Boy, you really cleaned up this town, didn't you? Will you have to leave now and go tame some other place?" The boy sounded excited to have heard about the shooting straight from Longarm's lips, but it was obvious that he did not like the thought that this real-life hero might soon leave.

"I didn't come here to clean up Manitou," Longarm told him. "Marshal McLanahan has that under control just fine. He's a good officer, and the town is lucky t' have him. All this with Newcomb and them . . . it just sort of happened. Nobody wanted it to, but I reckon it did. It's like that sometimes." Longarm got up and went to fetch a refill from the stove. And another kiss from Tish.

"Could I ask you sumpin?" Will asked.

"Sure."

"Why are you here if it wasn't to shoot those bad guys?"

Longarm shrugged and told Will about Earl Shiver and the threat of Indian warfare in the mountains.

"For real?" Will asked, wide-eyed.

"I'm afraid so. I wish it wasn't true, but it is."

"And this Shiver guy murdered an Indian girl and a white miner too?"

"It looks that way."

"Can you prove it?"

"I think so, son. I got a look at Blue Quail Singing's

fingernails. She managed to scratch the tar outta whoever attacked her. I figure when I catch up with Shiver the marks she left on him will be enough to convince the Indians that I've got their man. Of course the problem is that if I was gonna make it back up there in time to keep their warriors from raiding the mining camp I ought to be riding up the pass right this minute with Shiver along for proof. As it is . . . ," he shrugged again. "As it is, I've failed. Oh, I'll find Shiver eventually. But I don't see how I could do it in time now to avoid bloodshed up there."

"Wow. That's awful." Will shivered, then returned to something of more immediate interest to him. "Did you say that Mr. Randisi is still alive but he's dying?"

"He was alive the last I saw of him, which was around midnight. No telling if he's passed on during the night. Of course I've seen men hang on for days with a belly wound like that. The lucky ones die right off, for the longer a man lasts with a hole in his gut the worse it pains him and the louder he screams. You'll know it if Fats is alive another couple days. The whole town will hear him begging for a bullet to put him out of his misery, and there won't be anybody kind enough to do it for him."

"Both of you stop that sort of talk at the table, will you?" Tish protested. She snatched the oven door open and used a pot holder to pull a pan of biscuits out. "Anyway I've got your breakfast ready. Now hush up and eat what I've cooked for you."

"Yes, ma'am," Will said meekly.

"Yes, ma'am," Longarm echoed him.

The biscuits and gravy, he discovered shortly, were mighty damn good too.

148

Chapter 37

Longarm removed his hat and held it in one hand while with the other hand he held the door open. The woman who emerged from the town marshal's office was thin, her face deeply lined. He would have guessed her to be in her forties except for the infant on her hip and the cherubic little girl of three or four who clung wide-eyed to her skirts.

The woman had been pretty once. He could see that. Maybe even as pretty as her little girl. A hard life had beaten the prettiness of youth out of her now though. Some fading bruises suggested that it wasn't only life that had beaten on her. Some human hand had contributed, he would've wagered.

"Mornin', ma'am."

She glanced at him and gave him the briefest of nods. She did not smile. Longarm guessed her man was locked up inside. Perhaps she'd just brought him a treat for breakfast. More likely she'd brought him hell on the hoof. This little woman did not look to be real happy this morning.

Longarm stood for a moment watching her walk away, wondering what she was like, wondering how much different she could have been had things gone her way a little more. There was something in her appearance, in her clothing and the children's clothes and in the way she carried herself—and in those bruises—that said she'd had a long, hard row to hoe. And that she wasn't done with the chopping.

"Good morning, Long. Come to check on your prisoner?"

"Mornin', Tom," he greeted Marshal McLanahan. He smiled. "I know the prisoner is all right in your custody. I was more hoping that you might've heard something about my boy Shiver. I should already be riding up the pass if I expect t' make it back there in time."

"I wish I could help you, but I don't know a thing. Still keeping an eye out for him, of course, but I've had no luck so far."

Longarm nodded. It wasn't unexpected. But a fellow could always hope. "You say Reasoner is all right."

McLanahan smiled. "Except for having a strip of hide torn off his sorry ass. That was his wife that just left. I closed the door to give them some privacy but even so I could hear that she was giving him holy hell back there."

Longarm grunted. "Why is it that men will do this sort o' shit but then it's their women that have to suffer for it. I suppose he's her only means o' support."

"Of course."

"So with him locked up, the kids will be hungry."

"Naturally."

Longarm sighed. "Kinda makes me feel like an asshole sometimes, you know?"

"Yeah, I know. Do you want me to turn him loose, Longarm?"

"To tell you the truth, Tom, I'd of been tempted to do exactly that if it was only about the one assault. I can forgive a man that much. But he came at me twice, and last night he had his gun out and would've shot me if he'd had the chance. No, this one I'll be taking back to Denver in irons when I get back down out of the mountains. I believe in cutting a man some slack, but I don't figure to throw him the whole damn rope so he can hang me with it. I'm sorry for his kids, but I'm not crazy enough to give him a third crack at me."

"I'm not blaming you," the marshal said.

"I tell you what you can do though. I assume him and his family come from someplace else. I mean, hell, everybody around here does. The country hasn't been civilized all that long."

"Indiana," McLanahan said. "The family comes from Indiana, I think it was."

"When I get back, Tom, I'll stop at the railroad station over in Colorado Springs and arrange a pass so they can travel back there if she's of a mind to. Her man is gonna be away three years at the very least. Could be as much as ten. And hard as life in the prisons can be, he could end up with a sharpened spoon handle between his ribs and never come out. You never know. So if maybe she has family to go back to . . ." He shrugged.

"I'll talk to her about it, Longarm. Let you know when you come through again. It's good of you. I'll tell you what though. She's loyal to the son of a bitch. God knows why, the way he treats her, but she's loyal to him something fierce."

"I hope he knows what he's wasted there."

"I doubt it. The man is a drinker and a brawler, long on friends but short on sense. You probably know the type as well as I do."

"Afraid so." Longarm ran a hand through his hair and settled the brown Stetson in place. "Sure wish you knew something about that Shiver though."

"If I hear anything I'll send for you. Count on it. You want to go back and see Reasoner this morning?"

Longarm looked at the door that led back to the jail cells. He grinned. "No, that old boy took enough grief this morning. I guess it'd be too much to make him see me walking around unharmed."

"If you'll forgive me for saying so, you don't look exactly unharmed. Why, there's a bite mark on the side of your neck there. Did you go and get yourself into another fight after I saw you last night?"

"I, uh . . . walked into a door in the night." He remembered Tish's squeals but he hadn't realized that she bit him too. Certainly didn't know that she left tracks behind.

151

He tugged at his shirt collar.

"Don't bother. It still shows."

"Oh well." He hoped Marshal McLanahan wasn't much for gossip. Longarm did not want to ruin Morticia Grampion's reputation. But that was not the sort of thing that he could come right out and discuss with McLanahan. He unfastened the top button again. If he couldn't cover the mark anyway he might as well be comfortable.

"Care for a cup of coffee?" the town marshal offered. "I was just about to walk over to the café. Be glad to buy you a cup of their finest."

"Thanks, but I'd better pass this time. I have to get on down to Colorado City, maybe over to Colorado Springs too today. That bastard Shiver has to be someplace. I just don't know where."

"Good luck then. Check in with me later. Noon or after. Maybe I will have heard something by then."

Longarm paused to consider. He was going to be late getting up the pass. There was no way around that. But he had to get up there, with or without Shiver.

What he supposed he should do would be to keep looking this morning. Then come back around midday to collect his horse and get moving. Traveling by himself and pushing the horse hard . . . he still wouldn't make it. But the horse was a good one and it should be rested by now. He shouldn't miss the deadline by too awfully much.

Maybe he could talk Bear Killer and the young men of the band into giving him more time to bring in Blue Quail Singing's killer.

Maybe pigs could fly too.

But he had to try, dammit. He had to try.

"I'll be back about noon then," Longarm said. He stepped outside into the morning sunlight and tipped the Stetson low to keep the glare out of his eyes, then headed for the train station.

Chapter 38

Longarm was in a foul mood when he reached the Grampion house. He'd just come from McLanahan's office after spending the morning on a fruitless search in Colorado Springs. No one at the mainline railroad station there had seen Shiver, and the local police knew nothing of the man either.

McLanahan didn't have any news for him, and Longarm was beginning to despair of any hope he might have had to stop Bear Killer and the other young warriors from attacking the nameless mining camp.

About the only thing he could do now, he thought, was to collect his horse and then haul his ass up that pass just as fast as he could push.

It just about made his day complete when he reached the shed behind the Grampion house and found no sign of the horse there. Well, none other than some straw and manure that had been collected from inside the spanking clean and sweet smelling stall and stacked tidily beside the back wall. The stall floor was five inches deep in fresh straw, and the feed bunk that hung on the back wall was already filled with an armload of bright, clean hay.

Longarm should have been pleased that the boy was taking such good care of the bay. Instead he was pissed that the animal was not there for him to get on now and begin riding.

He grumbled his way to the back porch and tapped

lightly on the door that led into the kitchen. Tish opened it with a smile and a welcoming kiss.

"What's wrong?" she asked when Longarm did not respond with his usual ardor.

He gave her a brief rundown on the way his day was going and concluded with, "And now Will and the damn horse are missin' so's I can't get a start up the pass like I need to."

"Then you might as well sit down. I'll give you something solid to put in your stomach, and I can pack the leftovers for you to carry with you. That way you won't have to stop to cook."

"I'll still have to stop to let the horse blow every now an' then," he complained.

"I'm sure you will, but I can't do anything to help with that. I can help with your food, and I intend to. Now sit down. Will won't be long. He doesn't like to miss any meals, and I told him you might be back for lunch."

"How'd you figure that?" Longarm asked as he pulled out the chair that had become "his" in this household. He dropped his hat onto the floor and sat.

"Wishful thinking," she said with a smile. "You wouldn't have time for a little, um, roll in the hay before you leave, would you?"

"In the shed? What happens if the boy comes home before we're done?" Longarm asked with mock innocence.

Tish wadded up the dish towel she was holding and threw it at him. It struck him in the face and wrapped around his ears. He sat there, wearing it, as if he hadn't noticed.

"You clown," she accused. She removed the towel and replaced it with a long, passionate kiss.

"You know I won't have time for that," he said regretfully. "But whatever happens up there, when I'm done I got to come through here on my way home. Got to pick up a prisoner to carry up t' Denver with me."

"Will you stop here then? Overnight, I hope?"

Longarm smiled. "It might could take me two, even

three days to get the paperwork complete on that prisoner. And there'll be forms to fill out for the town. You know. For Reasoner's board bill an' like that. Yeah, I'm thinking I might be here for some days once I get back down from the mountains."

"I hope you will be," Tish said. She bent down and gave him a hug. She smelled of yeast, he thought. The scent was pleasant on her. Almost homey. It occurred to him that Manitou was not all that terribly far from Denver. Just a few hours by rail. He could pop down pretty much anytime he had a few days off. Just to, um, help out with things that needed fixing around the house. Like that.

Tish was cleaning his ears for him. Or something. She was using the tip of her tongue to do it.

Then Will got home and she had to leave be. The boy came rushing in, all full of excitement.

"I found him. I mean . . . *we* found him. My pals and me."

"What, the horse got loose but now you found him again?"

"No, not the horse. He's tied to the roof post right out back here. He was with me. I took him down to the creek to wash him and cool his feet. You know. And I seen . . ." he looked at his mother and corrected himself, "that is, I *saw* some of the guys there. And we was . . . I mean, we were talking an' I told them about that Shiver fella, and then we all wanted to go over to Doc's place to see was Mr. Randisi still alive an' was he screaming his guts out yet, so we done that. Did that, I mean. We went over and did that. And he's still alive, all right. His wife was there and his kids. They were all of them crying. Him too even though he's a grown man and oughtn't to do stuff like that. And then Doc, he went into another room to take care of another patient he had in there, and a couple of us went with him, mostly so we wouldn't have to see Mr. Randisi laying there crying, and Doc's new patient . . . he was just brought in this morning early . . . he was laying there crying some too, so that wasn't no better. . . ."

Longarm hoped the boy would get to the damn point

soon, but Will was surely wound up about this, whatever the hell it was, so Longarm gave him room to run with it for another minute.

"So anyway, I seen on the floor beside his bed these packs wrapped in old canvas, kinda dirty too, and tied on the outside o' one was this gold mining pan like men are all the time carrying through here on their way up the mountain prospecting, and there was a pack saddle too. That had real narrow bars, real narrow. And I asked, and Doc said it came off a mule.

"And you'd told me this Shiver fellow, the murderer you're after, you said he had a mule. And so I asked the man what was his name, and he said it's Earl.

"And that's when I realized that we'd gone and found us a real-life murderer. And so I came back here while the other fellas went to tell Marshal McLanahan." Will was grinning from ear to ear. "Did I go good."

"Lord Almighty, son, you did damn good."

Longarm leaped out of his chair and raced outside and around to the street. He was halfway down the block before he realized that he had not the least idea where the doctor's office was, with Earl Shiver lying in one of the rooms there.

He stopped and looked around and Will, apparently realizing the problem, came running to catch up with him and lead the way.

Chapter 39

"The man is dying," the doctor said.

Longarm knew that the instant he walked into the room. Earl Shiver stank. And it was not with sweat or simple filth. He stank of gangrene, which was probably a killer worse than any bullet ever invented. The stink inside the doctor's room indicated the rot that was eating into Shiver was well advanced.

The man was so weak it was amazing not that he had taken so long to get down the mountain, but that he had managed to get here at all. No wonder Longarm had not been able to find him. Shiver had been languishing along the trail, able to move only at a snail's pace.

"How long has he been like this?" Longarm asked.

The doctor shrugged. "Days, I'd judge. Maybe a week."

Which would put the time of the injury well before the date when Shiver murdered Ford Fargo.

It just could be, Longarm mused, that Blue Quail Singing killed her own murderer when she scratched him. Those simple wounds festered and the gangrene set in.

Fargo might have noticed. Either saw Shiver's wounds or smelled them. He could have said something to Shiver about the girl's murder, and that very well could have led to his own.

"How long does he have left?" Longarm asked.

"It's hard to say," the doctor told him. "Two or three days perhaps. Certainly not longer than a week."

Longarm nodded. He looked at the packs on the floor. "Will, I'd like you to take those home with you and put them in your mama's shed. I'll collect them when I get back in a few days."

"Yes, sir."

Some of the other boys were still milling about in the doctor's office, dividing their time between gawking at the man who was dying from a bullet in the belly and making faces at the stink in the room of the one who was dying from the poisonous flesh that was eating him alive. Will looked more than a little proud to be given an important assignment by the famous deputy U.S. marshal. He strutted and preened a little and delegated the actual carrying of Earl Shiver's packs to two other boys.

Something occurred to Longarm and he turned to the doctor for advice. "D'you happen to know who is running the livery now that Newcomb is dead?"

The doctor scratched behind his ear and said, "No, come to think of it, I haven't heard. Hadn't thought about that until this minute." He removed his spectacles and peered at one of the boys who was underfoot. "Bubby. Do you know who is handling the livery now?"

"I don't think nobody is, Doc."

"Are you sure? Have those horses not been fed?"

"I don't know who woulda fed them if they was," the chunky kid called Bubby said.

"Tell you what, son, I'd like you to do something for me," Longarm said.

"Me? Yes, *sir*!" Bubby seemed almighty pleased that Will Grampion was not the only one who was being recognized by the tall deputy marshal. "You just name it, sir. I'll see to it. You can count on me."

"I was hoping that I could. What I want you to do, son, is go over to the livery. There's a brown cob there that looks pretty stout. I want you to put a saddle on him. Pick out the biggest saddle they have there and use that. But I don't want a bridle on him, I want a lead rope. Bring him and my horse . . . you can find my bay over at Will's house . . . bring the both of them over here. Oh, and put my gear on the bay, please. Me and this gent here got us some serious riding to do."

"What gent here are you talking about?" the doctor demanded.

Longarm pointed at Shiver.

"I am sorry, Marshal, but that man is far too sick to be moved. I've already told you, he is dying. You can't throw him on the back of a horse and . . ."

"Doctor," Longarm interrupted, "what is gonna happen to Shiver if he lays in your bed here?"

"Why, he is dying, of course."

"Uh huh. And what will happen to him if I put him on a horse and haul his ass up that mountain?"

"He will . . ."

"That's right, doctor. He will die. Whether he stays here or goes with me, he's gonna die. At least if I take him up that mountain there's a chance that we might get there in time to avoid other men dying. White men and red alike. They're gonna die for certain sure if I can't get Shiver up there and give them that young girl's murderer."

"I cannot permit you to take him, sir. I'm sorry," the doctor said, "but I took an oath to alleviate pain and suffering. I will not allow you to walk in here and take my patient away like that."

"Doc, let me make somethin' clear. There's no way in hell you can *stop* me from takin' that man outta here. Now, Bubby, you'd best get moving. Do what I told you, and do it quick. Then when you're all done delivering those two horses to me here, I want you to go back and take care of those other animals at the livery. There oughta be some hay in the loft. Fork some down so they all can get to it. And make sure they all have water. The goats too, all right?"

"Yes, sir."

"I don't have time to worry with this today, but I'll pay you when I get back down. You can ask Will. I pay pretty good."

"Yes, *sir!*" The boy took off like shot out of a cannon with two other kids behind him eager to pitch in.

"Now, doctor," Longarm said, turning back to the gentleman in the sleeve garters and eyeglasses, "if there's anything you want to do or any medicines you want to give to Shiver here to make him as comfortable as possible for the trip up that pass, you go right ahead. I figure you got ten, fifteen minutes to do that before the boys get back with those horses. Then Earl and me are going for a little bit of a ride."

Longarm paused. "And God help the dumb son of a bitch that tries to slow me down or get in my way."

The doctor scowled. But he had sense enough to keep his mouth shut. He checked to make sure the bandages that covered Earl Shiver's gangrenous chest wounds were secure, and he dug into a chest full of pills and brown bottles to find a pair of yellowish horse pills that he forced down Shiver's throat. Once that was done he handed one of the bottles to Longarm.

"This is laudanum. Are you familiar with it?"

"Yes, of course." The opium extract was as good a painkiller as Longarm knew of.

"Give him as much as it takes to relieve the pain," the doctor ordered. "Don't worry about giving him too much. Even if you kill him you won't have taken much time away from him, so concentrate on keeping him free of pain. That is the best anyone could do for him now. Just be . . . the man is my patient, sir. I'll not have him suffer any more than he truly has to."

"I'm not tryin' to punish him, doctor. I reckon God will do that soon enough. I just want t' get him up there so I can show him to the Utes and stop a war."

"Very well then. But mind now. Give him all it requires to keep him out of pain. In fact . . . I can get more laudanum. Take these bottles too. I don't want you to run out of it."

"I'll do that much for you, doctor. Thanks."

"I wish . . ." The doctor shook his head. "Never mind. It doesn't matter what I wish about this, does it."

"No," Longarm agreed. "But then it don't much matter what I'd wish for neither. We'll all of us do what we can, the best we can, an' let the chips fall wherever they fly."

He stuffed the doctor's bottles of opiate into his coat pockets, then went to Earl Shiver's bedside.

He hoped Shiver lived long enough to make it to Iron Ax's camp. And in a way he hoped every bit as much, for Shiver's sake, that the fellow died along the way so he would be spared that much suffering. Bad as his condition seemed to be, riding lashed onto the saddle of a horse was going to be viciously hard on him.

Longarm wrinkled his nose as the full impact of the gangrene stench hit him, but he bent and picked Earl Shiver up with a gentle care that approached tenderness. No, he did not want to punish the murderer. He only wanted to stop more bloodshed, and it was Earl Shiver's tough luck how that had to be done.

"Let's go, fella," Longarm said to the semi-conscious man. "We got some miles to put behind us now."

Chapter 40

Longarm stopped . . . he didn't know what the hell time it was. Sometime between can't-see and can-see. Sometime in the small hours. He did not want to stop, but he had no choice about it. The bay was still moving well at the pace Longarm set, but the big horse, the heavy-bodied cob, was lathered so bad it was almost pure white to look at, and it was paddling with the forelegs. If he did not let the brown rest it would drop on him, and then where the hell would he be. Tough as the bay proved to be it would not be able to carry both Longarm and Earl Shiver the rest of the way through.

The rest of the way. He had . . . he did not know for sure. Thirty miles? Something like that. Call it half a day's ride. For a fresh horse that wasn't already worn out.

Longarm glanced over his shoulder toward the east. He wasn't sure but thought the sky looked a little pale off in that direction. Another hour, two at the most, and the eighth day would have dawned.

Right now, damn it all, Bear Killer and the warriors could be slipping into position ready to attack the miners at the first break of daylight.

This was the morning of the eighth day, and all hell could be breaking loose. Longarm did not have Blue Quail Singing's killer there for the Utes to see. Did not have him there to keep his promise. Did not have the man ready to hold to account for the murder of an Indian girl.

They had given him until now, and Longarm had failed to meet his pledge.

Wearily, his butt hurting and his knees shaking now that he was out of the saddle and on the ground again after all those hours, Longarm unfastened the cords that held Shiver in the saddle. He dragged the unconscious man off the leather and onto Longarm's shoulder, transferring Shiver's deadweight to the ground beside a gray, gritty boulder.

Longarm lay Shiver there, then went back to pull the saddles off both animals and hobble them.

A thin creek ran close by. He turned the bay loose on a patch of grass close to it but kept the brown cob walking for a while until it cooled some before he allowed it the freedom to roll and to drink.

While the horses rested Longarm built a small fire and put some water on to boil, then measured out a quart of mixed corn and oats for each horse. He found a poke of already ground coffee in his saddlebags and dropped a handful into his pot, then went back and checked each horse's feet and legs while the coffee cooked.

Lordy, but it did smell good. Even better than the coffee he'd been having down at Tish's house. It was a funny thing about that. Most foods are best cooked on a proper range and served at a table, but coffee is by God at its best cooked and enjoyed outdoors in the chill of the morning.

He poured himself some and wrapped his hands around the enameled tin cup, then hunkered down close to where Shiver lay so he could enjoy it.

"I . . . could I have . . . a taste o' that java?"

Longarm like to jumped out of his skin. Shiver had been so far out of things that more than once during the previous afternoon and through the night Longarm thought he was dead. Now he'd roused enough to speak.

"Yes. Sure." Longarm shifted over to kneel at the dying man's side. He lifted Shiver's head and let him sip the hot coffee.

"That . . . good . . . thank . . . s."

163

"You're welcome." Longarm let him drink some more. Between them they finished that cup and then another.

"What . . . where . . . are we?"

"Somewhere short of the Ute camp. I'm not for sure how far we have to go yet."

"Why . . . there?"

"Huh?"

"Why . . . go . . . Injun camp?"

"So they can see Blue Quail Singing's killer."

"Somebody . . . kill . . . a quail? So . . . what?"

"No, not somebody killed a quail. Blue Quail Singing was the name of the Indian girl that you killed, Shiver."

"Blue . . ." The miner shuddered. Longarm thought he was dying then, but after a moment he roused himself. "Didn't kill . . . no fucking . . . Injun."

"Why deny it, Shiver? You killed her and then you killed Ford Fargo when he figured out that you'd done it."

"Killed that . . . loudmouth . . . bastard . . . Fargo. I . . . done that . . . you bet. Didn' kill no . . . stinking Injun."

Longarm shrugged. Funny sons of bitches, murderers. They might confess to one crime but deny another just like it. Longarm really couldn't figure the bastards out.

"You want the last of this coffee?" he asked.

There was no answer. Shiver seemed to have gone back into his stupor. Just to be sure, Longarm tipped about a quarter of a bottle of laudanum into his mouth. That was enough to knock him out and probably the brown horse too. But it would keep him from hurting, and that was the idea.

Longarm finished the coffee himself, then left Shiver lying there while he went to saddle the horses again. They'd had all the rest he figured he could give them.

Off to the east the sun was rapidly approaching the horizon.

Off to the west there might well be people dying in the dawn of this new day.

God help them, Longarm thought. Red or white, God help them all.

Chapter 41

The cob was stumbling in the bright noontime sun. Longarm could hear its labored breathing and felt the constant pull on the lead rope as it lagged behind. His bay was having to help pull the bigger horse along.

Then the end of the rope was torn out of his grip completely as the large brown went to its knees. The horse was feathered with thick, ropy lather. Its eyes walled so that the whites showed, and the animal slowly rolled onto its side.

When the brown sprawled onto the ground it carried Shiver down with it, dumping him onto his head and right shoulder and then lying half on top of him when it settled into place.

"Oh, no!" Longarm dropped to the ground, his own legs shaking, and just turned loose of the bay's reins. It was something he almost never did, knowing that a loose horse is all too frequently a runaway. In this case he doubted the bay would take one step that it didn't have to. God knew Longarm did not want to go any further than he must.

He hurried back to the downed brown and his prisoner and discovered that he no longer had a prisoner. What he had back there was a corpse. Earl Shiver had expired sometime during the past hour or so, sometime since Longarm last stopped to loosen the cinches and let the horses breathe easy for a few minutes.

Dammit anyway, he mumbled, then cussed a little under his breath as he cut Shiver's body loose from the saddle and pulled on the lead rope to help the brown stagger back onto its feet.

Without Shiver's weight the horse was able to rise. It wobbled and shook and was likely ruined for the rest of its life so far as wind and endurance were concerned, but at least he hadn't killed it. Yet.

Longarm took a moment to get his own breath, then unfastened the cinches on the brown and pulled the saddle. He dropped the saddle beside a clump of soapweed and stripped the halter and lead rope off the big horse too. He added those to the pile and stood there for a moment trying to work out just what he was going to do with Shiver now that the SOB was dead and how that was likely to affect the Utes and their plans.

"Dammit!" he roared just about as loudly as he could manage. The sound of his voice startled the bay. The worn-out brown horse did not so much as flinch. But half a dozen pine jays fluttered loudly out of the branches of a nearby pine tree in response to Longarm's frustrated cry.

Not that he had a whole hell of a lot of choices left here.

He pulled his belt knife out, cussing himself a little for not packing all his camp gear along for what was supposed to be a quick, light run down the mountain and back up again, then began hiking toward a nearby stand of aspens.

It was going to take him more time than he really had in order to cut down some of the young trees and fashion a travois to haul Shiver's body into the Ute encampment.

It was damn near dark by the time Longarm made it into Iron Ax's camp. The bay was limping, its head down and its feet dragging. But it made it. Carrying Longarm and pulling a dead man behind, the horse made it. Longarm had turned the brown loose a couple hours back. He did not know if the big horse would survive to make its way back down the mountain to the comforts of the Manitou livery and at this point he was just too tired himself to really care. Either way he was sure the government would be stuck with a bill for the cost of replacing the horse. At this point he figured it was Marshal Vail's problem. Or Henry's. Longarm just was too stinking weary to worry about it.

Heads popped out of lodge flaps as Longarm came slowly inside the circle of tepees toward the ashes of the council fire that lay at the center of the camp. People began to emerge, leaving the supper fires inside the lodges.

He could see several of the young men whom he would have thought would be away raiding now if a war had started.

On the other hand, dammit, it was so late in the day that the raids could already have taken place. The Indians might well have already decimated the mining camp and now be home for a bite to eat and a romp with their wives before going off to work tomorrow . . . to slaughter a few more white intruders and bring back more scalps to make the little lady proud.

Bear Killer stepped out into the open.

So did Iron Ax.

And there, close behind Iron Ax, was Harry Baynard.

Longarm had completely forgotten about sending Harry over here to keep an eye on the Utes. It looked like Harry had as good as made himself part of the band from the comfortable way he was standing there.

Longarm let his reins go slack and the bay came to a grateful halt a rod or so short of the scalp pole that stood in front of Iron Ax's lodge.

Iron Ax's young, pretty wife came outside. She chose to stand close to Harry, Longarm noticed. He suspected Harry was getting some of that. And likely enjoying it every bit as much as Longarm had. Sweet girl. Good fuck too.

Longarm lifted his heel over the cantle of his old Mc-Clellan and sat there for a moment, resting sideways on the seat to collect his breath before he allowed himself to slide off the saddle and to the ground.

"Iron Ax. I have returned. I said I would come. My word is good. I tell you only truth."

"This white man. He is the one?"

"Yes, Iron Ax. This is the one."

"He is dead."

"Yes, he is, old friend."

"How he die?"

"Blue Quail Singing killed him. He attacked her. She fought. When I saw the body of your daughter Blue Quail Singing I looked at her fingernails. Here." He showed his own nails to Iron Ax. "I saw red meat there. She scratched the man who attacked her. She scratched this man. The wounds festered and turned rotten. It was the rot that killed him. It was Blue Quail Singing who killed him."

"That is good, but how do I know this?"

"Look for yourself, Iron Ax. You will be able to see the scratches under the bandages that the white doctor in Manitou put on this man."

Longarm motioned for Harry to help him. He cut the strings that bound Shiver to the travois and dumped the body unceremoniously onto the ground.

"Son of a bitch stinks, don't he?" Harry grumbled.

"You get used to it."

"You lie too, Long."

"Well for God's sake don't tell them that."

Longarm pulled open Shiver's shirt, exposing a band of white linen that was tinged yellow and orange with pus that had seeped through the bandages. Harry was right. Up close like this Earl Shiver stank pretty bad.

Longarm drew his knife. He hesitated for a moment before using it. He knew damn good and well Shiver wouldn't feel anything even if he jabbed the point of his blade into the dead man's eyeballs. But it . . . well, it just didn't seem right.

Still, he did not want to go to all the bother—and the smell—of unwrapping yards and yards of linen bandaging. He ran the blade down Shiver's ribs, slicing through the loosely woven cloth and splitting the bandages apart.

168

"There," Longarm said grandly, pointing to the wounds on Shiver's chest.

They were, he saw now, deep knife cuts, not the fingernail scratches he'd been expecting.

Earl Shiver told him that he hadn't raped the girl, and dammit it looked like for once in his miserable life Shiver hadn't been lying.

Someone other than Blue Quail Singing put those cuts there and ultimately killed Shiver. Ford Fargo perhaps? Longarm would never know.

The problem now was that Iron Ax, Bear Killer and the rest of the Utes did know.

They knew that this was *not* the man who murdered Blue Quail Singing.

"Oh, shit," Longarm said. "This is the wrong man, Bear Killer. There's no scratch marks here. I don't know what t' say. I . . . I'm sorry."

"Tomorrow," Bear Killer declared. "Tomorrow we will kill all the white men. Then we know we have the one."

Chapter 42

The bay horse had been taken quietly away while Longarm was paying attention to Earl Shiver. His Winchester was taken with it, of course.

He still had his Colt and if it came to that the derringer in his vest. But it was pretty clear he was not going to fight his way out of the Ute camp. About the only thing he could do now was put on a pretense of normalcy.

For the time being. Sometime between now and daybreak tomorrow he had to warn the miners about the impending attack.

Dammit it all anyway. He'd been so *sure* that Earl Shiver was the killer.

And he'd been wrong.

"We eat," Bear Killer announced when the fire was built up. "Then we dance. Tomorrow is time enough for war."

"Yes, my friend," Longarm said. "Tomorrow." He wondered if he was up to making a run on foot all the way to the mining camp in time to deliver the warning and get the miners prepared to fight.

"Good," Harry said. "They're killing some of them dogs for the feast."

"Jeez, Harry, you like dog meat?"

"Not 'specially, but I hate to hear the damn things barking all the time."

Bear Killer went off toward his own lodge. Longarm

and Harry wandered over to the fire, which was being built to huge proportions.

When they were well clear of any of the Utes, any of whom might well speak English whether they chose to acknowledge the fact or not, Longarm asked, "What's gone on here, Harry? I thought they were going to start the war this morning. I probably killed one horse trying to get up here in time and came close to killing this one too."

Baynard grinned. "Oh, I had some words with 'em," the little thief said. "I told them I was s'posed to make sure they gave you all o' today too before they did anything. That Bear Killer, he said this morning was s'posed to be it. I told him that mayhap you got confused but it was today you was aiming at all along so it'd only be fair for them t' wait until you got your man here. Of course at the time I thought you'd be bringing the right man. Or be smart enough to stay the hell away and go straight to the mining town instead of coming here."

"I guess I wasn't that smart. But thanks for giving me the extra day," Longarm said.

Baynard only shrugged.

"You getting along all right here?" Longarm asked.

"All right? Hell, I like it here. I even like most of the food. Not the bugs. But I like the other stuff."

"Bugs?"

"Ants. Grubs. Shit like that. They use red ants for like a spice. Like a Meskin would use peppers. And they roast the grubs. I can't quite go that far. But the other stuff is pretty good."

Longarm shuddered. "Grubs. Shit."

"Yeah, that's what I think too. But I got to tell you, Long, I never had so much pussy in my life. Never had better neither. These Injun girls are hot stuff, let me tell you."

Longarm did not say anything. Technically speaking, Indians being wards of the same government that he represented, he was not supposed to know anything about

171

how hot an Indian girl could be. But he had no cause to disagree.

"Tell me something, Long."

"Mmm hmm?"

"Tomorrow morning. You figure we'll go under the scalping knives first?"

"Actually, Harry, I think if you stay here inside the circle of these tepees you'll be safe. Their idea of hospitality would demand it. You're here as a guest, never mind that you're a white man. Of course if they catch you over there with the miners you're fair game, and they'd brain you as quick as anybody else."

"Then I think it's a good thing we're here and not there, right?"

"Absolutely," Longarm agreed.

"So tell me. You're gonna try and sneak out and go warn the miners, right?"

"Uh . . . yeah. I reckon I am."

"You're a crazy son of a bitch. You know that, don't you?" Baynard asked.

"I've never denied it."

The little man sighed. "So how're we gonna get out of here? And when? I wouldn't think it'd be safe to try until everybody is asleep. But that wouldn't give us time to make it on foot. We'll have to steal a pair of horses, won't we?"

"Uh huh. Tell me, Harry. You've been living here for a while. Do you think it would be possible for the two of us to steal *all* the horses?"

"So . . . like . . . the Injuns couldn't ride over and raid the miners?"

"Yes."

"No, Long, I don't think we could. Most of Bear Killer's young men are already sleeping with their best ponies tied on long cords to their wrists and at night now they're putting hobbles on all the ones that are turned out to graze. There's no way we could get them all. Not even most of them, I think."

"It was a thought," Longarm said gloomily.

172

"Think it over, Long. Whatever you come up with, count me in."

"You're safe if you stay here, Harry. You know that. And if the Utes take me under tomorrow morning, you're safe from prison too. Later on some time you could slip away easy and no one would ever be the wiser."

"Yeah, I already thought of that."

"So do you still want to sneak off when I do?"

"O' course I do."

Longarm smiled. "For a useless, no account crook, Harry Baynard, you aren't half bad. It's gonna grieve me to put your ass behind bars again."

Baynard grinned. "I wouldn't want to cause you no grief, Long. Feel free to forget about that warrant you have on me."

"I wish I could, Harry. I swear that I do. Uh, it looks to me like the feasting and the fun are gonna start. How are you at war dancing?"

"Say, I can do any kind of a dance. Did I ever tell you that I was a professional entertainer once? It's true, Long, true as I'm standing here. Why, I've performed for the President of the United States and Queen Victoria. Though not at the same time, I hasten to add. Yes, sir, it was a dance troupe, but we also sang a little. Acted some lines. I wish I had my chest handy so I could show you some of the handbills advertising the show. Why, I remember one time . . ."

Harry Baynard rattled on spinning his windy. Longarm ignored the little man and brooded about how he might be able to slip away and make it to the mining camp in time to save a few lives.

Some people were going to die though. That seemed inevitable. Someone was going to die. And it might or more likely would not be the person who really did murder Blue Quail Singing.

Lordy, but the thought of a murderer getting away with his crime did gravel Custis Long's guts.

Chapter 43

Longarm chewed slowly on a piece of slightly sweet, very fine grained and extremely tender meat. He should have liked it but he didn't. There was just something about the idea of eating dog that didn't set well with him.

The serious war dancing hadn't started yet. People were still filling up on the foods. But over across the fire from where Longarm sat, Harry Baynard and a sloe-eyed girl who looked like she couldn't be more than fifteen were doing some sort of a dance.

The truth was that Harry was pretty good at it too. He had the footwork down right well but the hand and arm and upper body movements were a little awkward. The girl seemed willing to teach him for however long he needed.

He was one popular fellow here, Longarm saw. After a while Harry and the girl disappeared into the shadows. When they came back there were grass stains on the back of the girl's dress, and Harry looked mighty relaxed.

But then Longarm supposed it was only reasonable that a man would want to die with his balls empty. Come to think of it, he kind of hoped Iron Ax would send that young wife to Longarm's bed this evening.

Harry came over and dropped into a cross-legged position next to Longarm. He reached for a bowl and a little girl of twelve or so filled it for him, then scampered away all proud of herself for being that close to one of the strange white men.

"I took a look at the horse herd," Harry said out of the corner of his mouth while pretending to concentrate on the dog-meat stew.

"Anything interesting?"

"Your horse and mine have been moved in close where somebody can keep an eye on them, but some of the scrubs are over yonder where they can be got at. You ride bareback?"

"Of course."

"Good for you. But it's a knack I never caught on to."

"I told you before you don't have to go."

"If you go I do too. I wouldn't feel right otherwise."

"These horses you say we can get at. Are they good animals? Broke decent and ready to run?"

"Nope. I told you a'ready they're the scrubs. Half wild sons of bitches mostly."

"So if we jump onto one it's apt to blow up under us."

"Kinda makes it interesting, don't it," Harry said. He helped himself to a cup of something that was in a pottery jar.

"What's that?"

"You don't wanna know. I wish I didn't."

"But you're drinking it anyway," Longarm observed.

"It's like a crooked card game. When it's the only game in town . . ."

"Yeah, I know. If it's all you got you might as well give in and enjoy it."

"Uh huh. I . . . excuse me."

Longarm hadn't seen her approach, but Iron Ax's younger wife was over by Iron Ax's scalp pole. She was motioning for Harry to join her.

"Aren't you too old to be going for seconds this quick, Baynard?"

"So I'll get her to play with it a while first. Lemme go see what she wants now. Maybe I can put her off for a half hour or so until I get my sap up again. Be right back."

Longarm couldn't help but smile in spite of all their troubles. Harry Baynard was irrepressible.

Harry put his arm around the girl's waist, and she went

175

onto her tiptoes and whispered something to him. Longarm thought Harry looked surprised. He leaned down and said something to the girl, then she spoke again at some length. She spoke looking down at the ground. Longarm thought she seemed ashamed about something. Or perhaps frightened. Harry was solemn when he returned to Longarm's side.

"You speak the language, Harry?"

"Naw. But you know how it is with bed talk. You find a way. She has a little English. I picked up a smattering of Ute. Her and me, we get along real good. You know?"

Longarm suspected if Iron Ax wanted to get generous with his women tonight it would be the old crone who came slipping under Longarm's buffalo robe while Harry got to romp the pretty one.

"I got something to tell you, Long, but you got to promise me that you won't tell anybody exactly how this here knowledge came to light. You got to, Long, because I promised her that an' I wouldn't want to go back on my word."

"All right. Unless I'm under oath in a courtroom or something. Whatever it is, I won't go and perjure myself."

"It isn't in a court that would matter. It's here. Tonight."

"All right, but what is it?"

"Scratches. You said whoever raped that girl . . . what was her name . . . Blue Quail something?"

Longarm nodded.

"Whoever did her got himself scratched up some by her. Is that right?"

"Yes. I saw the evidence of it before her body was taken away and hidden someplace."

"Well it might interest you t' know then that a warrior named Rides Far is scratched pretty bad. There's marks still on him though not like they were to begin with, of course."

"Are you sure about this?"

"Muskrat is."

"Muskrat?"

"The girl. That's her name. Well, something sorta like that. I'm not for sure what it really is. Anyway, that's what she just told me. She said . . . this is why you gotta be careful what you say about it . . . she said Rides Far raped her when she was young. He likes it rough. Thing is, she likes it kinda rough too. She's married to the old man now, but she still likes to sneak around and get a little of what Rides Far carries between his legs. That's how she's seen the marks where he was scratched. She said they were put there fresh right about the time that Blue girl got killed."

"Which means . . ."

"Yeah, I expect it does. She knows that too. But she don't want old Iron Ax to know anything about this because it's one thing for him to loan her to whoever he wants, but it'd be a big insult for her to go off an' hump some buck without him telling her to. She says he'd likely cut her nose off and divorce her, an' then where would she be."

"Shit," Longarm said. "So who is this Rides Far fellow?"

"You see that big guy over there with the gray squirrel fur wrapped around his braids? That's him."

Longarm sat for a moment staring into the fire and thinking.

Then he stood and walked out into the middle of the dance ring where the revelers were getting ready to go on the warpath come daybreak.

Chapter 44

For what seemed a very long time Longarm stood motionless in the firelit ring, head down and arms hanging at his sides.

After a bit he began to tremble, almost to vibrate.

He looked up at the starlit sky and raised his arms.

In a deep, husky voice he began to have a conversation of which observers could hear only one side. Longarm said, "Ick kaebla boo sistimus bekoko."

He stopped and listened a while, then said, "Quirdit mongo fibibint deohaw." He nodded and said, "Kindo mai." Then he listened again for quite some time, still with his arms lifted high.

Eventually he lowered his arms and said, "Kindo lee."

At that his chin dropped toward his chest and he stood as if in a trance. By then he had the full attention of everyone in the band, young or old, male or female. They stood in silent awe until Longarm once again lifted his face to the sky.

He began a low chant and a short, stomping dance, turning in slow circles, then faster and faster until he was whirling around as fast as he could propel himself.

Finally he let out a screech and dropped to the ground as if in a dead faint.

No one approached him. No one tried to touch him. He lay there until eventually his eyes opened and he climbed back onto his feet.

He held his hands up, palms outward, and loudly announced, "I have heard from a spirit. A new spirit, one I do not know. The spirit has spoken to me. The spirit has given a message to me. The spirit asks me to open the eyes of its favored people. The spirit asks me to fulfill the word I gave to The People. The spirit asks me to bring the killer of Blue Quail Singing to justice as I once promised to do." Longarm's eyes drooped as if he were in a trance, and his voice deepened. "The spirit says the murderer is here among us. The spirit will direct me to the one. The spirit . . ." He broke off the words and barked like a dog, shaking and trembling and jerking his limbs.

He heard murmurs of fear and the shuffling of moccasins in the grass as the people moved back away from him into the night.

"The spirit wants all to come close," Longarm said loudly. "The spirit wants the children here." He pointed. "The spirit wants the unmarried here. The spirit wants the old to be here. The spirit wants the warriors to come here. Here. Here. Here." He motioned in small circles around and around on a spot close by the big fire. "All. Here. No one of The People is to . . . is to . . . all must be here. And here. And here. The warriors must be here."

He did the jerky dance again, and this time he heard the people moving close around him, moving to where the unknown spirit was supposed to have said.

Longarm waited until he heard no more movement before he again opened his eyes.

He dropped onto his haunches and like an organ-grinder's monkey sprang on all fours along the row where the children were seated. He came into a crouch and half shuffled, half danced his way through the young unmarrieds and then past the women and the old people.

Finally he came to the warriors. He stopped. Threw his head back and tilted it as if listening once again to the voice of the spirit.

After that he walked slowly past the warriors one by one, pausing before each of them to lay the palm of his left hand onto the warrior's right shoulder. With each of them he would squeeze lightly and shake them. Then drop his arm and move to the next.

He touched the shoulder of Iron Ax. Of Bear Killer. Of each of the warriors.

Until he reached Rides Far.

And this time when he touched the man's flesh Longarm screamed and jerked his hand away as if he were burned.

"Ayyyyyyyiiii!"

Rides Far spun around and ran for his life, disappearing into the night within seconds.

Longarm fell to the ground . . . which was not an entirely bad idea anyway. He was still so damned tired he thought he would shit.

The warriors of the band stood in shocked silence for a heartbeat. Then with wild cries they went pounding into the night in pursuit of Rides Far.

After a bit Harry edged over beside Longarm and knelt down close to his ear. "The coast is clear, Long. I think you can get up now. You an' that spirit."

Longarm opened his eyes. He looked puzzled. "Spirit? What the hell are you talking about a spirit for, Harry?"

"Long!"

Longarm laughed and winked at him. "C'mon, Harry. I don't know about you, but I'm wore down complete. I got to get some sleep now or die for the lack of it."

Chapter 45

Longarm and Harry Baynard rode slowly along the creek that would eventually bring them to the mining camp where men would still be waiting in anticipation of an attack that, thankfully, would not come.

They rode very slowly because it would take days for Longarm's bay to recover from the punishment he'd put it through. But then he figured he could give the horse plenty of time to rest up once he got down to Manitou. After all, he had a lot of paperwork to do down there before he could collect his prisoner.

Thinking of prisoners, Longarm turned to Baynard. "Y'know, Harry, it's a damn shame I can't trust you to stay out of trouble."

"Trouble, Long? I don't know what you mean. I'm innocent as a lamb, I tell you. And as inoffensive. Wouldn't harm the hair on a pretty girl's ass, I wouldn't."

"Pretty girls don't have hairy asses, Harry."

Baynard beamed. "See? I told you I wouldn't. And I don't."

"You, Harry, are incorrigible."

"Sad, but true." After a moment Harry brightened. "Whatever happened to Rides Far last night? Did Iron Ax tell you?"

"He didn't offer to say, and I didn't ask. Just like they didn't ask anything about that spirit I heard from. Whatever it was, they're satisfied with it. That seems good enough to me."

"And there won't be no war."

"And there won't be a war," Longarm agreed. He yawned and stretched. He still had some sleep to catch up on. But he supposed that could wait too until he reached Manitou and had better company than Harry Baynard while he was doing it.

"You know," Longarm mused aloud, "it's a damned shame what happened to that prisoner of mine."

"What prisoner?"

"Guy by the name of Baynard. Harry, his first name was."

"What the hell are you talking about, Long?"

"I'm talking about poor Harry Baynard. I had him in custody. Then that asshole Earl Shiver came along and murdered him. Put a knife into his gizzard slick as you please."

"What? But . . ."

"Yep. And so it will say in the report I'll be turning in when I get back to Denver. My warrant got served, but the miscreant was murdered by that Shiver fella before I could get him back to face the court.

"Of course that will save the taxpayers the cost and the bother of a trial. But it's a shame nonetheless."

"But you . . ."

"Reckon I should also mention to my boss what a big help that fine upstanding citizen Ford Fargo was, helping me keep Iron Ax's band of Utes quiet. Placing himself in jeopardy of his life to do so. Yep, he's quite a fellow is Ford Fargo."

Longarm gave his companion a long, level look. "Isn't that right, Mr. Fargo?"

Baynard . . . or rather Fargo . . . waved his hand. "You can call me Ford. All my friends do."

Longarm began to laugh. He was still laughing when they reached the outskirts of the little no-name mining camp beside the no-name little creek far back in the Front Range mountains.

Watch for

LONGARM AND THE PIRATE'S GOLD

306th novel in the exciting LONGARM series
from Jove

Coming in May!

**Explore the exciting Old West with one
of the men who made it wild!**

J. R. ROBERTS

THE GUNSMITH

parked outside the gate and walked up to the courtyard. I thought I'd take a few minutes for myself before
I went in and became what you thought me to be." His
lips twisted. "Haven't you heard that music soothes the
savage beast."

"I believe the quote refers to 'savage breast'."

"I've always thought that my way was more appropriate. And you probably do, too. We've been together during
many occasions when my true nature came to the fore-
front. Isn't that what you see when you look at me, Jane?"

It was true. They had known each other for a few
years, and Caleb had seemed to appear whenever she was
involved in a situation that was threatening. She had a
sudden memory of a time when they had been together
in the Alps and Caleb's throwing a body down before her
like a savage giving a gift to his mate. The man he had
killed had been attacking them, but all she had been able
remember was the savagery and pleasure in Caleb's
e.

He laughed. "You're having to think about it. Are
afraid you're going to hurt my feelings? You're no
ally so diplomatic."

You're not a beast. You do have your primitive side
n't know what you are, Caleb. I don't believe yo
me to know. I do know you're intelligent, complex
an be amusing. I know I owe you my life when yo
to me in the hospital."

d you may never forgive me for that." His smi
ne, his tone fierce. "You wanted me to let you d
you could join your lover in the great beyond?
about to let that happen. I won't let you go, Jane
gave me an invaluable gift. It doesn't matt
I wanted it or not. I still have to be grateful f
did." She smiled faintly. "And I'm sure th

I said, it's all about the music." She was only a few yards
away from Cara, and she deliberately moved into her field
of vision and stopped.

It still took Cara a few minutes to notice she was there.
And a moment more to reluctantly lift the bow and stop
the music. "Is it time to go in?"

"I'm afraid it is," Eve said. "It's been a long day. Time
to get to bed."

She nodded and got to her feet. "I like it here, Eve. The
music is stronger here than I've ever felt it. Even when
I'm not playing, I can hear it."

"I know what you mean." Jane came closer to her and
sat down on the edge of the fountain. "I'm no musician,
and I can almost hear it. Some places seem to make their
own music. The Highlands are like that. I think you'll
like Gaelkar."

Jock nodded. "Aye, wild and wonderful things have
happened there, haven't they, Jane?"

She met his eyes. "And how would I know? I've never
been there. But it's deep in the Highlands."

"Well, we should be there by tomorrow night and she
can judge for herself." He took Cara's hand. "May I es-
cort you inside, mademoiselle?"

"Much better than chick," Eve murmured.

She watched as Jock and Cara walked back to the front
door. The beautiful, strong young man and the small,
fragile young girl. There was something very touching
and old-world about the protectiveness that Jock was
showing the child. She glanced at Jane as she started after
them. "Coming?"

"In a moment." Jane dipped her hand into the water
of the fountain and let the drops slowly fall back into the
water. "I'll be in soon."

Eve stopped. "Okay?"

"I should be asking you that," Jane said. "I just want some quiet time."

Eve nodded and started up the steps. "I'll see you upstairs."

"Eve."

She looked back at her.

"I'm glad you came to me. I'm glad you trusted me to help." She smiled. "We'll get that little girl through this."

"Yes, we will. We can get through anything together." She blew her a kiss. "Family."

Jane watched Eve disappear into the castle and close the front door.

She stayed there, her eyes on the door.

Waiting.

One minute passed.

Two minutes passed.

"Dammit, what are you doing, Caleb?" she said impatiently as she turned to glare at the shadows of the stable across the courtyard. "What game are you playing?"

"No game." Seth Caleb strolled out of the shadows toward her. He was wearing a black turtleneck sweater and khakis, and the moonlight glimmered on the white thread in his dark hair and lit his high cheekbones, deep-set dark eyes, and full lips. "I was just admiring you in the moonlight. I don't often get a chance to observe you without your getting nervous. How long ago did you realize I was here?"

"I don't know. Not right away. Maybe I saw a movement."

"Then why didn't you sound the alarm?"

"Because I knew it was you."

"How?"

"You sent me a message you'd be coming tonight."

"Yes, I did." He stopped before her. "So it was en reasonable that you'd come to that conclusion. smiled. "But reason had nothing to do with it, did it felt me here."

"Think what you like, Caleb."

"Oh, I will. I just want you to admit it to your not to me. We have a connection. It's been ther the beginning. Electricity?" He tilted his head along with something, deeper, less civilized. I se all the time when you're anywhere around me."

"I don't want to talk about this."

"Then be honest, Jane."

"It . . . might be possible. You gave me bloo was hurt and you have that . . . thing with bloo

His brows rose. "Thing?"

"Hell, what else can I call it? What are we to call it? I'm sure it doesn't have any technic don't know anyone else who's able to ma blood flow of anyone he's close to. It's too dangerous, she thought. It wasn't only he could control if he chose to use that talen She had seen him do it, and that power "And you have to admit it's hard to desc

He nodded. "Unique, as far as I can d my family. A small gift, but my own."

"Well, it evidently worked for me since I don't have any idea how it wo subject to some kind of residual— anything." She stared him in the ey something else? Like what you we shadows while Cara was playing?

"I wasn't lurking. Is it too muc want her to stop when I arrived playing while I was still drivi you're arrogant enough to believe that you have control of my life, but forget that. I'll run my own life. I have no intention of dying. I was wrong. There are people who need me. And two of them are in that castle." She got to her feet. "I didn't want you to come because you're always disturbing. But you're here, so make yourself useful. The only thing I want from you is for you to keep Eve and Cara safe." She added deliberately, "And not to get in my way while I'm trying to do it. Do you understand?"

"Of course. You're always very clear with me. Much more clear than you are with anyone else. It's as if you think I'll step outside bounds if given the excuse." He was smiling again. "I'll be very careful not to do that. I'll let you ignore me as much as you're capable. I'll be wonderfully helpful and make certain that all goes well with your world."

"And what are you going to get out of all this, Caleb?"

"Opportunity." He headed for the front door. "It's all I need . . ."

Eve had thought she would be tired enough to sleep, but she realized after an hour of tossing and turning that wasn't going to happen. Not surprising. She was still charged from the flight from Atlanta, and it seemed that every moment since then had been full of renewing relationships, making sure that Jane was okay with what was happening, and Cara was comfortable in this new environment. It was like a new and different life from the one she had left behind her in Atlanta.

And she should be grateful that life appeared to be so different. Talk of ancient ruins and treasures instead of bombs and threats of death at every turn. She *was* grateful. She just wanted to be back with Joe and working to have this nightmare over. It might be safer for her, but what about Joe?

Don't think about it. Do her job as Joe was doing his.

Cara.

She got out of the huge bed and padded across the room to the adjoining room, where Cara was sleeping. She quietly opened the door and peeked at the girl in the bed across the room.

She was fast asleep. It was clear Cara had not had the same problem as Eve. But then children usually slept well. She remembered Jane had no problems until she was in her teens, and Bonnie had been able to curl up anywhere and drop off. Eve had found her so many times in the hammock in the yard with her hand tucked beneath her cheek and her red curls mussed from play.

Bonnie . . .

Eve quietly closed the door and went over to the casement window that she had left thrown wide when she went to bed. She looked out at the forests and the hills beyond.

"I haven't heard from you, and it's beginning to scare me, Bonnie. You told me once that you might not be able to come to me anymore," she whispered. "Is it because you don't think I'll need you? I'll always need you. I want this child. It's a miracle. But I can't let you go. We've been together too long. It would be like losing you all over again."

Silence.

She touched her abdomen.

Hey, tell Bonnie we need her. I don't know if she had anything to do with making you come into our lives, but she might have. She's pretty special, and it wouldn't surprise me if she has influence. But we have to make sure that she sticks around for us, okay?

No answer there, either.

Of course not. What did she expect? The baby was trying to survive and become the child it was meant to be. It was Eve's job to handle everything else. She was being ridiculous, and she should go to bed and try to sleep.

She got as far as settling down in bed again. Then she was reaching for her phone and dialing.

Joe answered immediately. "What's wrong?"

"Nothing," she said. "Everything. I just wanted to hear your voice and know that you were all right. We're going to start off tomorrow trekking through some castle in the Highlands. I feel a million miles away from you right now."

"Me, too." He paused. "You're feeling okay?"

"Strong. Very strong. I could lift mountains."

"Exaggerating a bit?"

"A bit. But not that much. I remember I felt like this when I was pregnant with Bonnie. It was as if she was giving me her strength, too. The only problem was a few weeks when I couldn't keep anything down. So stop worrying. Everything's working out well with Manez?"

"Hell, yes. He's giving me more than I expected. Perhaps more than he expected. It may be a break for us."

"What are you talking about?"

"Just rumors right now. I'll let you know when I can confirm them." He paused. "I got a call from Les Carmody at the Forensics Department a couple hours ago. They wanted to assure me that they were making progress and should be able to tell me something fairly soon."

Not good. "I thought you said that it might be another day."

"I'm a cop." He grimaced. "They're trying their best to help me out. There's a good chance they're already suspecting the truth since they can't have recovered any trace of body parts yet. They just don't want to raise my hopes."

"And Salazar will probably know almost as soon as you do that there was no one in that car."

"I'd bet on it. And I'll be glad when you manage to lose yourself in those Highlands." He changed the subject. "How is Jane doing?"

"Better. Not as good as I'd like to see her, but she's healing. We can't ask for more than that right now."

"Does she know about the baby?"

"Not yet. I'm waiting. She's already trying to protect me. I don't want her worrying any more than she is already." She added teasingly, "And have her ask every time she talks to me if I'm surviving this pregnancy."

"Was that aimed at me?"

"Gently. Lovingly."

"I'll accept both with thanks. On that note, I'll let you go so that you can get some sleep. Don't overdo it tomorrow while you're trekking over that ruin, even if you think you can lift mountains."

"Joe."

He laughed and hung up.

She was smiling as she put her phone on the nightstand and turned over in bed. The news had not been all good, but merely talking to Joe made her feel a sense that they were on the move . . . and together.

Don't think that any minute Salazar and Franco might find out that they had been fooled.

They would still have to find out where she and Cara had gone. That would take time.

Lord, she hoped it would take enough time.

Joe hung up from talking to Eve and stared down at his phone. She had sounded good, but she would not have phoned if she hadn't needed to touch base with him. Eve's career as a forensic sculptor dominated her life, and she was used to working nonstop. She would never have chosen to uproot herself and go on this outlandish treasure hunt in the wilds of Scotland.

But he had chosen for her, and she was trying to adjust and make it work for them.

At possibly one of the most crucial points of her life.

He wanted to be *with* her, dammit.

Calm down. They were already involved and had involved Jane and Cara. It had to work.

But push it along, make it happen sooner.

He picked up his phone again and quickly dialed Manez.

"Don't you ever sleep?" Manez asked sourly when he picked up the phone. "You may be driven, but I need my rest after a day of dealing with this scum."

"You promised me an address."

"That was less than twelve hours ago. Nothing moves fast down here unless you want to end up hanging from a bridge without a head."

"Bullshit. You're just as driven as I am. I'd bet you dove into squeezing all available informants the minute you hung up with me."

"That doesn't mean I was able to tap into information that was accurate."

"Were you?"

"Maybe. I'm still exploring the—"

"Give me an address."

"I'd prefer to verify first."

"We may be running out of time. I need to get a handle on this."

"I don't want you jetting down here and causing a blowup before I'm ready."

"I need that address."

Manez was silent. "Very well, but you don't move without me."

"As long as you don't drag your feet."

Manez sighed. "You're a very difficult man, Quinn. The address is one forty-five El Camino Road."

GAELKAR CASTLE
SCOTLAND

"Good God, MacDuff. It's magnificent." Eve was gazing out the window of the Land Rover at the staggering beauty of the amethyst-slate mountains in the distance as they neared the castle. The dramatic towering starkness of the peaks, the barrenness that was the vast glens took her breath away. The sun was shining, and yet these Highlands still retained their moody, almost stormy, grandeur. "You didn't tell me."

"It's always best to be surprised." He smiled at her. "You think Cira chose well for her new kingdom?"

"You'd have to ask Jane. I think it probably suited her. There's a wildness here that I can see her appreciating."

"I refuse to ask Jane. She won't want to commit herself."

Eve looked back at Cara, who was sitting beside Jane. "Do you like it, Cara?"

She nodded, her eyes fixed dreamily on the mountains. "So much music . . . And did you see the eagles?"

"I'm afraid I didn't notice either of those things. I was just taking in the general impact." She turned back to MacDuff. "How long before we get to the castle?"

"It's just around the curve up ahead. It may disappoint you."

"It's ruins, for goodness' sake. Low expectations."

But she still found herself eager to see that castle built so long ago at the dawn of this land.

"There it is." MacDuff pulled to the side of the road and got out of the Land Rover. He looked up the hill at the ruins of the castle while they waited for Caleb and Jock, who had opted to come in Caleb's car. "It's not very large, but it's in better shape than you would imagine for the lack of repair. That one wall of the battlements is as strong as when they built it. The dungeons are still entirely intact. Once the family left, they abandoned it. They were moving up in the world and concentrated all their energies on building their new home on the coast."

"MacDuff's Run, the castle where you grew up?" Eve asked, as she and Cara got out to stand beside him. "I'm certain that anyone would agree it's much more impressive than this one."

"I like it." Cara's gaze was fastened on the broken walls and tumbled stone of the castle. "It's . . . nice."

MacDuff chuckled. "You constantly amaze me. You criticize my humble hunting lodge, which granted is not in wonderful condition, but you're besotted with this ruin."

"I just think it feels like home," Cara said simply.

"Providing your home has a dungeon." He turned to Jane. "What do you think? Does it feel like home?"

"That's a leading question." She smiled at Cara. "But a castle can be a home as well as a fortress. When I was still trying to find out everything about Cira, I went on archaeological digs in Herculaneum. We had to be very careful not to destroy anything that would indicate how the people lived or died. We worked with spoons, carefully sifting."

"Is that what you're going to do here?" Cara asked eagerly.

Jane glanced at MacDuff. "It's how I'd prefer to do it. It's surprising what secrets can be revealed by using a spoon instead of a shovel. Since we have no idea where we're going with this, it might be a good idea to see if we can get a clue." She added, "But then, I'm not in charge."

"And you think I'm going to use a battering ram because I'm too impatient?"

"I know about impatience," Jane said. "I've been there. Ask Eve. It's your show, MacDuff."

He nodded. "And maybe we'll try a spoon . . . for a little while."

"Good." Jane turned to Cara. "Then would you like to grovel in the dirt with me? Warning. You'll have an aching back and bruised knees unless we can find someplace that sells knee pads."

"Could I do that?" Cara's face was lit with excitement. "I saw a show on *National Geo* that had one of those college digs. It looked like fun."

"Like I said, sore knees. But I found it worth it. There's no guarantee that we'll find anything, but there's always a chance." She looked at Eve. "You're invited, too."

"I didn't expect you'd leave me out. It will give me something to do. I'm not accustomed to sitting around twiddling my thumbs." Eve stood looking up at the hill. "Those people who built that castle didn't know the meaning of twiddling their thumbs. You can almost sense the energy and determination. I wonder how much was done by hand."

"It was Cira's home," Jane said. "Her first taste of real freedom and power after being born a slave. She would have gotten down on her knees and laid those tiles herself. She would have rigged a pulley like the Egyptians to drag those stones in place. She probably loved this castle."

"Then why would she have left it?" Eve asked.

"She didn't, it was her descendants who finally decided they needed to take the next step. She built this place as a kingdom, but I'm sure that she instilled that thirst for power in those who came after her. She grew up in Herculaneum realizing how weak a woman could be if she didn't have wealth and influence. She did the best she was able, became a famous actress, and gathered what wealth she could. Then, when the volcano erupted, she fled with everything she owned." Jane smiled. "And some things she didn't own. She probably hid out in the Highlands for a long time after she first arrived here until she thought she was safe. Then she decided it was time to start to build."

"Well, after her descendants decided to abandon this place, they apparently never looked back on what she'd built," MacDuff said dryly. "We have no record of any of her family returning here after they reached the coast, where they built MacDuff's Run."

"They might have looked back," Jane said. "They liked money; you say the family earned their title by raiding and robbing along the border. If they didn't take those coins with them, then I can see them going back to get them. Unless there was a reason not to do it."

"Can we find out?" Cara asked.

"Maybe," Jane said. "If they left us a clue one way or the other."

"The spoon?" Cara grinned.

"The spoon," Jane said solemnly. She turned back to the Land Rover. "Let's start unloading our bags and supplies and get them up to the castle. I assume you didn't arrange for help here either, MacDuff?"

He nodded. "Jock and I will come back for the tents and camping supplies. Privacy appeared to be everything when Quinn called and asked me to take you. And it's a good rule to follow when you're going after a treasure trove, too."

"I can see that," Eve said. "But that hill looks like a climb." She was grabbing for her backpack. "Let's get to it."

"I'll do it." Cara was already helping Jane with her backpack. She was moving with alacrity, and her expression was eager. Eve was glad to see it. There was nothing better than purpose to make time pass quickly and give one a sense of worth.

"There's Caleb," Jane said as she watched his car come down the road toward them.

Eve was aware that Jane's easy casualness was abruptly gone. All she needed was to have Caleb show up on the scene, and she was charged, wary.

Jane looked at Eve and shrugged. "What can I say?"

"Nothing. I was just thinking that tutoring Cara in the art of the dig might be good for you, too." She started up the road, letting the barren beauty and austerity of the hills around her reach out and touch her, take her into the misty earth and blue sky. For this instant she could almost believe she belonged here.

Work.

Distraction.

It could be a solution for all of them.

Son of a bitch!

"It's not possible," Franco said through his teeth. "It's not true." He hung up, breathing hard as the fury tore through him. But it was true and he knew it. Jessup, that greedy bastard in Forensics, wouldn't lie to him. He knew what would happen to him if he did.

So what did he do now?

No choice.

He dialed Salazar. "We have a problem. Forensics found no body parts in the Toyota."

Silence. Then Salazar began to swear.

"You fool. How could you make a mistake like that?"

"I'm not a fool."

"You're worse, you stupid prick. You're worse than Walsh ever was. Quinn played you. You lost the kid *and* Duncan."

He had no defense. He was humiliated. But he was going to kill Salazar for talking to him like that. "Not for long. I'll go after Quinn and find out where he sent them. I won't let him do this to me."

"He's already done it." Salazar's voice was harsh. "You've been keeping track of Quinn?"

"Of course, you wanted him dead."

"It's good that you didn't kill him yet. He's the only one who knows where the kid is. Is he at the Lake Cottage?"

"He left there to go to the precinct where he works. I followed him, but he didn't come out. He'll probably be back this evening."

"Probably? Find out for sure. I'll cut your heart out if you lose him, too." He hung up.

He meant it, Franco knew. This last mistake had made his position impossible. Salazar might cut his heart out anyway no matter what he did. He would try to make amends by butchering Quinn, but he had to prepare for the worst-case scenario. Salazar would more than likely send one of his primo killers to make sure that everyone knew he was a failure and what was done with a man who failed him.

Get ahead of the game. He was smart. He could find out where Quinn had sent Duncan and the girl for safety. Then he could either tell Salazar or go ahead and take care of them himself.

Then he would dispose of Quinn in the most brutal way possible, a true *rematar,* a bloodbath.

And then he would start planning how he would rid himself of Salazar without having to contend with the other members of the cartel. He was in a better position to do that than ever before.

He had an ace in the hole.

It would all come together. He just had to move fast. First, find Eve Duncan and Castino's brat.

"I need to talk to you," Salazar said. "Tonight at ten." He hung up.

He hadn't wanted to do this. This meeting was a risk when he didn't need any more risks.

He had no choice. Franco's failure had put him in a corner. He might need help, and he wasn't going to go through this alone.

It would be all right, they'd work it out.

All this hell would be worth it.

He got to his feet and moved out onto the patio where his children were swimming in the pool. Beautiful children, he thought with satisfaction as he watched his son, Carlos, race across the pool. Three fine sons.

Castino had never been able to produce sons, just those two puny daughters, who had caused him such a headache during these last years.

But one child was dead and the other would soon be

totally out of the picture, too. And then he would have his reward.

Yes, and the meeting tonight would be worth the risk.

MEXICO CITY

One forty-five El Camino Road was an elegant creamy-tan stucco hacienda surrounded by trees behind a tall wrought-iron fence.

And the fence wasn't electrified, thank God, Joe realized, as he pulled himself up and over. He jumped to the ground, then darted behind the trees and made his way toward the house.

A soft glow issued from the windows at the rear of the house. Salazar?

There was no telling if Salazar would come to this house tonight, but, if what Manez said was true, there would never be a more likely time for him to show up. That was why Joe had jumped on a plane to fly down here when he'd been told the results from the Forensics Department.

He crouched behind a bank of large shrubs near the driveway, every sense alert.

Be patient, he told himself.

When you're playing a hunch, you have to be prepared for it not to pan out.

But that hunch was strong and burning bright. He needed a break, and this might be the one.

No one seemed to be moving around inside. There were no cars in the driveway.

But they could be parked in the back. The trees were so

thick that any vehicles wouldn't be seen unless you were right on top of them.

So stake out the house.

And wait for lightning to strike.

Headlights from the sleek black Mercedes entering the gates, not surreptitiously as Joe would have thought, but boldly, recklessly.

The car was coming fast and was approaching the driveway in seconds.

A screech of brakes as the car stopped, and the driver's door flew open.

Come on, Joe thought, let me see you. Is it true?

Then the driver jumped out of the car and was striding toward the front door, every step emotion-charged and full of explosive anger.

Joe stiffened. Oh yes, it was true.

Moonlight fell on sleek dark hair.

And the beautiful face and winged brows that were so very like her daughter, Cara's.

Natalie Castino.

CHAPTER
7

Salazar flinched as the door slammed after Natalie came into the house.

"I see you're in fine temper," he said as he strolled out of the bedroom. "And you drove right up to the house instead of parking in the trees. Not smart, Natalie. The only way we've survived so far is to be careful. Do you want to get us killed?"

"I'd see that I wasn't the one killed." Natalie threw her handbag on the couch. "I'd just tell everyone that you lured me here to offer me information about the kidnapping of my little girls. A mother is always desperate and willing to take chances when it concerns a child. Of course, I'd have to shoot you so that it would make the story stick." Her eyes were glittering with anger as she strode toward him. "But I'm not desperate, I'm furious, because I think that you're going to tell me that you've made another mistake. Isn't that right?"

"Duncan and Cara weren't in the car. Franco doesn't know where they are."

"I knew it," she said through clenched teeth. "I could see it coming when you told me that Duncan had taken Cara to Atlanta. What are you doing about it? You're not relying on that stupid prick to find them?"

"I haven't taken him out of the action. I may be able to use him."

"What are you doing?" she asked again.

"I've tapped Jose Domingo, my distributor in Atlanta and told him to check out airline manifests on commercial airlines for the last two days. He's checking out train and bus, too. But I'd think that Quinn would want Duncan and the kid to go far and fast to get them to safety. So far, no records of them have surfaced. So Domingo is checking private and charter flights."

"How long before you'll know?"

"Only a few days. I have to be careful about pushing Domingo. His contacts are valuable to me. He doesn't want to make waves with ATLPD by any overt moves. After all, he could deal with any of the other cartels."

"Then go after Quinn," she said impatiently.

"We're getting there. He's been off the radar for the last several hours since we've heard about the forensic report. But Franco will locate him."

"Maybe he's gone to join Duncan and Cara."

"He went to the trouble of staging that elaborate red herring. He won't chance being followed and giving their hiding place away. He knows we're watching him. Franco will gather him up if he doesn't get another lead before that." He held up his hand as she opened her lips. "I know, an incompetent fool."

"You seem to hire no one else, first Walsh, now Franco. This entire thing has been bungled. You *promised* me. I trusted you." Her hands clenched into fists. "I gave you my daughters. You said that it would be over in a heartbeat, and no one would ever know."

"We've gone over this before. It didn't work out." He was sick to death of her attacking him. He just wished he was sick of her. He'd thought in the beginning that he'd grow tired of her and would be able to find a way to dispose of her and make his position more secure. It hadn't happened. He only had to see her, touch her, and he had to have her. Just thinking about her, and he got hard. He wanted her now. "And you wanted those girls dead as much as I did. I did you a favor."

"No, I told you I wanted them kidnapped. I didn't say you had to kill them."

"You knew that was the only safe way to handle it. You just closed your eyes. Why else were you so angry when I told you that Cara and that nurse got away?"

"Because at that point there was nothing else to do. I couldn't go back. I had to go on with it."

He slowly shook his head. "You wanted it." He moved closer to her. She smelled of vanilla and that exotic Russian perfume she'd worn since the day he'd met her. She'd told him her father sent it to her every year. Whether he screwed her or not, before he left her he always had to shower and get her scent off him before he went home to Manuela. His wife knew he had other women, but she couldn't know about Natalie, and that perfume was too distinctive. "And you wanted me. You still want me."

"Not now," she said impatiently.

"Now." He put his hand on her breast. "You're not sleeping with Castino. You need it. I can feel your nipples hardening." He rubbed at the sensitive tips through her silk shirt. "I'm doing everything you'd want me to do about the kid. It won't be long and you'll be safe." He unbuttoned her shirt. "But I need encouragement . . ." His tongue touched her nipple. "Give it to me."

"I don't need you." She was starting to breathe hard. "There are other men."

"None that I wouldn't kill if I caught you with them." He bit down hard and felt the shudder that went through her. "Like I did when I heard you were screwing that chauffeur you hired to take you around to your fancy parties. Do you remember what I did to him?"

"Yes. It was . . . bloody."

"You liked it. You liked knowing that you'd caused it. That you had the power. It was difficult for me to do it in a way Castino wouldn't suspect had a connection with you." He pushed her away and took off her blouse and bra. "So I set him up to be caught in a Federales raid near the border. I protected you then, too, didn't I?"

"And yourself."

"It's the same thing."

She looked at him challengingly. "You only want me because I belong to Castino."

"Not only. You know better. It might have started out that way, but we're both caught now."

"Not me." She stared fiercely up at him. "I'll let you have me only as long as you amuse me. When I get bored, I'll walk away."

"I haven't bored you yet." His hands tightened on her breasts. "Get in bed."

She didn't move. "That's not why I came here."

"It's why I came here. Sometimes you're so concerned someone will find out about this place that I can't get you to come. But you came tonight, didn't you?"

"Let me go."

"Get in bed. Why not? We're here now. You're hot,

you need it." He added thickly, "And I need you. I'll make you scream, Natalie."

She smiled. "Perhaps."

"Are you teasing me? That's very dangerous."

"I've heard nothing but what you want." She took off the rest of her clothes and stood there naked. "I want to hear what you want to give me." She took down her chignon and her hair flowed around her shoulders. "Oh, I'll scream for you." She came toward him. "And I'll make you scream. But I came here for a purpose, and you'll give me what I want."

"I told you that I was working on it. I have to be careful."

She rubbed against him like a cat. "Not good enough. I don't care about being careful any longer. I want a promise that you'll keep." She reached down, caressing him. "And you'll give it to me."

Her breasts brushing against him. The scent of her . . . "Shit."

"I need it to happen. You either give it to me, or I'll find someone who will."

"I'll kill you."

"No, you'll give me Duncan and Cara, and it won't be in a few days. You'll know where they are tomorrow. I don't care if it causes problems with your distributor in Atlanta. You'll do what you have to do." She went to the bed and lay down. "And before you leave here tonight, you're going to promise me that no matter what you have to do, I'll know where to find them."

"You?" He was over her, tearing off his clothes.

"Me. I can't leave it to you any longer." She gazed up at him as he came into her. "I have to make sure it's done." She whispered as she started to move, "Now promise me . . ."

3:15 A.M.

"Come back to bed," Salazar said thickly as he watched Natalie dress. "I'm not done with you."

"I'm done with you." She slipped on her shoes and went over to the mirror on the far wall. "You were right, I needed it. You were very entertaining." She ran her fingers through her hair. "We may have to arrange things so that we can do this more often. Would you like that?"

"I'd like to stay alive more," he said dryly. "Too dangerous."

"That's what I always say, but I'm beginning to think we should explore the possibilities. We need a change." She touched up her lipstick. "If you find me exciting enough?"

She knew damn well the effect she had on him. "Stop playing games and come back here."

"You don't have time. You have calls to make, don't you?" Her smile was brilliant as she turned back to him. "And I have arrangements to take care of, too. Changes . . . Salazar." She headed for the door. "I can hardly wait."

He watched the door close behind her and cursed low and vehemently. He was still horny as hell, and that wasn't his only frustration. He didn't like it that Natalie was being so demanding, but he knew it had been coming. He had barely been able to restrain her for the last few years.

He looked at his phone on the bedside table. Those calls Natalie had spoken about were against his better judgment. Not good business. It was clever to stay beneath the radar and not do anything to disturb either the Feds or the police department and make them pay too much attention to his operations. But if he didn't meet

Natalie's deadline, she would be even more likely to become difficult.

What the hell, he thought recklessly. He was ready for a change, too. He was tired of being careful. How many years had it been since he had been like Franco and taken what he wanted and made everyone around him fear him? He wanted that heady feeling again.

He picked up the phone and dialed Franco.

"I need to know where Duncan and the kid are by tomorrow night. Do you have any possibilities?"

Franco hesitated. "Your man here in town said that he'd discounted all the commercial airlines and narrowed it down to four or five private airlines. Three Quinn has used in the past nine years. I thought I'd check those out. I'll be careful. Domingo said you wanted us to be discreet."

"I want to know tomorrow night. Screw being discreet." He hung up.

3:35 A.M.

Joe watched Natalie Castino drive out of the gates and waited another fifteen minutes for Salazar to leave. He didn't come out of the house. The lights in the bedroom went off after another five minutes. He probably felt safe as long as Natalie wasn't with him.

You're not safe, you bastard.

He moved quickly toward the wrought-iron fence, and, a few minutes later, he was over the top and dropping to the grass.

A shadow in the bushes to his left!

He whirled and gave a roundhouse kick that hit the

man in the throat, then moved in for the kill as he was falling.

"No!" Manez moved out of the bushes. "*Madre de Dios,* you've caused enough trouble, Quinn. I won't have you killing my men."

Joe stopped, breathing hard, trying to calm the rush of adrenaline. "Then you shouldn't have men who set themselves up to be taken out. I saw him the minute I hit the ground."

"Pedro is a very good man." Manez helped the man to his feet. "You're obviously just better. Go back to the car, Pedro. I'll take it from here."

Pedro gave Joe a glowering glance and turned and walked away.

"And you shouldn't expect me not to react if you don't tell me you're going to be on stakeout, Manez." Joe gazed after Pedro. "How much does he know about this house?"

"Why? Would you go after him and finish the job?" Manez said sourly. "He knows nothing. No one knows about this house but you and me and the prisoner who gave me the information. I just thought I might need backup."

"Against me?"

"Against Salazar. I'd be an even greater target than usual if he saw me here. Though I had an idea you might be popping in and causing trouble." He turned. "I need to get you off the street. I'll walk with you back to your car."

"I checked it out before I went to the house. Are you trying to protect me, Manez?"

"Only because I don't need you blowing the only lead I've had since—"

"I'm not blowing it," Joe interrupted. "I just had to verify so that I knew where I could go with it. I had to see what was happening."

"You should have left it up to me. I was going to bug the place and make sure that I had all I needed."

"This is Salazar and a woman he's been screwing for years. They both know the consequences. Do you think that he wouldn't take precautions? I had a listening device, and I should have been able to hear through the glass of the window and couldn't do it."

"So you found out nothing?"

"I found out that she went in angry and came out looking very sleek and satisfied. I don't know the dynamics, but they're definitely lovers." He stopped at his rental car. "And presumably have been lovers for a number of years according to your informant. The question is if she's his accomplice. I'd bet that she is."

"I'd . . . hesitate. A mother doesn't kill her children."

"We both know that's not true. It depends on what the stakes are and the personality of the mother." He paused. "It's the most unnatural crime imaginable, so the personality would have to be twisted beyond belief."

"Perhaps . . . she doesn't know?"

Joe looked at him.

Manez shrugged. "The idea offends me. What can I say?"

"You can say that you'll give me all the information possible on Natalie Castino. I suppose you got photos of her going through the gate?"

"I thought it might be useful."

"To stage an uproar between Salazar and Castino that would put the coalition in chaos? Not yet, Manez."

"I'll be the judge of that."

"No, not until Eve and Cara are safe." His lips tightened. "Salazar will have put precautions in place to make sure he's not connected to this place or Natalie Castino. That photo will mean nothing. Even if Castino makes a move on Salazar and takes him out, it won't be good for me. Then he won't be able to give the order to stop Franco and whoever else he's put on tracking Eve down. Let me take care of him myself."

Manez shook his head.

"You gave me a week."

"That was before Natalie Castino appeared on the scene. I can use her, Quinn."

"A week."

Manez shrugged. "Five days. Subject to change if I find it necessary."

"Done." Joe got in the car. "You won't find it necessary. I believe Salazar's attention is going to be focused away from anything to do with the cartels for the time being. He's going to be doing everything he can to find Eve and Cara."

"And what are you going to do?"

He pulled away from the curb. "Get back to Atlanta and make sure he comes up against a stone wall."

"I like this." Cara dug her spoon into the stony dirt of the courtyard and smiled at Eve. "I kind of thought Jane was joking about it, but she really gave me a spoon."

Eve chuckled. "I believe it's more of a way of teaching patience and care than necessity. I remember when she was digging at the site in Herculaneum, she was very impatient. She must have learned an important lesson."

"But MacDuff hasn't learned it." Cara's gaze went to the area where the Laird was working with Jock. "I didn't think I'd see an earl with his sleeves rolled up and sweating. And he has a shovel."

"It's his idea of a compromise. He let us have spoons and he's going for the big stuff. He believes that the chest might be in the dungeon area. It would take a long time

for him to get down there with a spoon. We're only looking for possible clues, keys, boxes, scrolls, or anything else
written by family members. They're looking for the chest
itself." She put her spoon aside. "But I'll have to leave you
to it by yourself for a while. I have to go and take a look
around the surrounding area and get my bearings."

Cara nodded. "It's a new place. Elena always used to
look around the neighborhood when we moved to a different place. She said it made it safer for us."

Eve nodded as she got to her feet. She should have
known Cara would not be alarmed. Her life had been one
long flight for survival. "Stay close to Jane."

"You're going alone?"

"Jock was going to go with me, but he appears to be
busy with MacDuff. I'll be fine."

"Yes, you will." Caleb was suddenly beside her. "But
Jock thought that you'd be even better if you had someone to keep you company. He asked me to take his place."
He grimaced. "A great compliment since he really doesn't
trust anyone but MacDuff. I don't think he trusts me either, but he knows I can take care of you, and he knows
where he can find me if he has to go after me."

Cara laughed. "But Jock wouldn't hurt you."

"Not if I could help it." He smiled at Cara. "You like
him?"

She nodded. "He wouldn't hurt anyone."

Caleb looked at Eve. "I believe that's our cue to leave."
He took her elbow to help her over the rocky terrain toward his car parked on the road. "I'll keep her safe, I
promise, Cara."

Cara nodded and went back to her digging.

"Jock has her completely fooled," he said quietly. "She
thinks he's some kind of Boy Scout. Are you going to tell
her about him?"

"Not if I don't have to do it."

"Because she's a child?"

She shook her head. "She's not really a child. Because she's half-right, he wouldn't hurt anyone he didn't have to hurt. He is what she believes him to be. He didn't try to fool her, he was just being himself. I don't want her to think everyone she reaches out to is a threat."

"Well, I don't have that problem with Cara." He opened the car door for her. "If you've noticed, she regards me with the same wariness that everyone else does. I'm surprised that she permitted me to take her Eve away without her."

Eve glanced at him, her eyes twinkling. "But you were vouched for by Jock. That makes you totally acceptable."

He started the car. "Until she reaches the age of intimidation. Then I'd have my work cut out for me." He glanced at Jane sitting on a rock and going through a box of papers. "Wouldn't I, Eve?"

"Yes," she said bluntly. "But even Jane allowed me to go off with you without protest. She either trusts me to take care of myself, or you've made inroads on her trusting you."

"Which do you think?"

"I have no idea. I know you usually don't give a damn about anyone's trusting you. But Jane may be different." Her gaze narrowed on his face. "Is she different for you, Caleb?"

"She's a beautiful woman."

"Are you going to answer me?"

"So that you can rush to protect her?"

"I'll always do that."

"She's . . . different. I won't hurt her . . . if I can help it."

"That's not good enough."

He suddenly smiled recklessly. "It's all you'll get from

me. It's more than I've ever given before. She fights me, and that makes me . . . angry."

"That's not what you were going to say." Her gaze was still reading him. "I think you were going to say it hurts. Were you?"

"Me?" He shook his head mockingly. "Why would you think I would succumb to that particular weakness? No one else believes that I would ever be that soft."

"I know you would never admit it. I don't know why I asked."

"Neither do I." He took out a folded paper from his pocket and handed it to her. "Jock gave me this map. He thought you might want to look it over. He told me to take you to the lake. It's the only area that has access from the north. From the south, anyone coming would be easily spotted."

She unfolded the map and checked it out. "By all means, let's go to the lake."

Gaelkar Loch was large, deep, crystal blue, and surrounded by craggy hills that fell steeply to its green banks. The north bank was bathed in thick gray mist that not only shadowed the lake itself but obscured a good fourth of the massive hills that hovered over it.

Eve felt suddenly small and overwhelmed as she stood on the edge of the steep slope nearest the road and looked out at the blue water and that ghostly mist. "What is it?" she murmured. "I've been to the Alps and I never felt . . ."

Caleb nodded. "It's principally that heavy fog. MacDuff tells me that it never goes away. Most unusual. It makes the place seem a bit menacing. It's easy to imagine that anything could happen in those mists. There are all kinds of legends about it. The locals say that it could hide the beginning or the end of the world."

He shrugged. "Some people feel it, some people don't. It does manage to capture the imagination. These Highlands have been battlegrounds and full of pain and savagery for centuries. I'm sure that Cira was a part of those battles."

"But you feel it? You weren't born here either, were you?"

"No, my family settled in Italy centuries ago." He grimaced. "Much to the dismay of the villagers who were there before them. It seems my ancestors were far more intimidating than I am, and the villagers didn't understand the gift that was passed down through the family."

"Imagine that," Eve murmured.

"But I do have a home a few hundred miles from here now. I like the wildness of the Highlands." He smiled. "I think I would have bonded with Cira."

"I believe you would, too." She looked back at the lake. "MacDuff believes Cira is Jane's ancestor."

He nodded. "But that means nothing to me. I want Jane exactly what she is, what she's made of herself." He inclined his head mockingly at Eve. "What you've made her." His smile faded. "As usual, I have a number of purely selfish interests in coming here, but one of them is to help you, Eve. I won't let anything happen to you or Cara." Then the smile was back. "Jane would have my head, and that's not the part of my anatomy I'm interested in giving her."

Outrageous. Totally outrageous. But she still had trouble smothering a smile. "It depends on how you look at it. But I do thank you for any help. There are many reasons why I need everything to go smoothly while we're here."

"Smoothly. What a curious word to use in this case." He looked at her speculatively. "And you're usually very clear and concise."

"It's just a word, Caleb." She could have bitten her tongue. The word had come out of nowhere. Everything had to be smooth. She had to take every care so that the child would be able to survive these next weeks. But Caleb was sharp and intuitive, and he had caught that subtle inference. "Stop reading something into—" Her phone rang, and she breathed a sigh of relief. She took the cell out of her pocket and her relief was gone in an instant.

Joe.

"I've got to take this." She walked a few yards away from Caleb as she punched the access. "Is there a problem, Joe?"

"The forensic report came back yesterday. Salazar knows that you and Cara weren't in the car."

She drew a shaky breath. "We knew that was coming. Yesterday? Why didn't you call me when it first came in?"

"I was a little busy."

She stiffened. "I don't like the sound of that. Did Franco come after you?"

"He didn't get a chance. I made myself unavailable. Something else popped up, and I had to check it out."

"Joe."

"I'm going to tell you. That's why I'm calling. It may be a way we can manipulate the situation to keep Cara in the U.S. I was in Mexico City checking out a lead one of Manez's informants handed him." He paused. "For at least the past six years, Natalie Castino has been sleeping with Salazar. Probably longer than that, but that's the only time span Manez's informant knew for sure."

"What?" Eve was stunned. "There's got to be a mistake."

"I was at their little love nest in the hills outside Mexico City. I saw her. She was angry with Salazar. She'd probably just heard about the forensic report."

"Joe, that doesn't make sense. It had to be dangerous for her to conduct a liaison with Salazar. If her husband found out, she'd be killed."

"Maybe she thought it was worth it." He paused. "Or maybe she was caught in a trap and couldn't get out."

"You think that she helped him kidnap the girls," she whispered. It was almost too horrible to say the words. There was no child more helpless and vulnerable than when a parent was involved. They were automatically thought to be the protector, not the aggressor. "Why, Joe?"

"Manez is trying to find out. He's digging for more information about her." He added ruefully, "He didn't want to believe it. He's a tough guy, but he probably loves his own mom, and it's hard for him to make the connection."

"It's hard for anyone." She was having trouble herself. Though she had done a few reconstructions on children who she had later found out had been killed by their parents, it had almost always been an accidental blow. Or by the father to hide proof of molestation. She could remember only two murders committed by a child's mother, and the women had both been declared by the court to be insane. But then, maybe judges had the same problem as Manez about accepting that a mother could kill her own child. "I don't understand. It's not as if she had much to do with Jenny and Cara. You told me that nurses took care of the children, and she and Castino didn't see that much of them. I've seen photos of them while they were with their parents and . . . they were damn adorable." She had to steady her voice. "Why would she do it? Was it because she was so obsessed with her lover, Salazar, that she'd do anything he wanted?"

"It's a possibility, but I don't believe that's true. The

woman I caught sight of outside that house last night was no weakling. She exuded power, lots of power. What she was doing with Salazar was what she wanted to do." He added, "And I'd bet that if she was involved in the children's kidnapping, she wanted that, too."

"Did Manez give you anything more to go on?"

"He came back with a bare-bones report by the time I got back here to Atlanta. I'll forward it to you. Not much. She married Castino when she was eighteen and had Jenny only a year later. In Russia, she was Daddy's little girl and lived the life of a princess. Sergai Kaskov is a Mafia boss, but he evidently adored her and gave her everything she wanted. But maybe she didn't want to be a princess, she preferred being a queen. When Castino came to Moscow and she heard how powerful his cartel was, he seemed to be what she needed. For the first few years, her life in Mexico was ideal, parties, a husband who was crazy about her, designer clothes, the power she'd never had in Russia."

"It changed?"

"Not on the surface. She had another child, Cara, a few years after Jenny. The word was that she hadn't wanted to have another child, but Castino was insisting. He wanted a boy."

"And he didn't get one that time either."

"No. So he wanted to try again. Natalie suddenly became ill and flew home to Moscow to visit her father. She came back eight months later, and she was in fine form and absolutely radiant. Manez said that everyone who saw Natalie and Castino together during that period remarked on how she managed to dazzle Castino again. He wasn't pleased about her long visit to her father and had taken a mistress. But within a few weeks, he'd sent her away, and Natalie was queen again. She kept him so busy, in bed and out, that he wasn't pushing about her getting pregnant immediately."

"If she was that busy with her husband, she wouldn't have had time to seduce or be seduced by Salazar."

"I don't know, it depends on what spurred them to get together. Manez didn't give me any more details about that period."

"What about the girls? Would she have had an opportunity to help with the kidnapping?"

"The afternoon before Jenny and Cara disappeared, Natalie had taken Jenny to perform at the garden party at a friend's house in the hills. Cara stayed home, taken care of by Elena. Natalie said she and Jenny returned to the house at about six, and she sent Jenny and Cara to bed about nine. No one discovered they were missing until the next morning."

"She sent them to bed at nine," Eve repeated. "Her nurse would have put their nightgowns on them, wouldn't she?"

"Presumably."

"But Jenny wasn't found in a nightgown when they took her out of that grave. She was wearing a white eyelet dress and a black-velvet ribbon in her hair." She moistened her lips. "As if she'd gone to a party."

"You're saying you think that the girls were taken immediately after Jenny was brought back from that garden party?"

"It would give Salazar almost twelve hours more to whisk them out of Mexico before the search started." She felt sick. "Natalie gave him that time."

"But you still don't want to believe it." He said wearily, "Neither do I."

"I can't think why she would—"

"We'll find out eventually. We just have to accept

that's almost certainly what happened." He was silent. "And be on guard against her."

"On guard?"

"Manez told me that she boarded a flight for Moscow this morning. It seems her father is ill and wants to see her. Convenient?"

"Perhaps she's panicking and going to him for protection."

"Or perhaps she'll surface somewhere other than Moscow. I just wanted to warn you that she may be a factor." He paused. "How are you? Everything okay with Cara?"

"She's digging in the dirt at the castle. She's smiling a lot and having a good time." She drew a shaky breath. "And how the hell do I tell her that her mother might have been responsible for killing her sister and Elena?"

"You don't tell her, not yet. Let it play itself out. You didn't answer me. How are you?"

"I'm digging in the dirt, too. And right now I'm with Caleb, gazing out at a lake that the Highlanders say might have been created to hide the beginning of the world or maybe the end of it."

"Caleb? If he showed it to you, then I'd bet on the end."

"Maybe. I can never tell about him. But Caleb's been more accommodating than usual." She changed the subject. "What are you doing?"

"Trying to keep Franco and Salazar from tracing you. I got behind when I flew down to Mexico. I'm on my way to Gainesville now to contact Jeff Brandel, the pilot who flew you to Scotland. I'm going to give him enough money to go out of the country for a while. He should have arrived back in Gainesville by now." He was silent for an instant. "Look, yes, the idea of Natalie Castino's killing her own child is horrible, but look at the good side that we found out about it. How likely is it that Immigration would send Cara back to a mother who's suspected of murdering her sister?"

"But how long would it take to prove that Natalie did that? It's hard to believe, people push it away. She might persuade everyone that she's a victim."

"The glass half-empty?"

"I want hope for Cara, Joe. I just don't want to take chances. Not with her, not with you. I love you." She added unsteadily, "Take care of yourself." She hung up.

She gazed blindly out at the lake that had so intrigued her before. The beginning of the world, the end of the world. Mist and swirling waters and no one knew what was happening beneath that mist.

And no one knew what had happened to twist the heart of Natalie Castino, who should have loved and cared for her children and instead had tried to destroy them.

"Bad news?" Caleb was studying her expression. "Quinn?"

She nodded. "It looks as if Salazar will be on the move soon, if he's not now. I guess that's actually not bad news. We knew it was going to happen."

He shrugged. "You looked stunned."

"Joe just found out that Jenny and Cara's mother was probably involved in their kidnapping." She made a face. "I suppose stunned is the word, and sick, and bewildered. I can't understand it. A child's life is so precious. I can't see how any mother could do that."

"You're saying kidnapping, do you mean killing?" he asked bluntly.

"I'm having trouble saying the word when connected to Jenny and Cara." She deliberately said, "Killing. Because that was where it was going to end, and Natalie Castino must have realized that."

"I'm just being very clear." Caleb's lips turned up in a half smile. "No one minces words about me, and I generally return the favor." He tilted his head. "This is really disturbing you."

"You're damn right it does. I'm a mother. I instinctively want to protect any child." She added fiercely, "And I want to punish anyone who would try to hurt a child."

"Back to the primitive. I understand that concept though I generally operate from a different standpoint." Caleb looked out at the lake. "Have you seen enough? Would you like me to take you anywhere else?"

"No, we should probably go back to the castle." She started to turn away, and then realized he was studying her again. Why? Had she been too passionate about the idea of Natalie Castino's crime and betrayal? She couldn't have been anything else. Perhaps that wasn't why he was staring at her so curiously. He might not have even noticed how upset she'd been.

Though he probably had noticed and would analyze and bring it up at his leisure. Not that she couldn't just laugh it off. But she seldom laughed at whatever Caleb deduced about anything. He always came too close.

Face it now. She turned to look at him. "What? You're staring at me."

"I like looking at you. I like *you*, Eve." He took her arm and led her back toward the car. "I can see why you and Jane are so close. You're both painfully honest . . . most of the time. I find that infinitely refreshing." As they reached the car, his hands slipped down and he grasped her hands as he stood looking down at her. "Though it's usually not in the least complimentary to me. But even that's forgiven, I always know where I stand." He stared directly down into her eyes. "And here's where *you* stand. Don't worry, I'll make sure that you'll be safe. You have

Jock and MacDuff, who are the soul of everything bold and noble, but every little while you need someone who's not at all noble. That's me." He was smiling as he opened the car door for her. "I have an incredible number of dirty tricks at my disposal. And I'm putting them all at your disposal."

She stared at him in surprise. "What brought this on?"

He shrugged. "Occasionally something touches me, and I have to respond." He got in the driver's seat. "You seem to have hit it today." He started the car. "Don't tell Jane, she'll say I'm conning you."

"No she won't. She knows you better than you think."

He nodded. "But she'd still put up barriers and have me jump through hoops. She doesn't like the idea that I might do something that's not totally on the dark side. It confuses her."

"It confuses me, too." She paused. "What . . . touched you today, Caleb?"

His smile was mocking. "Now that would be a revelation. There's always a price for a revelation of my unique personality. You wouldn't want to pay it."

Would Jane want to pay it? Eve wondered.

"In time," he said as if he had read her thoughts. "If I prepared the way." He changed the subject. "Now tell me about Cara and that music that was luring me like a Lorelei the other evening. What do you intend to do about her when this is all over?"

GAINESVILLE, GEORGIA

Still no answer.

Joe frowned as he hung up the cell.

It was the third attempt to reach Jeff Brandel he'd

made since he'd gotten on the road today. Straight to voicemail on the first two calls, this time no connection at all.

He didn't like it.

Fifteen more minutes, and he'd be at the airport.

Nothing might be wrong.

But, dammit, he didn't like it.

CHAPTER
8

GAINESVILLE AIRPORT

"I need to see Brandel," Joe said as he strode into the small terminal that was more like an office. "Where is he?"

"In hangar Twelve E." A lanky young brunette woman in jeans and a plaid shirt looked up from the paperwork in front of her. "He's been there since this morning working on his plane. Should I call him for you?"

"I've been calling him." He left the terminal and strode out on the tarmac.

Hangar 12E.

And the metal door was pulled down.

It was a nice day, why the hell pull down the door?

Three minutes later he found out the answer.

Blood.

He stood there gazing at the man tied to the chair, who must be Jeff Brandel. It was impossible to tell because his face was cut and burned, and one eye was gouged out. His mouth was duct-taped shut.

"My God."

He moved closer and saw the drill beside the chair and the cuts on Brandel's body. The death wound was from the machete piercing his chest, and the blood was still flowing from it. He had gone through hideous torture, and had obviously tried to withstand it. He was a good guy and had probably not wanted to break and endanger Eve and Cara.

But there was no sign of the man who had done this so there was every chance that he had gotten the information he needed before he had killed Brandel.

He felt the anger rise as he looked again at the pilot. Anger and fear.

"Shit." He took out his phone and dialed Eve. "Brandel is dead. By the look of the body, he probably told them everything he knew."

"Dear God, no . . ." She was silent, trying to cope. "He had a wife. He told me he'd just gotten married two months ago. I . . . liked him."

"Yeah, so did I." He turned away from Brandel and walked to the open door. "But that's not important right now. Brandel talked. How much did he know? I only told him where he was to take you. Nothing else. Did you tell him anything?"

"No. He just said something about Cara and how he wanted kids and then about his wife."

"He couldn't hear anything you talked about with Cara?"

"No. The cockpit door was closed." She paused. "But he had to have seen Jane pick us up at the hangar. He was still sitting on the runway and hadn't pulled away yet."

Joe muttered a curse. "Even if he had no idea who she was, they'll be able to dig into our background and make a good guess fairly quickly."

"But that's all they'll know. MacDuff wouldn't have broadcast info about the hunt because he wouldn't want to have to deal with any other treasure hunters. Jane certainly wouldn't have talked about it. We arrived at the airport here in Scotland, then just vanished. It's not that bad."

"The hell it's not. They'll still be closer to you than I ever intended."

"But not closer than you thought might happen. I remember that remark you made about a Special Forces unit to protect us."

"*Might* happen. It wasn't supposed to happen." He looked back at Brandel. That wasn't supposed to happen either, a good man had suffered and died. "I'm going to call MacDuff and warn him what's going down. I wanted to tell you first."

"I can tell him. I'm almost back to the castle."

"Then go ahead and do it. I'll call him later. I need to phone the precinct and report Brandel's murder." He paused. "And break the news to his wife."

"I'm sorry. It's not going to be easy."

"None of it is easy," he said roughly. "And I don't want to stay here trying to heal wounds. I want to catch the next flight to you. I can't even do that because it's a sure thing I'm being followed. I can't risk leading anyone to you."

"Salazar and Franco," she reminded him. "I know you're feeling frustrated, but you might still be able to find them and take them down. Look how much you've already found out about Natalie Castino. We're safe for now, Joe."

"For now." He was gazing down at Brandel's bloody face. "I'll do what I can here. I don't know how long I'll be able to keep from saying to hell with it and just taking off. Watch everything that's going on around you. Take care." He hung up.

Only he should be the one taking care of her, he thought in frustration. He shouldn't be thousands of miles away. He couldn't stand it.

He had to stand it.

He punched in the number for the precinct. "Joe Quinn. I need a forensic team and the medical examiner out here right away. I'll give you the address . . ."

"Nasty. Real nasty." Detective Pete Jalkown shook his head as he gazed at the covered gurney as it was wheeled out of the hangar. "You knew him?"

"Slightly. I hired him for a job."

"It wouldn't have anything to do with Eve?" Pete asked. "You know, the captain is very curious about that explosion. She was happy that Eve wasn't in that car but definitely curious."

"She'll have to stay that way," Joe said. "I'll talk to her as soon as I'm free to do it."

"If it were anyone but you, Quinn, you'd be in that interrogation room on general principle." His glance shifted back to the medical examiner's van. "And this isn't going to make it any better. Serial killers are a big headache when the captain has to deal with the press."

"Serial killer?"

"Possible," Pete said. "Three hours ago we got a call from Travel-Rite Charter Service. They found one of their pilots, Zeke Dalkway, in the alley behind the terminal building. Worse condition than Brandel."

"Torture?"

"Four fingers missing and someone spent a long time on him before they killed him."

Because he hadn't been able to give them the information as Brandel had, Joe thought bitterly.

"The captain is going to jump on those cases with both feet," Pete said. "Much too visible and gory to ignore. It's like waving a red flag in front of a bull. Not smart."

Neither smart, nor discreet. Salazar had also jumped in with guns blazing. Nothing subtle about his attack mode. Patient for eight years of searching for Cara, but that patience had vanished overnight. He had gone for the jugular.

After he had spent the night with an angry Natalie Castino. Connection?

Blood and agony.

Two men ruthlessly tortured and dead because Joe had hired a pilot to help Eve and Cara escape. No more patience, no more careful planning to avoid confrontation. A complete change of modus operandi.

Yes, he could see a connection.

"I've got it!" Franco said as soon as Salazar picked up the phone. "You wanted it by tonight, I'm hours ahead of you."

"Where are they?"

"Scotland. Brandel delivered them to Ardland Airport outside Edinburgh."

"And where did they go from there?"

"He didn't know. If he'd known, he would have told me."

"I'm sure he would," Salazar said. "But I need more than you've told me. You've given me a city and country. I need an address. I need *them.*"

"I have the description of the woman who met them at the hangar. I think it might be Jane MacGuire. She's

Duncan's adopted daughter and lives in London. That's pretty close."

"An address."

"I'm on it. I'm taking the next flight to Scotland. I'll find them."

"If I don't find them first. I'll see you in Scotland, Franco."

Silence. "You're going to Scotland? You don't have to bother. I'll take care of it."

"That hasn't been my experience so far. I'm allowing you the opportunity to convince me. Don't disappoint me." He added with a touch of cool menace, "In the meantime, I'll be on the spot and making sure that doesn't happen."

Music, Eve thought drowsily. Faint, far away . . . beautiful . . .

Cara.

Far away?

Her eyes flew open.

Cara wasn't in her bedroll a few yards away!

Easy. If she was playing her violin, then there was nothing seriously wrong.

She drew a deep breath. Her pulse was gradually steadying. Okay, find Cara.

She crawled out of the tent and knelt there, trying to locate the sound.

The stone wall near the top of the ruin.

Cara was sitting there, her violin tucked under her chin.

And the magic coming out of that instrument was breathtaking.

Eve should tell her to come back to the tent. Cara

shouldn't be out there by herself. It was all very well for Eve to tell Joe that they had a window of safety, but she wanted to keep that window guarded and close to her. She'd have to go and disturb that magic and bring Cara back to the tent.

Or maybe not.

There was a familiar figure climbing up the stone blocks toward the top of the wall. Moonlight poured over his fair hair and slim, powerful body.

Jock.

She felt a surge of relief and sat back down outside the tent.

Jock would handle it.

Cara was safe with Jock.

There was someone there in the darkness, Cara realized vaguely. Someone was below her, climbing the stones. The presence was friendly, warm, and comforting.

Eve?

Instant guilt.

She probably shouldn't be doing this. She had thought if she got far enough away from the tent area that she wouldn't disturb anyone. Darn it, that must not be true if Eve had to get up and come after her.

She sighed and stopped playing. "I'm sorry. I didn't mean to bother anyone. I'll go back to—"

"As far as I know, you didn't bother anyone. I just thought you might want company." Jock Gavin climbed the last two stones and was standing there. He dropped down on the wall beside her. "Having trouble sleeping?"

She stared at him in shock. She hadn't spoken to him since that night in the courtyard, but it wasn't as if she hadn't thought about him. He always seemed to be some-where near, working with MacDuff, talking to Jane or

Caleb. He was like the music, beautiful, warm, moving in and out, simple, complicated . . . stirring. Even when she wasn't looking at him, she was aware of where he was, what he was doing.

"Cara?"

He was gazing at her inquiringly. What had he asked? Sleep.

"Usually, I sleep fine." She looked out at the hills. "But like I told you, there's music all around us here. Sometimes I wake up . . ."

"And have to go join the music?"

She nodded. "Crazy, huh?"

"Not at all. I envy you. How does it feel?"

"It . . . fills me. Whenever anything goes wrong, it makes me able to take it and go on."

"Everything?" he asked gently.

Elena. Jenny. Her index finger pressed hard on the violin string. "My sister and my friend were . . . killed. I didn't think anything would help. But the music was still there." She moistened her lips. "And somehow it became . . . part of them."

"That's a wonderful thing."

She nodded. "I was so angry. I wanted to reach out and hurt. I still do. I went to church and prayed, but it didn't help. But the music helps. Eve helps." She looked at him. "You help, Jock."

"Me?" His brows rose in surprise. "I'm happy to be of service, but I don't see how that ever came to be."

"You're beautiful," she said simply. "Like that Tchaikovsky I was just playing."

He threw back his head and laughed. "I wasn't expecting that."

"Why not? You know what you are. Lots of people must have told you." She made a face. "MacDuff even made fun of me because he knew I was sort of dazzled. But it wasn't because you were like one of those princes in Disney movies, it was because of what you are inside. It kind of . . . shines."

"Really?" He was silent. "I'm flattered, but I'm not sure what you mean. And what you call my 'shine' could never come close to what I heard tonight."

"It does for me." But she didn't know how to put it into words. She didn't know why it had tumbled out. Yet it was strange that she didn't regret it or feel embarrassed. Not with him. "There are so many bad people in the world who kill and do terrible things. But you wouldn't do anything like that. Inside, you're clean and bright and warm. Just being around you makes me feel like that, too. Like Eve. Like the music."

He went still. "Cara. I'm not at all like Eve. The only similarity I have to your music is that I truly love it. I'm not what you think I am."

"Yes, you are." Her gaze went back to the violin she was holding. "Seth Caleb said something like that about you, but I don't believe it."

"Believe it," he said quietly. "Look at me, Cara."

Her gaze lifted to his face. It was hard, intense, and unsmiling. "I don't know what you're seeing, but it's not the man you want me to be. I've been every bit as terrible and violent as the people who have hurt you in the past. I try to tell myself that I had excuses, and I was a victim, too." His lips twisted. "But in the end we all have to accept responsibility for our own sins and try to come to terms and maybe change. There's nothing beautiful about me, Cara."

She gazed at him for a moment and shook her head. "You're wrong."

"You're not listening to me."

"Because I'd be afraid of you if you were bad. I had to learn that bad doesn't always look like bad. I did learn that, so now I have to rely on what I feel. I'm not afraid of you, Jock."

"Good. I would never do anything to hurt you. But you're too young to be able to judge the entire picture. I've done terrible things, Cara."

"But you wouldn't do them now."

He sighed. "How can I convince you? Yes, I would do them. It's difficult to stop once you've had that taste on your tongue. But I hope I would only do it to protect. But that's not a certainty, Cara."

But how she was feeling was a certainty. She was trying to frantically adjust that certainty to what he was telling her. "Protect. That's like the police or the FBI or the army or even those knights who lived here in this castle. They all did bad and bloody things, but it was for a good reason. Right?"

"Wrong. You're talking about heroes. I'm no hero. But if I could be anyone's hero, I'd want to be yours. I'd like to be your big brother, your knight, anything you want." He added gently, "I wish I could tell you that I'd qualify. I'd like the idea of you finding someone in this world to trust besides Eve and your music." He smiled. "Try MacDuff. He has some heroic qualities."

She shook her head.

"Then you're on your own. Caleb would be insulted if I tried to tell you that he's a hero." He snapped his fingers. "But you have Joe Quinn. He should be more than sufficient."

"I'm not looking for a hero. Don't be silly. All I said was that I know you're a good man."

"Shining."

She smiled. "Now you're making fun of me."

He smiled back at her. "Because you took me by surprise, and I'm on the defensive." He dropped to the stones at her feet and linked his arms around his knees. "And I need soothing. Play me that Tchaikovsky that reminds you of me."

"I thought you were coming up to tell me to go back to my tent."

"Do you want to stop playing and go back down to reality?"

"No."

"Then play me that Tchaikovsky." He leaned his head back against the stones. "When you're ready, we'll go back."

She tucked her violin beneath her chin, then stopped. "You're not staying with me to protect me?"

"Why would I do that? That would be counter to everything I've been telling you. It would set me up to be a bloody hero." He airily waved his hand. "So let me be selfish and completely self-absorbed. Soothe me, Cara . . ."

She looked down at him and slowly lifted her bow. Not a hero? She still thought he was wrong about that. But she wouldn't argue with him anymore. He'd been so busy telling her all the things he couldn't be to her that he wanted to be. Big brother, knight, surely somewhere in that mix was . . . friend.

She started to play.

"You're awake," Cara whispered as she settled down in her bedroll an hour later. "Is that my fault, Eve? Did you hear me?"

"I heard you," Eve said. "You shouldn't have gone without telling me. It might not be safe. The only reason I let you go alone when we were at the hunting lodge was that I knew it was safe. I can't be sure of that here. I was going to come after you, but I saw Jock climbing the stones. I knew you'd be okay."

"It seemed safe," Cara said. "There wasn't anyone around. It was beautiful. This is a wonderful place. Do you know, sometimes I look out at the hills and mountains and I see something, a rock, a tree . . . and then an hour later it's gone. I know it's probably shadows, but it seems kind of . . . mystical. And when I'm up there on the wall, I can see forever."

"But would you be watching while you were playing? I've seen your face, and you're not aware of anything but the music."

"You're right." Cara stared into the darkness. "I guess I was stupid. I'm sorry to worry you. I won't do it again."

"Not without telling me. But you didn't worry me. I told you that I knew Jock was with you." She paused. "You couldn't sleep? Dreams?"

"No, I just needed to play. Sometimes everything gets all tight inside, and I have to let it out."

"And did you? You played for a long time."

"Yes, I was going to come back sooner, but Jock wanted the Tchaikovsky again." She smiled. "Or maybe he didn't. He knew I wasn't ready and wanted to give me the extra time. He . . . understood."

"I'm sure he did," Eve said quietly. "Jock is nothing if not empathetic. And I could tell he likes you very much."

"I like him, too."

"That's pretty obvious," Eve said dryly. "You were very definite about what a great guy he is when Caleb was mildly critical."

"Because it's true. Or you wouldn't trust him."

Eve hesitated. "That doesn't mean he was always trustworthy, Cara. When he was just a little older than you, he fell into the hands of Thomas Reilly, a terrible man who was chemically and psychologically experimenting with mind control. Reilly was involved in all kinds of criminal and terrorist projects. Jock became his prime subject. While he was with Reilly, he did . . . things."

"I know that. He told me."

"He did?"

"Oh, not about that mind-control stuff, he just told me that he'd been very bad. He said that I shouldn't think that he was anything good." She was silent a moment. "But he *is* good. That wasn't his fault, and it was a long time ago. He's changed now, hasn't he?"

"Yes, it took a long time and Jane and MacDuff working with him, but he's changed."

"Jane helped him?"

Eve nodded. "She wouldn't stop until he was on his way back."

"That was good." She was silent again. "But he's not all the way back, or he wouldn't think he's so bad."

"Sometimes you can't return to what you were, you just have to go on," Eve said gently. "Jock is doing fine, Cara."

"He's wonderful," she said with sudden fierceness. "No one should have hurt him. No one should have made him think he was—" She broke off. "You're laughing at me."

"Yes, I was just thinking that you may have your first crush. You're getting toward that age."

"No, you have crushes on movie stars and rockers. Heather had them all the time. That's not like this."

"What is it like?"

She frowned. "I don't like the idea of the bad guys always winning. Elena . . . . Jenny . . ." She paused, trying to work it out. "Jock. He still doesn't believe he's one of the good guys. He doesn't know about the shine."

"Shine?"

"Never mind. But he's still hurting, Eve."

"He'll work it out. It may take time." She added, "You can't do it for him, Cara."

She was silent.

What more could she say? Eve wondered. Cara had been surrounded by pain and loss since she was very young. Instead of growing callous, she had grown more sensitive to it. She had not been able to save the two people she loved most in the world, and now she couldn't bear to face Jock's being hurt. He had managed to reach out and touch her in a special way. Eve had known that when she had seen them together in the courtyard. "He won't appreciate your interfering in his life."

"I could try," Cara said stubbornly.

"Cara."

"Jane helped him before, but she's too busy now."

"Cara, he's a grown man, you're eleven years old. It should work the other way around. There's something wrong with this picture."

"That doesn't matter." She turned on her side and burrowed under the cover. "Jenny didn't think it was strange to tell me that I should take care of you."

"And one more doesn't make a difference?" Eve asked ruefully. "You're setting yourself up to take care of Jock Gavin?"

"Yes," she said drowsily as she rubbed her cheek on the pillow. "I'm going to take care of Jock . . ."

EDINBURGH, SCOTLAND

Salazar was walking toward the exit at the airport when he received a call from Franco.

"I'm in London," Franco said. "I've been scouting

around Jane MacGuire's apartment and gallery, and she's definitely not here. She didn't leave any information with her agent about where she was going. Her landlord said he saw her leave in her car about the time that would coincide with an arrival at that airport in Scotland."

"Now you've told me about where she's not. Can you tell me where she is?"

"Not yet. But I think I've verified that she was the woman who picked up Duncan and the kid. I'm doing a complete background check on Jane MacGuire and her known contacts in London and Scotland now. I should have something for you soon."

"See that you do. My patience is gone. It's time we cleared this mess up." He hung up.

It wasn't only his patience that was gone. He hadn't heard from Natalie since he'd texted her the message about Duncan's arrival in Scotland. But he knew that he would soon.

That was fine with him. His adrenaline was pumping, and he felt more alive than he had in years. He was on the hunt. He could smell the blood.

He stepped outside the terminal and headed for the taxi line.

A sleek black Mercedes slid to the curb in front of him and a chauffeur jumped out and opened the passenger door. "Mr. Salazar."

Salazar stepped closer to the car and he was immediately enveloped in the familiar scent of vanilla and Russian perfume wafting from the backseat.

Natalie.

He hadn't expected to see her this soon.

It seemed she was smelling the blood, too.

He stepped forward and got into the car.

2:24 A.M.
GAELKAR CASTLE

Jane closed the ledger after she'd finished cataloging the afternoon's finds and leaned back in the chair. She should really go to bed. She had deliberately stayed up and worked in the research tent so that she'd be tired enough to sleep. She wasn't sure if it had done any good. She had trouble sleeping anyway, and the news that Eve had told them after she had talked to Joe was too disturbing. Working in this castle surrounded by the hills and winds and silences that whispered of the past had taken Jane away from the thought of the ugliness and violence of monsters who killed.

As they had killed Trevor.

As they might kill Eve and Cara.

"You're working late."

She looked over her shoulder to see Caleb standing in the doorway of the tent. He was dressed in black jeans and white shirt, with the sleeves rolled to the elbow. The night breeze was lifting his dark hair away from his face, which was, as usual, slightly mocking.

Darkness, flames, pure sensuality.

Her hand tightened on the ledger.

More disturbance that she didn't need.

"I'm done now." She forced herself to release the ledger and push it aside. "Or as done as I can be. What are you doing here? You startled me." Her lips twisted. "Which completely belies your claim that we can always sense each other."

He smiled. "I said I can sense you. You might possibly miss a tick occasionally with me. Though I don't see how considering how wary you are." He moved into the tent. "Why the burning of midnight oil? Are you getting close to something?"

"We've hardly scratched the surface. Though MacDuff has discovered a possible opening beneath the dungeons that might lead somewhere. Or not. It's all too vague to even guess." She got to her feet. "A wild-goose chase. If there's a treasure, I don't believe it's here."

"Why?"

"It's not the first time that the family has searched these ruins. The first expedition was in 1927, and there was another in 1969. Surely someone would have found a clue, something . . ."

"MacDuff's not stupid. Why is he here?"

She shrugged. "Because he's MacDuff and he thinks that he has a destiny. Hell, he was almost more involved with tracking down the Cira story than I was all those years ago. That's probably why he wanted me along. He's got this idea I'm part of his destiny, too. It's bullshit."

"No sudden psychic flashes from Cira?"

"I never had psychic flashes. Stop making fun of me, Caleb."

"I wouldn't think of it. But I've been watching you since we've been here. You're feeling something." He suddenly chuckled. "But then so am I. It's the Highlands, after all. In the courtyard, you told Cara that you could feel the music. Did you hear her playing tonight?"

"Yes, I went and stood outside the tent for a minute. I was worried. But then I saw Jock with her, and I knew it was okay."

"Because, in spite of Jock's wicked past, he has an honorable soul?" His tone was mocking. "Like Trevor."

"No, not like Trevor. Trevor didn't have an easy life, but he didn't go through the hell that Jock did." She met his eyes. "And Trevor did have an honorable soul. Even you could see that."

"Crystal clear. I even liked him except when he was getting in my way." He added deliberately, "But I don't have to worry about that now. I thought when Trevor died that he might pose an even greater threat than when he was alive. But I'm working my way through it." His gaze narrowed on her face. "And so are you. Every time we come together, I can see it happening."

She could feel her heart start to pound just looking at his face, that sensual mouth. No, she wouldn't let him do this to her. She forced herself to look away. "I'm going to my tent. I have to get up and start working in a few hours." She turned off the lanterns and started for the door. "You might not understand that, since you're not sweating and digging in the dirt like the rest of us."

"I understand, but I see no reason why I should join you in your misery. That's not why I came on this hunt. My job is to watch and listen and, if necessary, to act." He stepped aside to let her pass. "You'll find me much more valuable in that capacity."

"And is that why you dropped in on me at this hour tonight? Are you watching, listening?"

"All the time. And the hour didn't matter, I function better at night. But that's not why I came by when I saw the light streaming out of the tent. I've been debating all day if I should talk to you. Very unusual for me." He was strolling beside her toward her tent at the end of the row. "As you know, I seldom hesitate about anything. But this may be something sensitive that I should stay out of." He shrugged. "But since when am I sensitive? So I decided to go for it."

"I wouldn't expect anything else," she said dryly. They

had reached her tent, and she stopped and turned to face him. Bright moonlight. She could see him almost as well as in the tent, and it was having just as powerful an effect on her.

Don't let him see it.

Get it over with and go into the tent.

"What is it, Caleb?" she asked impatiently. "It's been an upsetting day. I want to put a period to it."

"I know. You're upset about what Eve told you about Salazar closing in and finding out she's in Scotland."

"Dammit, of course I am. Aren't you?"

"Not as much as you. I knew it was going to happen. It was only a matter of time. I'll just make adjustments."

"I'm not that philosophical. I love Eve."

"Do you think I don't know that? But that love can be complicated, that's why I hesitated."

She stiffened. "It's more dangerous than she told us?"

"Not as far as I know. But she might want to save you worry. You'll have to make up your mind about that."

"I'm going into this tent in ten seconds."

"That's enough time." He smiled down at her. "Eve was upset when Joe told her about Salazar and Natalie Castino. Very upset. Particularly when she told me that Natalie might have killed her own children."

"Of course she was. Anyone would be upset."

"That's what Eve said, particularly anyone who'd had children, a mother who would never understand how anyone could do that to her own daughters. She was near tears, very passionate about it."

"What's your point, Caleb?"

"That Eve was so upset when she said those words that she reached down . . ." His hand moved to Jane's belly and put his hand on it. "Like this. Just for a second." His hand dropped away from her. "I'm sure that she didn't even realize she'd done it. Pure instinct."

Jane went rigid. "What are you saying?"

"It made me curious. It could have been nothing. Or it could have been something very important."

"It was nothing."

He shook his head. "As I said, I was curious. So when I took her back to the car I stood there and took both her hands while I talked to her. Like this." His hands grasped Jane's, his thumbs on her wrists. "Blood is powerful, it controls so many things. You can feel it pound through your body, can't you?"

"Yes." Her breathing was shallow. She felt his thumbs on her wrists, her pulse leaping more every second. Her skin hot, burning where he was holding her. "Let . . . me . . . go, Caleb."

"Soon. Only a demonstration. I made sure that Eve didn't feel any discomfort at all. But it's not really discomfort, is it, Jane?"

"Let me go."

"Reluctantly." He dropped her wrists. "I just wanted to remind you that I can do a few things with blood that other people can't." He grimaced. "Not entirely true. I wanted to touch you. I used it as an excuse."

She drew a deep, quivering breath. "What a surprise." She moistened her lips. "And why did you reach out and hold Eve's hands?"

"I believe you've already guessed. The blood flow in all of us is very powerful, it can tell so much." He reached out again and ran his index finger across the vein of her left wrist. "But at certain times, it becomes even stronger and more definitive. It's incredible during that time."

Her pulse was leaping beneath that finger. Her mind was leaping even more frantically. "During what time?"

He lifted her wrist and pressed his lips to the pulse point. "Eve's pregnant, Jane."

"No!" She jerked her wrist away from him. "That's not true."

He sighed. "I was afraid that you'd be shocked."

"You can't be sure. You just touched her."

"I just touched you. Blood responds. In different ways, of course, depending on the demand. I was analyzing with Eve. If I'd had a little more time, I could have determined how far along she is, but that wasn't important. You can ask her."

"Yes, I can ask her," she repeated numbly. She shook her head to clear it. "If I decide I believe you. Which I'm not at all sure I do."

"Entirely your choice. I thought I'd give you the option. You've taken Eve under your wing, I thought you should know you're responsible for more than you counted on."

"She would have told me."

"Would she?"

No, she might not, Jane thought. She and Eve were so much alike. Jane would not have wanted to lay an additional burden on her, and neither would Eve. "It might not be true. For God's sake, you're not a doctor."

Caleb was silent.

But he had saved Jane's life in that hospital only a few weeks ago when all the doctors had given up on her.

"How certain are you?"

"Very. Some of her blood is being directed to a different place. It's very interesting."

"Interesting?" She rubbed her temple. "Yes, I'd say that it's interesting. However, I'm not in any shape to examine or comment on it. I think . . . I'm scared, Caleb."

"You? Our brave, bold Jane? Nonsense."

"Screw you. This is Eve. It's important. I don't know what she's feeling. She's got to be . . . I don't know."

"Which is why I told you. I could have kept it to myself and let Eve play her own game as she wanted. But that would have cheated you." His lips tightened. "She wouldn't have meant to do it, but in the end, you would have been cheated. I won't allow that, even from Eve."

"It's not your call. You have nothing to do with this."

"But I appear to be very much involved, don't I? It comes from that habit of inserting myself whether I'm wanted or not." He reached up and stroked her cheek. "I find I can't do anything else with you. Now, go to bed and try to sleep. Though I've probably robbed you of that option."

"Almost certainly," she said unsteadily.

"I just want you to remember while you're tossing and turning that there's nothing to be afraid of. I told Eve that I'll be there, and I meant it." He made a face. "That sounds sickeningly noble. Forget I said it. Just remember that I hate to lose. I won't lose this either." He turned and strode away from her.

Leaving Jane staring after him with clenched hands and a chaotic collection of feelings. Trust Caleb to destroy any possibility of serenity this trip might hold.

She wasn't being fair. She wouldn't have wanted him to hold that information back. His presentation had been quintessential Caleb, a combination of sex and charged emotion, but he had given her what he thought she needed to hear. But it didn't alter the fact that he had thrown her a curve that had taken her breath away.

She went into her tent and dropped to her bedroll. She would get ready for bed later, now she had to sit and let that stunning news sink in. There were all kinds of ramifications of Eve's being with child. She wanted to solve them, help her, but how could she when she didn't even know how Eve felt about it?

Or how she felt about it.

This wasn't Eve taking in a lost child as she had with Cara. This was Eve with a baby that might dominate her life as her Bonnie had done.

That had the potential to hurt her as Bonnie's death had done.

No! She felt an instant rejection at the thought.

But she wanted above all for Eve to be happy.

She sighed and laid her head back on the pillow. She obviously would have to work her way through this bewilderment before she talked to Eve . . .

"Are you sure you want to do this, Cira?" Antonio moved to stand behind her. He put his hands gently on her shoulders, and whispered in her ear. "You don't have to say farewell to him here. We can go back to the castle and have the priest give the Gods' blessings and bury him near us."

"No." She looked down at the small casket she'd had the carpenters craft with such care. "I want it to be here by the lake. Marcus liked it here." She could feel the tears sting her eyes. "He told me someday he was going to go into that mist and bring me gifts of gold and jewels fit for a queen. I told him not to be foolish, that I had all the riches I could possibly want already." She looked over her shoulder at Antonio. "It's true, you know. This is a hard, wild land, but we've made it our own. I have everything I ever dreamed about in those days when I was a slave in Herculaneum. I have a husband I love who gave me five strong sons and two daughters who may be even stronger."